Born and educated in London, Michael Maguire's first writing success came early at the age of eleven when he submitted an episode of a children's serial which was accepted and broadcast on ITV.

After working as a journalist, he became a successful full-time novelist of both adult and children's books. *Swiftly* is his eighth published work, and the rights to two of his children's novels were bought by Disney.

SWIFTLY

When an injured Irish greyhound named Degsey arrives at Oyster Gables Animal Shelter, the lives of everyone who works there are dramatically affected. The dog seems to possess a mystical sixth-sense which can influence people's actions and alter the natural course of events. Horses are being stolen from various locations in Devon, and Sky Patakin, female manager of the Oyster Gables, plus trainee Shack Skinner and new assistant Daniel Rusk, find themselves in a great deal of danger as they attempt to discover the culprits. It takes all of Degsey's special powers to protect the people she loves, and things are never quite what they seem . . .

Books by Michael Maguire
Published by The House of Ulverscroft:

SHOT SILK
SLAUGHTER HORSE
SCRATCHPROOF
SCORCHER

MICHAEL MAGUIRE

SWIFTLY

Complete and Unabridged

ULVERSCROFT
Leicester

First published in Great Britain in 1998

First Large Print Edition
published 2002

British Library CIP Data

Maguire, Michael
　　Swiftly.—Large print ed.—
　　Ulverscroft large print series: general fiction
　　1. Scottish deerhound—Juvenile fiction
　　2. Horse stealing—Juvenile fiction
　　3. Children's stories
　　4. Large type books
　　I. Title
　　823.9′14 [J]

　　ISBN 0–7089–4669–0

Published by
F. A. Thorpe (Publishing)
Anstey, Leicestershire

Set by Words & Graphics Ltd.
Anstey, Leicestershire
Printed and bound in Great Britain by
T. J. International Ltd., Padstow, Cornwall

This book is printed on acid-free paper

Inspired by Lucy

1

Marshwood Stables. Two a.m. on a cold, grey damp Saturday in July. Martin Griggs reluctantly opened the cab door of Ryker's travelling horse-box and shivered as the fresh south-westerly wind tore hungrily at his leather jacket.

'I hate the early mornings,' Griggs muttered, accepting a head collar, halter and a pair of bolt-cutters from Tony Ryker's outstretched hand. 'They always give me nosebleeds.'

'Stop moaning.' Ryker sucked on a thin cheroot and let a spiral of smoke curl towards the windshield. 'Just go for the nags in the first four boxes. They're the livery horses. The rest are racehorses and we don't want them ... too much trouble. There are no stable security lights and no alarms. It'll be like taking candy from a baby.'

Griggs didn't reply. He knew what he had to do and his cheekbones looked sharp and projected as he adjusted the face-hugging material of his ski-mask. He was 26 years old, small and scarecrow thin with pale olive skin, curly fair hair and regular almost feminine features. He made his way cautiously forward, his long bony fingers unclipping a flashlight from his belt.

Marshwood Stables were set back from a narrow lane and screened by trees and thick evergreen shrubbery behind a high stone wall. Large ornately carved stone gateposts supported heavy wrought iron gates.

Tony Ryker waited for Griggs to reach the gates before crushing his cheroot into the cab's overflowing ashtray and pulling on his own ski-mask. He glanced quickly in each of the side mirrors, checking for light or movement before slipping the catch on the driving door and dropping to the ground. He made his way to the rear of the vehicle.

All quiet. Perfect.

Tony Ryker had done this operation many times before. Between them, he and Griggs were responsible for the theft of more than five hundred horses from the South West of England. It was a profitable trade. Steal up to ten horses a week and keep them out of sight in a deserted Devon warehouse. Then, when the trail had gone cold, sell the younger ones at horse markets in other parts of the country. The unfortunate old stagers which nobody wanted to buy were shipped via Harwich to continental abattoirs for horse meat.

It was a sleazy business, but it had made

Ryker a very wealthy man. Not that his current lifestyle reflected it. For six months of the year he lived in Martin Griggs's rented mobile home in the Devon hamlet of Hele, near Ilfracombe. It was a ramshackle dwelling, far away from the tourist trail and mostly ignored by local people. The mobile home sat in six acres of straggly undergrowth which doubled as a paddock and backed on to a derelict fertiliser warehouse.

Very handy. Total isolation.

The ideal hideaway for horse rustling and shady business dealings — a far cry from Ryker's respectable, alternative lifestyle as a law-abiding husband and father who owned an elegant Tudor house in Berkshire.

'Gotcha,' Griggs murmured, as the bolt-cutters sliced effortlessly through a thick padlocked chain which shackled the main gates. They opened smoothly, and Griggs wasted no time in streaking across the stable compound to the first of the loose boxes.

'Well done, Griggsy,' Ryker mouthed the words, allowing himself a satisfied smile as he watched Griggs's flashlight wink twice. Ryker reached up and slid the metal pegs from their keepers, then took the strain with both arms outstretched as he slowly lowered the vehicle's ramp.

Rolls of fat bulged through his shirt at his

stomach, but he was still in reasonable shape for his 42 years. There was a great amount of power in his neck muscles, in his broad shoulders and thick wrists.

Ryker was the one with the aggressive character, the backbone, whilst Griggs was the born follower. They'd met three years ago at Exeter racecourse. Ryker was there winning money; Griggs was there losing it. The partnership had been formed the moment Griggs had foolishly tried to steal Tony Ryker's wallet. The big man knew all the tricks of the pickpocket trade and he had immediately caught Griggs's thieving fingers in a vice-like grip. Griggs pleaded for his freedom and Ryker (subject to conditions) had duly granted it.

The conditions were met and the alliance was cemented. Ryker needed a sidekick, a gopher who would be at his beck and call, and Griggs needed this big, dominant businessman's know-how. They also both shared one common interest . . . Easy money.

Some of that was about to be earned now as Griggs took the bolt-cutters to each flimsy padlock securing the first four loose boxes.

A shrill whinny speared the early morning air.

'Easy, easy,' Griggs whispered through clenched teeth as the padlock fell away and he entered the first box.

A large bay mare flared her nostrils and backed up as Griggs carefully fastened the head collar he had with him to the horse. 'That's my beauty,' he breathed, running a soothing hand over the mare's muzzle as he wrapped the halter round his arm. 'No noise. Be a good girl for Griggsy.'

Ryker waited well out of sight by the ramp. Muscles rippled in the mare's hindquarters as Griggs whispered comforting words to coax the horse towards the travelling box. A well-practised routine now followed:

Ryker took the halter from Griggs's hands and led the mare up the ramp and into the first of a dozen wooden stalls. Griggs grabbed another head collar and halter from a row of hooks and quickly retraced his steps back to the loose boxes.

This time he emerged with a black colt and the system continued. Horse to Ryker . . . collect head collar and halter . . . back to loose boxes. He worked with clockwork dexterity. The last two horses quickly followed, a washy dun gelding and a piebald mare. Speed was the key to success and in total the whole operation had taken less than eight minutes.

Ryker glanced at Griggs as he fastened the ramp. Through the ski-mask he could see

Griggs's mouth sucking in air as he puffed with exertion. 'You look done in, my little ferret,' he sniggered. 'You need building up. For lunch you can cook us both some nice steak and chips.'

Griggs was an excellent cook, and Ryker being wifeless on his Devon trips exploited this expertise to the full.

'Make it horse meat and chips if you like,' Ryker said with sour amusement as they both climbed back into the cab. 'Lots of protein if you cook it rare. Tastes best if you have your chips floating in half gravy, half blood.'

'You're disgusting.' Griggs pulled off his ski-mask.

Ryker did likewise, giving a throaty laugh as he selected reverse gear. The travelling horse-box eased its way out of Marshwood Lane and onto a narrow country road.

'We'll stick to the back doubles,' Ryker stated, lighting a cheroot with a book-match. 'Less chance of meeting the police.'

Griggs gave a grunt.

Ryker scratched at the scorpion tattoo on his right forearm. 'I'm well pleased with tonight's work, Griggsy. I reckon we'll get a thousand a piece for the bay, the black, and the dun — and maybe up to fifteen hundred for the piebald.'

'S'pose.'

6

'Come daylight and the owners are going to be weeping buckets. Bet some of them belong to a load of posh kids. Heart-breaking, isn't it? Their loss is our gain, eh?'

'Yeah.'

Martin Griggs's eyes were closing. Ryker leaned sideways and launched a trail of smoke doughnuts towards Griggs's face.

'Pack it up and watch the road! It's a miracle that smoking hasn't killed you!'

'Now don't go all moody on me just 'cause you're tired. Worse than a whining old crone you are.'

Griggs controlled his irritation with visible effort.

'I love horses,' Ryker continued relentlessly. 'I can't get enough of 'em, my little ferret. I'm greedy, Griggsy. I'm a greedy man who likes to be satisfied.'

Griggs said nothing. He'd heard it all before. Many, many, times before. Ryker loved babbling on after a successful job. He couldn't help voicing his ego, mainly at Griggs's expense. Any minute now he'd make his usual crack about video machines, Griggs thought.

As if on cue, Ryker gave another throaty laugh and said with relish, 'Sure beats stealing videos, eh Griggsy?'

Griggs offered a bored grunt.

7

Tony Ryker's big hands swung the wheel this way and that as he went through the gears with practised ease. The travelling horse-box cruised through the tiny villages of Sherwood Green, Huntshaw Cross and Brownscombe. Griggs was hunched down in his seat, dozing.

Time passed. Four more cheroot butts found their way into the ashtray. Ryker kept to his plan of avoiding the main roads and the vehicle bypassed the A39 and skirted the picturesque hamlet of Westleigh.

Suddenly Ryker's forehead puckered.

The piercing beam of the headlights had illuminated a movement in a nearby piece of moorland. Ryker applied the brakes a touch too fiercely sending Griggs catapulting against the dashboard.

'What the heck's going on!' Griggs flared.

The travelling horse-box coasted to a halt in a lay-by.

'There's a shaft-horse tethered over there.' Ryker indicated a piece of moorland. 'It's just begging to be taken, Griggsy.'

Griggs cursed under his breath and pulled himself up to look. His sleepy eyes focussed on a gypsy caravan and a heavy-shouldered chestnut cob of about fourteen hands standing peacefully under a clump of trees. Its back was slightly bowed and its leg joints appeared stiff and swollen with age.

'What d'you want that for? Looks twenty years old at least.'

'I told you, I'm greedy.'

'Crazy more like.' He sniffed and pulled out a handkerchief. 'Just let me rest. I can feel a nosebleed coming on.'

'You're always getting nosebleeds.'

'I'm a born sufferer . . . always have been. Let's get off home. We can do without another broken-down old hack.'

'That hack's worth four hundred pounds on the continent. We've got five back at the mobile, so we need one more to make up the batch. They go over from Harwich in sixes, right?'

Griggs thought for a moment. He didn't like the old horses. They were kept in the paddock at Hele, and they were prone to problems. Unlike the weekly markets for the warehoused young horses, the Harwich shipments for the old crocks were monthly — and that meant extra work. Water troughs to be filled, the odd bit of hay to top-up the outdoor grazing, and, because of their age, the very real risk of illness.

'I hate the old nags,' he whined to Ryker. 'If they get sick it's always me who has to sort out the problem.'

Ryker played with his diamond-studded

signet ring, twisting it round and round his finger. 'Stop complaining. What do you expect me to do, run up a bill with a vet? You've only got to keep them fed and watered until they've left for the knackers yard.'

Griggs shifted uncomfortably and looked at the old cob again. 'What about that gypsy caravan?'

'What about it?' Ryker consulted his watch. 'It's ten past three in the morning. They're not going to worry about us, they'll be sleeping.'

Griggs considered carefully. Doubt, apprehension, confusion flashed across his eyes. He sensed something. He wasn't sure what at first, but as the tiredness cleared, he knew exactly why he was feeling uneasy.

He sensed trouble.

★　★　★

The greyhound stirred. The snap of a twig underfoot sent tiny electrical impulses racing to the nerve ends of Degsey's ears. The ears lifted, then pricked as she listened. There was an uneasy thumping inside her rib-cage as she heard a shuffle of feet outside the caravan. No human would have picked up the noise, but to Degsey's hypersensitive hearing it sounded loud and threatening.

She didn't want to leave the three greyhound puppies snuggled warmly against her breast, but the outside noise had prompted her instincts to race ahead of her rational thoughts. She stood up carefully, easing her long, long legs from under the soft little six-week-old bodies and stretched her muscles, shaking the drowsiness from her body.

Seamus Horrigan was sleeping. A huge patchwork quilt covered most of his face leaving only his pink scalp showing between the thinning strands of grey hair.

Degsey's liquid-brown eyes turned towards her master. She knew Seamus was fast asleep, and recognised the signals. She watched as the quilt rippled with his breathing; saw his chest rise and fall; heard the deep nasal sound of his snoring. She thought about waking the old Irishman with a quick nudge of her muzzle, but dismissed the idea as the voice of Griggs warranted urgent attention.

'Stupid rope,' he was muttering to himself, 'tied with a load of granny knots.'

The chestnut cob named Mister Rafferty looked at Griggs with guarded curiosity as his thin fingers worked at the knotted fibres. Slowly they began to loosen and the rope worked free, rattling the brass ring attached to the tethering stake.

The noise fired Degsey's muscles into action. Her powerful haunches flexed and she sprang through the hinged, flap-like aperture in the caravan's front door, built by Seamus exactly for an emergency such as this.

It was like a bullet leaving a gun. Degsey powered her way through the flap and sailed over the caravan's front wooden steps. Her sleek body speared the early morning air and she landed softly, now treading delicately but purposefully through the lush grass.

Degsey's colour was predominately white, with three irregular small splashes of dark brindle on her body. Her head was a combination of white and brindle, as was her tail — hardly the best of colours for camouflage.

Griggs heard her exit. The flap had banged against its housing and he went rigid, his fingers stiffening around the rope halter. He turned towards the noise, expecting to see gypsies and the twin barrels of a shotgun being levelled at him, but the only movement came from the scurrying clouds in the almost black sky.

Degsey had dropped low, sinews relaxed, eyes fixed unblinkingly on Griggs. It was a proven fact that a grey-hound had the best eyesight of any dog, and Degsey would now use this gift to the full.

Tony Ryker was getting impatient. He'd

lowered the ramp and was gesturing to Griggs to hurry up. A cheroot smouldered fitfully in his mouth.

'C'mon! C'mon!' Griggs urged, clicking his tongue at Mister Rafferty.

Degsey looked from Griggs to Ryker to the travelling box. She glimpsed the other four horses. Three were weaving their heads in obvious distress whilst the fourth blew a fine mist of moisture from nostrils that flared red as it whinnied uncertainly.

With the strange telepathy which existed between beasts, Degsey was aware that the whinny was a cry for help and the same awful fate that had befallen the other horses would soon befall Mister Rafferty unless she acted quickly. She instinctively knew, in her much-too-human soul, that Griggs and Ryker were evil.

'Greyhound!' Ryker yelled, as Degsey broke cover. She veered towards Griggs, every nerve screaming with adrenalin-induced urgency.

Griggs began to run, the broken shambling gait of panic. He still had a firm grip on the rope halter and this forced Mister Rafferty to follow at a rather lumpy trot.

Degsey's lithe body slashed Griggs's legs causing him to stumble awkwardly. He staggered, slithered and swayed, but he didn't release the halter. The manoeuvre caught him just below the knees, but the impact had left Degsey momentarily winded. She fought for breath, spinning round on her front paws, sending damp little divots of grass flying into the air.

'It's coming at me again!' A pulse pounded in Griggs's throat as he appealed to Ryker.

Ryker disappeared into the travelling box, then reappeared brandishing a pitchfork.

'Leave the dog to me,' he instructed, his eyes flashing, his thick hair lifting as he tossed his head in emphasis. 'Just get that horse up the ramp!'

Degsey's lean, muscular form shot towards Griggs. She didn't intend to bite him — it wasn't in a greyhound's nature to be savage — but she would try to use her speed and agility in a bid to make him drop the halter.

She homed in with long, fluid, purposeful strides.

Ten metres.

Five . . .

Ryker was suddenly there, standing between Griggs and the greyhound, holding the pitchfork like a javelin and ready to launch the twin spikes at Degsey's fast-closing body.

She saw him and swerved. The muscles in her forelegs and thighs caused a braking action and the pads of her feet splayed out in an attempt to stop. She very nearly somersaulted, but somehow her thick toenails managed to gouge enough of a grip in the soft turf to keep her upright.

The pitchfork left Ryker's hands . . .

It was a powerful throw. He had been aiming for the shadowy outline of the greyhound's neck, but her sudden manoeuvre had changed things drastically.

Degsey felt a little rush of air on her cheek as the deadly prongs whooshed past her face . . . then a thick clotted cry bubbled in her throat as she felt pain.

Both prongs had briefly lanced her left shoulder, tearing through skin, muscle and sinew and causing blood to streak her leg and puddle in the clefts of her paw. She stood still, dazed slightly, as the pitchfork continued its flight before thudding into the ground.

'Got the dog!' Ryker seemed jubilant. 'Shoulder, I think. Switch on your torch.'

Griggs was still fastening Mister Rafferty into a free stall. He wiped a sheen of sweat from his brow, then bounced back down the ramp. 'Did you kill it?'

'Not sure . . . Can't see properly.'

As Ryker raised the ramp, Griggs unclipped the flashlight from his belt.

Degsey had tucked herself behind the roots

of an upturned tree. She'd flattened her body against it, moulding herself into the tangled wooden tendrils. She gathered both her strength and her wits as she coaxed saliva over her shoulder wound with her long rasping tongue.

Griggs snapped on the flashlight letting the beam rake the grassland around him. It illuminated a patch of turf where Degsey's blood still glistened wetly. The fringe of the beam feathered briefly across the shaft of the pitchfork.

'Can you see the greyhound?' Ryker asked, looking over his shoulder as he fastened the ramp with the little metal pegs.

Griggs had already dashed forward to retrieve the pitchfork. 'No, but I'll find it . . . and then I'll stick it — properly!'

'We haven't got time for games,' Ryker made an impatient gesture. 'Get in the cab before we wake the gypsies. If the greyhound's gone, it's gone.'

Griggs ignored him. The yellow beam from the flashlight rippled over the bark of the upturned tree. Suddenly Degsey was framed in its blinding glare.

'Gotcha!' Griggs's tongue circled his lips.

'Leave it!' Ryker motioned towards the cab. 'You told me earlier not to push *my* luck, so don't push yours.'

No words were going to stop Griggs. He moved forward smelling blood-lust, the pitchfork wavering menacingly in the greyhound's direction.

Degsey watched him come. She didn't move. Her muzzle was drawn back in a quivering vicious snarl, her lips shimmering pinkly as a warning growl began to build in her throat.

Griggs suddenly stopped . . . rooted to the spot.

Something in Degsey's lower jaw was glinting in the beam of the flashlight. It held Griggs mesmerised. Was it a tooth? A sharp canine? His thoughts reeled wildly. Gold. Was it a gold tooth? It was so bright he had to screw up his eyes. He felt a sudden tightness in his chest. His palms were clammy, his throat dry.

Degsey held Griggs's mystified gaze. Her growl deepened as spittle bubbled and drooled over her gums, and down her two lower canine teeth.

Griggs stood transfixed, unable to look away. It was as if the gold glint had a life-force of its own. The pitchfork fell from his fingers as he shielded his eyes with a quivering hand. The tooth, the gold, or whatever, was blinding him, sapping the strength from his body. The glint seemed to bounce into the glare of the flashlight, willing him to extinguish the beam.

He fumbled for the 'off' switch. 'H-help me,' he stammered.

His fingers clawed at the flashlight and the piercing glare flickered and went out. Degsey was plunged into shadowy darkness.

Griggs backed away. Sweat was coursing down his backbone and his legs felt leaden. He paused for a moment, hawking air in his lungs.

Gradually . . . very gradually, things began to stabilise. As he stumbled back to the road his head cleared, the tightness in his chest eased, and he felt his strength begin to recover. He tried desperately to compose his thoughts as he made his way round the back of the travelling horse-box to the cab.

Ryker was behind the wheel. He puffed meditatively on a cheroot. 'Well?' he asked, 'Did you get it?'

'No . . . I didn't.' Griggs slumped wearily into the passenger seat. 'Just drive.'

'You look scared witless.' Ryker engaged a gear and the travelling box moved off. 'I heard the dog growling. Did it go for you?'

'I don't want to talk about it.'

'Frightened you, eh?'

'Not in the way you think. It was weird, Tony, very weird.'

Ryker laughed. 'You're the only weird thing around here, my little ferret.'

Griggs gave a hostile, stubborn stare. 'I'm telling you! That's some sort of devil dog. It's got supernational powers.'

'Supernatural,' Ryker corrected.

'Yeah, that as well. It was spooky. It stopped when I switched off the flashlight.'

'Well it is a gypsy dog,' Ryker said mockingly. 'Maybe it's carrying a gypsy curse.'

'I think it's got a gold tooth . . . I think that's what gives it the power.'

'Gold tooth? What gold tooth?'

'Sharp bottom canine. Left one I think.'

Ryker's face now showed a mixture of amusement and exasperation. 'I suppose the greyhound's now got its slippers on and is reading a paper in front of the fire!'

Griggs's jaw bunched. 'Take the mickey, I don't care, but I know what I saw. And I never want to see that blasted dog again!'

Ryker's brow creased as he glanced in his off-side door mirror. The reflection showed Degsey running at full stretch, keeping pace with the travelling box.

'Looks like you will see it again, Griggsy,' he let the words out gently. 'I don't believe it, but it's following us. Must be after that gypsy horse!'

Griggs gave a grunt of irritation. 'Yeah, very funny, Tony. Ha, ha!'

'Look for yourself.'

'I'm not stupid. Stop trying to be clever.'

'I said *look!*' Ryker's left hand grabbed Griggs's leather jacket and he heaved him across his own body, pushing his face towards the off-side door mirror.

Degsey was still there, muscles rippling, legs just a blur of speed as she kept astride of the vehicle's rear end. Her face showed an intensity of single purpose.

Griggs's lips were bloodless as he glanced from Degsey to the dashboard instruments. 'L . . . look at the speedometer,' he stammered. 'That dog's injured but we're still clocking 38 miles an hour!'

This fact hadn't escaped Ryker's attention. His mind was working overtime on how he could put Degsey's speed and stamina to personal use.

'Flapping tracks.' Ryker scratched meditatively at the growth of bristles on his chin. His jaw had been broken sometime in the past and was lumpy and out of line with the rest of his face. 'A dog with that sort of speed could beat any opposition and make us a pile of cash.'

'Count me out,' Griggs replied without enthusiasm, hunching back in his seat. 'That dog's jinxed.'

Flapping tracks were not registered under the National Greyhound Racing Club and therefore rules and regulations counted for very little. Meetings were held up and down the country, and unlike licensed tracks you didn't have to prove that you were the legal owner. It was done in the name of sport, but large amounts of money changed hands if you had a successful greyhound.

Ryker was driving with fingers steepled, tapping a spoke of the steering wheel with his thumbs. 'I'll be coming back for that dog,' he mused. 'I've got plans, Griggsy.'

'Coming back! When?'

'Tomorrow, maybe. We know it belongs to the gypsy caravan, and that won't be moving far without a horse.'

Griggs shifted his bony shoulders angrily but remained silent.

'That dog's going to make me rich,' Ryker added with a satisfied smile. 'Oh yes, my little ferret. That little beauty is going to make me a fortune.'

As the travelling horse-box negotiated a long bend in the road, Degsey decided on a woodland short cut. She left the tarmac and veered right, slicing through a tangle of bracken, and spanning the width of a hawthorn hedge. An elderly badger crossed her path as the smells of the forest teased her nostrils — the pheasant, the fox, the hedgehog, the rabbit and the hare. She identified each one by its own characteristic scent, remembering all the delicious, secret places where they would be hiding. But this was no time for giving chase or playing games. A voice was pumping in her ears, prompting the same message, over and over again . . . Save Mister Rafferty . . . Save Mister Rafferty . . . Run . . . Run . . . Run . . .

She scooted over wild honeysuckle, heather and prickly gorse, dipped through tractor ruts and across open farmland. She ignored the needle-sharp pains in her lacerated left shoulder and tried to disregard the sticky blood that was drying on her leg. Her thoughts now turned briefly to the love for her three puppies, and her heart gave an involuntary leap. She tried to reassure her motherly instincts that all the frenzied activity at the caravan would have woken her master. Seamus would be comforting them, she convinced herself. They would be safe. Safe, snug, and warm.

'Dog's burned itself out,' Ryker said to a disinterested Griggs. 'No sign of it.'

The travelling horse-box had covered the two miles from Westleigh to the small Swiftly turnoff which led to the beach. Ryker increased acceleration, sticking to the main

22

road which would take him through Barnstaple and on to the hideaway at Hele.

Suddenly, without warning, Degsey launched herself over a five-barred gate and into the path of the travelling horse-box. She stood stock still, panting, staring hypnotically at the faces behind the cab windshield. She was illuminated by the headlight beams like a piece of bizarre theatre.

'Hellfire!' Griggs covered his eyes.

Ryker jammed on the brakes, and the vehicle's suspension groaned noisily as the tyres screamed for traction. He swung the wheel left in a frenzied slide, mounted a grass verge and uprooted some newly planted saplings.

Griggs felt the vehicle right itself and once again pick up speed as it trundled back onto the road. He also heard Ryker exhale in a sigh of relief. Slowly he opened his eyes.

'W-where's the dog?' Griggs peered into the near-side door mirror, blinking uncontrollably. He saw that Degsey had given up the chase and was now padding across the road to the grass verge. 'You shouldn't have swerved,' he stated irritably. 'You should have run it over while you had the chance.'

Ryker increased acceleration. 'What, and kill the goose that might lay the golden egg?'

'I told you it's a devil dog.' Griggs vibrated

with exasperation. 'What's the use, you don't understand.'

'I *understand* you're talking nonsense.'

'Did you see the gold tooth? It must have showed up in the headlights. Did it glint? Is that why you swerved?'

'I told you, I swerved to miss the dog.'

'The tooth *made* you swerve.' Griggs mulled this over as things began to snap clear, like a lens focussing in his head.

'Think, Tony. Did you see anything glint?'

Ryker shrugged and looked uncomfortable. He had seen something shining in the dog's mouth but he wasn't going to admit the fact to his partner. His voice lacked conviction as he said, 'The disc on the collar, maybe. I don't know. I can't remember.'

Griggs shook his head in a slow, exaggerated movement.

'What?' Ryker asked, looking defiantly at him. 'What's up with you now?'

'The greyhound wasn't wearing a collar.'

'Then I don't know.' Ryker's patience was wearing thin. 'I suppose I didn't see anything . . . Alright!'

The big man lit another cheroot and concentrated on the road ahead. He threw a glance that told Griggs if he was nursing any thoughts of pursuing the subject then he was in very real danger of being thrown from the cab.

Griggs breathed a sigh of frustration and tilted his head back as he staunched the beginnings of a nosebleed with a handkerchief. 'Gypsy devil dog,' he muttered.

Degsey watched the fast-diminishing rearlights of the travelling horse-box. It cruised smoothly past Horseshoe Coppice and negotiated the brow of a hill. Then it was gone.

She stood in an exhausted stupor. A pulse was pounding in her throat and she could hear her own ragged breathing. She was weak through the loss of blood; far too weak to make the journey back to the caravan. With her head hanging limply, almost touching her hugely muscled shoulders she took the beach road that led to Swiftly village. She padded very slowly, taking one carefully placed step at a time. Her thoughts centred around Mister Rafferty. She couldn't remember a time without the old cob horse — he had been there when she was a puppy, and there again when she had puppies of her own. He had pulled the caravan mile after mile, strapped proudly between the shafts wearing a harness and huge collar that glittered with silver mountings. He was a true friend to her and her master Seamus. Loyal and faithful.

Solid as a rock. Staunch and dependable. Now this friend had gone out of her life and she felt an overwhelming sadness. She also blamed herself for letting it happen.

She walked. Minutes dribbled away.

To the right of her were sprawling sand dunes studded with tufts of grass which rippled when caught by the wind, and beyond these was the sea and a few flickering lights of human habitation. Degsey's nose twitched as she padded past the dunes. The scent of a hundred or more rabbits sleeping in sandy warrens plucked at her finely tuned senses.

The early morning air smelled salty fresh as she paused at the Swiftly quayside. She passed one cottage, then another, feeling herself inextricably drawn to a large two-storey creeper-covered house where a red chimney protruded boldly on either side, promising warm, cosy fireplaces in winter. It stood in three acres of land which sloped gently down to the beach and lay well back from the road, with a pair of enormous conifer trees flanking a driveway to the front door.

Degsey stood at the entrance, lifting her neck painfully so that her eyes could focus on the latticed white-shuttered windows and their gable-shaped canopies. They were overlaid with oyster shells, pearl side up, and shimmered with a luminescent brilliance in the moonlight.

This was the place to rest.

She sensed it, smelt it, felt it.

Each step was becoming more and more laboured as she made her way past the trees and shrubbery to the porch. She walked under a hanging sign which proclaimed: *'Oyster Gables Animal Shelter'*.

Little pools of orange light seeped from beneath the front door, making her welcome. She lapped gratefully at water from a courtesy bowl placed nearby ... then exhaustion took over.

She folded her legs under her and sank down onto the porch mat. The blood on her shoulder had streaked and caked to a brittle crust, but the pain began to run beyond the wound, surging hotly, then icily, then hotly and icily again, in flashing repetitions that made the heat and the cold feel the same.

She tried to ignore it, telling herself that in a few hours her strength would recover and then she would walk back to her master. Seamus would make things right ... he always did.

She closed her eyes.

Slowly, blissfully, sleep finally engulfed her and she tumbled down the long corridor to oblivion.

2

'Don't they make alarm clocks with bells in them any more?' Sky Patakin asked, her eyes dark and direct.

'Sorry.' Jonathan yawned an apology and took his place at the well-scrubbed pine breakfast table. 'It's only eight o'clock.'

'Spring was down at seven,' Sky continued, looking briefly towards her younger sister. 'We have rules at Oyster Gables, and the animals come first.'

Jonathan was twelve, tall and slender, with short springy fair hair and mischievous blue eyes. 'It's no wonder you haven't got a boyfriend,' he said. 'You're always complaining.'

'There's more to life than boyfriends. They just complicate things. Besides, I'm very lucky to have a job which provides me with a home. Running an animal shelter takes up all of my time.'

'It's not natural. You're nineteen.'

'And that's old is it?'

'Old enough. I've already noticed a few wrinkles.'

Sky made a disapproving face. 'When I

want your opinion, Jonathan Patakin, I'll ask for it.'

The sweatshirt she was wearing matched her tawny hair. She had good bones, a generous mouth and uncompromising eyes. There was a wiry strength in her build, a warm suppleness as she moved purposefully to the old coal cooking range. She broke two eggs into a frying pan alongside the sizzling bacon, tomatoes and slices of frying bread.

Scooter, the shelter's pet boxer dog was having problems ignoring the delicious aroma. He lazily uncurled himself from his basket, padded across the stone-flagged floor and rubbed his face against Sky's legs. He was a fawny red with a flashy white chest, and he had the habit of drooling whenever cooking smells alerted his taste buds.

'Stop slobbering, Scooter ... *No!*' Sky dropped the soft syllable with gentle but absolute finality.

Spring had finished her bowl of muesli. 'Have we any releases today?' she asked Sky, helping herself to orange juice. 'If Beethoven's fit to go, I'd like to help.'

'We could release him today.' Sky flipped over the bacon with a spatula. 'His neck wound's healed nicely, but the badger has the most powerful bite of any wild British mammal ... so I'd rather wait for help. A job like that needs two adults and the new assistant manager should be here shortly.'

'His name's Daniel.' Jonathan pursed his lips to avoid grinning. 'I wonder how big sister will cope with a man about the house?'

Jonathan had seen an official-looking letter pinned to the notice-board in the outside office. The shelter was administered by a charitable trust, and the letter notified Sky that the trustees had appointed Daniel Rusk to fill the temporary live-in vacancy. Not that Sky was too pleased with the decision. She'd hoped for another female to replace her usual assistant, who was away on maternity leave.

'How old is he?' Spring asked, helping herself to toast.

'Eighteen,' Jonathan piped up before Sky could answer. 'He's taken a year out between school and university to gain work experience. He's already spent six months at a safari park.'

'Anything else you'd like to tell us?' Sky flicked back a strand of hair from her forehead and fixed Jonathan with a penetrating gaze. She wore her hair coiled on top of her head in a loose disorderly mass that threatened to come undone at any second.

'He has A-levels in zoological and biological stuff . . . and he's coming from Brighton.'

'Bristol,' Sky corrected, dodging round an

ever-hopeful Scooter and handing Jonathan a plate of eggs and bacon. ' . . . and in answer to your original question, I've no qualms about having a man about the house. It'll make a change . . . It'll be different . . . A new face, and all that.'

Jonathan said nothing, just picked up a fork and took a healthy mouthful of his breakfast.

Spring, who was vegetarian, clicked her tongue dubiously. 'You're turning your stomach into a graveyard.'

'It's my stomach.'

'It's unhealthy.'

'If we were meant to be carrot crunchers we'd have been born with long floppy ears and we'd be hopping everywhere.'

'One in five people in this country refuse to eat meat,' Spring stated.

'Well I'm one of the four who does.'

The opening of the back door quashed further argument as Shack Skinner entered the kitchen. He wasn't very tall but he was stocky and muscular. He was clad in jeans which were beginning to wear thin and fray at the knees, black training shoes, and a tattered denim jacket emblazoned with animal rights badges. He had very direct hazel eyes and curly brown hair and carried himself with a careless ease, his face full of confidence.

This was Shack's third week of a six-month

Job Skills training scheme at Oyster Gables. He was sixteen, currently out of work, and had been sent to the shelter by the Employment Centre at Barnstaple. Sky found him hardworking, flexible, compliant, anxious to learn. He hoped eventually to join one of the mainstream animal welfare groups, but until then he was glad to be getting valuable hands-on training.

'I've mucked out the stables and the donkey pen,' he told Sky. 'And I've checked the aviaries and the animal recovery cages — all okay.'

'Thanks, Shack.' Sky replenished the old cooking range with some more coal. 'Like a coffee?'

'I'd better not. It's my morning to attend the animal husbandry class at Bideford College, so I best be off.' He collected his crash helmet from a wall peg and motioned towards the front door. 'See you after lunch.'

He tucked his thumbs into the waistband of his jeans and grinned engagingly as he passed Spring and Jonathan. 'Bet you two are glad to be away from your mum and dad?'

Spring smiled, crimping her eyes. Jonathan lifted a knife in a sort of acknowledging salute.

Sky busied herself at the sink. 'When you've finished breakfast,' she began, 'I'd like you to feed the small mammals first, then . . . ' She broke off on hearing Shack talking to somebody, or something, at the front door.

'Is everything all right?' she called out.

'You've got a visitor.' Shack's voice came and went, as if he was moving about.

Sky pinched her lips tight before murmuring, 'Oh, good lord, not Daniel Rusk . . . it can't be . . . not this early.'

'A dog,' Shack called back, quelling her fears about Daniel. 'A greyhound bitch. I think she's been injured.'

There was a clatter of cutlery as Spring and Jonathan hurriedly left the breakfast table. Sky unhooked Scooter's collar and lead from a hook on the wall, and all three headed along the hall to the front door. Scooter lumbered behind.

Degsey swayed uncertainly, looking dazed and bewildered as she sniffed gently at Shack's hand. Her body movements were sluggish as she raised doleful eyes towards Sky.

'Out of the way, kids,' Sky ordered, and took over.

Scooter's collar was immediately buckled around Degsey's neck and the lead handed to Shack. Sky ran a practised eye over the greyhound's conformation, her gaze settling on Degsey's injured shoulder. She took a pinch of neck skin between thumb and forefinger and watched as it stayed peaked instead of springing quickly back. A brief examination of the dog's gums revealed a sickly paleness rather than the normal deep pink colour. Her tongue was dry, her eyes sunken and her pulse weak — all signs of fluid loss.

'Has she been hit by a car?' Spring posed the question.

'No, she's been pierced by something sharp . . . probably last night. Two small puncture wounds.' Sky indicated without touching. 'She's dehydrated and weak through loss of blood.'

'Bet she's been dumped,' Jonathan stated. 'Where's the owner?'

'Goodness knows, but we can't worry about that now. She needs warmth and fluid replacement.'

'An intravenous drip?' Shack suggested. 'Dextrose and saline?'

Sky nodded and tapped her forehead with the heel of her hand. 'Can she walk, Shack, or will she need carrying to the treatment room?'

The question was academic. Shack had already cradled one beefy forearm under Degsey's bottom, and the other around her chest. 'She's a big girl,' he said, getting his balance before making his way back down the hall. 'She's incredibly muscular. Must weigh around thirty kilos.'

Sky walked quickly ahead, her thoughts concerned only with giving Degsey correct and speedy therapy.

Oyster Gables Animal Shelter had been set up solely as a haven for sick or injured wild mammals and birds, and Sky was far more familiar dealing with creatures of the forest than administering treatment to domestic animals. As a general rule callers with injured dogs or cats were always referred to the vet's surgery or the animal welfare clinic. This was an Oyster Gables regulation.

Two livery horses and two donkeys were the only exception to the 'wild-life-only' rule. The horses brought in additional income to the shelter in the form of rent; and the donkeys, both now unwanted and formerly used for seaside rides, brought in tidy sums when hired out for local fund raising events.

Sky wasn't used to stray dogs spending the night on the shelter's doorstep. Badgers, foxes, squirrels or barn owls she could handle . . . a sick greyhound posed more of a problem.

★ ★ ★

35

Daniel Rusk had made good time. He'd left Bristol at eight a.m., journeyed via Bideford, and was now turning east onto a minor road which would take him to the Swiftly turn-off. The wheel was smooth under his hands and the tarmac hummed as the tyres cruised over it. He glanced at his wristwatch. It had taken just under two hours to cover the one hundred miles.

Rich, rolling farmland flanked the narrow country road as Daniel's elderly grey Volvo estate car negotiated a roundabout and skirted the hamlet of Westleigh. The sky was blue and cloudless, tinged in the east with a soft pastel hue. The sun shimmered against the windshield eclipsing Daniel's face with a study of contrasts — high tanned forehead, broad cheekbones, and intelligent brown eyes. His dark hair was combed straight back off his forehead and ran to small black curls which lapped over the line of his collar.

He was looking forward to the challenge of Oyster Gables. From working with the largest form of wildlife, he'd now be working with some of the smallest.

'Please report to Shelter Manager Sky Patakin' his job confirmation had said. He'd never worked for a female before. He grinned at the prospect. Sky Patakin. He repeated the name twice, saying it out loud. It sounded nice, unusual.

He didn't mind that the vacancy was only temporary. It suited his plans. In another six months he would be going to study at Exeter University where he hoped to graduate with a degree in zoology.

The road ahead curved into a bend. Daniel was only half concentrating as a pheasant darted out of the undergrowth, and streaked in front of the Volvo. He took evasive action, swerving slightly, clicking his tongue as he watched the bird dive into the cover of a hedgerow . . . then something else flickered at the corner of his vision.

Through some brown-fringed gaps in the hedgerow he could just make out the colourful outline of a gypsy caravan parked in the middle of moorland, and an old traveller sitting on one of the shafts, his head buried in his hands.

Daniel cruised the Volvo into a lay-by and applied the handbrake. He guessed the old man was in need of some sort of help so he made his way towards the caravan.

Seamus Horrigan looked as if his world had just crumbled around him. The shock registered in his pallor, in his obvious distress and the equally obvious effort he was making to control his emotions.

He looked up at Daniel, fluttered his hands in a gesture of helplessness, and asked simply, 'Have you seen them?'

Daniel caught the strong inflection of an Irish accent. 'Seen who? What's happened?'

'Me family. Missin' so they are.'

'Can I help?'

''Tis too late, boy. I've been lookin' since daybreak.' He sighed and fingered a large gold earring which pierced his right ear. 'Mister Rafferty and Degsey be gone . . . 'Tis an awful, awful day in me life.'

Daniel studied the old gypsy's features. It was a pleasant, country face with the winds of the Irish glens etched upon it in a hundred separate wrinkles which mapped the surface of his skin. His thinning grey hair was tied back in a ponytail and a ragged moustache sat above his generous lips. His eyes were flinty blue, quick and perceptive.

'Degsey would never leave the wagon,' he went on. 'Not without reason. Y'see she has the babbies to look after.'

'Babies?'

''Tis so.' Seamus climbed up the wooden steps to the caravan's footboard and opened the top half of the porch doors. He beckoned a perplexed looking Daniel to join him. 'See, there they be. Little lost souls without their mammy.'

Daniel followed him onto the footboard and gazed into the caravan. The Venetian-style shutters to the side and rear windows were closed against the morning brightness causing the linoleum floor to be lined with alternate slats of sun and shadow.

'The wee ones.' Seamus indicated. 'Right next to the policeman in the corner.'

'Policeman . . . ?' Daniel's mind was reeling.

Seamus rasped the bristles on his unshaven chin and managed the semblance of a smile. 'The ole brass Colchester stove there. Sorry, boy, I see so few folk that I be forgettin' you're not used t'travelin' talk.'

Daniel craned his neck towards the stove. There was a locker seat just beyond it and this was covered with a Sheepskin rug. Three pairs of inquisitive eyes turned to face him.

'Jeez, puppies!' Daniel grinned broadly, showing very white, even teeth.

''Tis so, Degsey's babbies so they are.'

'And I thought . . . ' Daniel sheepishly rubbed his nose with the back of his hand. 'So Degsey is a dog?'

'She be a very special sort o' dog. The most beautifullest greyhound bitch to ever walk God's green earth.'

'And Mister Rafferty?'

'Ahh, me old cob horse. Pulls the wagon so he does.'

There was a glint of amusement in Daniel's eyes. He looked at the pups and they looked back at him making tiny squeaky noises. An all-white one licked an all-brindle one's ear, whilst another which was mostly white with three brindle patches screwed up its face, curled its tongue and yawned, before giving a wheezy little bark.

'I can help,' Daniel said. 'I'm on my way to Oyster Gables at a village called Swiftly. It's an animal shelter. We could take the puppies there, and then make enquiries about Degsey and the cob.'

'I'll not be leavin' me wagon.' Uncertainty seemed to flicker in Seamus's eyes. 'Could mount t'days before me animals be found.'

'But you can't stay here . . . you're stranded without a horse. Supposing Mister Rafferty doesn't come back?'

He exhaled slowly, feeling the muscles tighten at the back of his neck. He said nothing.

'Leave the caravan here, locked up,' Daniel suggested. 'Stay at Oyster Gables until the horse is found. They're bound to have a spare room. There won't be a problem.'

' 'Tis kind, but I be the problem,' he said. 'I couldn't do it me boy. Ah sure no, not

40

sleepin' in a proper bed, and washin' wi' new-fangled plumbin' an' tings. Ay, I remember 'em before me travellin' days . . . brass taps wi' hot and cold wrote on those little twisty tings. I'd be a young 'un workin' on a farm at Ballinalacken, a few mile west o' Lisdoon.' He paused, adding with gloomy finality, 'I'll be too old now t'be doin' wi' change. I have me habits y'see, so I'd be fair twizzled stayin' in a proper house wi' me own room an' tings.'

Daniel told him he understood. He thought for a long moment before inspiration hit him.

'Of course.' He pressed his lips together, looking triumphant. 'We'll take the caravan to Oyster Gables. Park it in the grounds.'

'And how will we be movin' it boy?'

'I'll figure that out once we're at the shelter. Perhaps we can tow it . . . I'm not sure yet.'

' 'Tis me home. I'll not live anywhere else.'

'Trust me. I won't let you down.'

The passive resignation had gone from his face; his hands were no longer trembling; his eyes were direct and steady. 'Ay, I trust you me boy. Take us to this shelter of yourn.'

Daniel nodded, pleased with the arrangement. Seamus collected an old corduroy jacket and his pipe from a locker then

41

scooped up the three puppies and handed two to Daniel. His face was immediately caressed by pink tongues which felt like sandpaper as the pups smothered him with moth-like fluttering kisses. For such small creatures they seemed to have legs that went up to their ears. Long, lanky, and dangling.

Seamus secured the porch doors and both men made their way across open moorland to the parked Volvo estate car. Daniel shifted his two pieces of luggage, erected the dog-guard, and set the puppies down on a car rug.

Seamus was having trouble with his front seat-belt. He explained that he'd never worn one before, adding, 'The most mechanicallest ting I've ever driven is a tractor . . . and that was more than fifty year ago, so it was.'

The Volvo's exhaust burbled sweetly as they headed towards the Swiftly beach road. The fair weather; high, scattered clouds and warm temperatures had brought the tourists as well as the locals out in force. They paraded at leisure, cameras hanging from their necks, guidebooks in their hands.

Daniel and Seamus talked during the brief drive. They discussed odd, unrelated things about themselves which fused together to help build a mutual respect. The love and welfare of all kinds of animals was the special link — an ongoing scrapbook of stories filled by both their lives.

'Oyster Gables,' Daniel announced, indicating right before swinging the estate car across the road and between the pair of large conifer trees. He parked beside a motor-cycle and a white Escort van which displayed the name of the shelter in gold lettering.

''Tis the most whimsicallest place I've ever seen,' Seamus admitted, his eyes wide with curiosity as he gazed at the glittering pearl-oyster shells which chequered the gables. ''Tis fine, very fine.'

Daniel nodded sagely, seeing the shelter for the first time. He looked beyond the house to the smooth, golden beach, breathing in the salty, slightly fishy air as he listened to the lapping waves.

'Hello!' Spring's voice brought him out of his happy reverie. Her hair was the golden colour of ripened wheat, long and thick and with a sheen that fell to the lower edges of her shoulder blades. She was bouncy and exuberant and looked slightly older than her eleven years. Her whole face was alight with energy as she asked, 'Are you Daniel Rusk, Sky's new assistant manager?'

'Yes, I am.' Daniel exited the Volvo, prompting Seamus to do likewise. 'And you must be . . . ?'

'Spring Patakin. Sky's sister.'

'Then I'm very pleased to meet you.' He snapped open the estate car's rear door and reached in for the puppies. 'Can you help me with these little rascals . . . they belong to my friend Seamus.'

'Hello, Seamus.' Spring shot the old gypsy a winning smile and gathered two of the puppies into her arms. 'Oh, they're bigger than you think. Are they greyhound pups?'

'T'be sure they are, missie,' Seamus said, lifting the third pup from the car rug. 'Do y'like greyhounds?'

'I like all dogs. We have Scooter, he's a boxer, and then we have . . . well I don't know what her name is, but she's a greyhound. She was badly wounded in the shoulder. We found her this morning.'

Her words made Seamus feel a sudden, almost superstitious fear of asking the most obvious, relevant question.

Daniel had no such fears. 'What colour is this greyhound, Spring?'

'The same colour as the pup that Seamus is holding.'

Seamus was cradling the white pup with the three irregular splashes of brindle. He breathed out long and hard, experiencing a great wave of thankfulness. Dry-mouthed, he said, ' 'Tis Degsey. You've found me darlin' Degsey. Praise be to God and Mary,

44

Peter, Paul and Patrick!'

Wrinkles furrowed Daniel's brow. 'This is marvellous news. What an amazing coincidence.'

'Ach no!' Seamus said, hugging the pup tightly. 'This be no coincidence, boyo. I tink this be Degsey's doing.'

'I don't understand?' Spring glanced questioningly at Daniel. He leaned against the Volvo, his brown, bare forearms folded against the whiteness of his shirt.

'How can it be Degsey's doing?' he asked Seamus.

'Did I not tell you she was a very special dog. Special enough to arrange for you and me t'meet. Special enough to bring us both t'Oyster Gables . . .'

'But I was coming here anyway. The fact that I met you on the road was just a fluke. Call it fate if you like.'

'You didn't have to stop.'

'No, but a pheasant shot out in front of the car . . . and then I saw you . . .'

''Twas Degsey's doing. She can influence tings like, with her mystical powers 'n all. She's had them since she was a wee babby.'

Daniel looked sceptical. He fingered a tiny scar on his forehead which was all that remained of a victorious school rugby tackle.

'We were meant t'find her,' Seamus went

on. '´Twas serendipity, Danny me boy. Oh ay, Degsey leads an enchanted life.'

'What's serendipity?' Spring's eyes sparkled with curiosity.

Seamus said nothing, just lifted his bushy eyebrows into secretive half-moons.

Daniel felt a smile coming to his lips and fought it down. 'I think,' he said slowly, giving a sideways glance to Spring, 'that we've just been listening to some good old-fashioned Irish blarney.'

The front door opened and Sky stepped out into the sunlight. She was wearing a white surgical coat and her long, elegant fingers cradled a mug of steaming coffee. Her skin was shining where the sun had caught it the previous day, highlighting the smattering of freckles across her cheeks and the bridge of her nose.

'I'm Sky Patakin,' she announced, looking Daniel over with sceptical thoroughness as she crossed the forecourt. The words had an educated articulation combined with a vibrant self-assurance. Her smile seemed stiff and formal.

Daniel gave Sky a strong, brisk and no-nonsense handshake. 'Daniel Rusk, I'm very glad to be joining you.'

She saw the greyhound puppies and tilted her head back. 'This seems to be my day for greyhounds. I've just left one in the recovery room. She's supposed to be woozy from the anaesthetic, but she's pining and snuffling at the door . . . It's most peculiar.'

''Tis Degsey.' Seamus's voice sounded relaxed and amused. ''Twas I not just sayin' that the wee darlin' dog knows I'm here.'

'Are you the owner, Mr . . . er . . . ?' Sky queried.

'Horrigan, ma'am. Seamus Horrigan. And Degsey's owner so I be.'

'Well, she can't possibly know you're here, Mr Horrigan,' Sky continued bluntly. 'Not unless she possesses some kind of telepathy. The recovery room is at the back of Oyster Gables. It's soundproofed and has no windows.'

Seamus looked at Spring and winked as he tapped the side of his nose with a forefinger.

'Serendipity,' Spring murmured, remembering the word. Daniel slowly shook his head in confused disbelief.

'The wound,' Sky asked, 'do you know how it happened?'

'I be tinkin' it must be poachers,' Seamus said. 'Me wee girl must've disturbed 'em.'

'And do the three pups belong to Degsey?'

'Ay,' Seamus nodded. 'They be her little 'uns.'

'Then perhaps you'd like to reunite Degsey

47

with her puppies and Mr Horrigan.' Sky turned to Spring. 'Maybe that will calm her down.'

Spring cradled the two pups in one arm and took hold of Seamus's roughened hand. She led him, holding the other puppy, towards the front door. Relief showed in the old gypsy's grizzled features and there was a definite bounce in his step as he tilted his face towards the heavens and muttered some indistinct prayer.

'Is Mr Horrigan a friend of yours?' Sky asked Daniel, brushing a trailing hair back from her forehead.

'No, we met by coincidence. He'd lost his horse and his dog and I just happened to be in the right place at the right time . . . ' He paused, swallowed. 'At least that's what I think happened.'

'Only think?'

'It's all a bit strange . . . especially when you mentioned telepathy. Seamus would have us believe that his greyhound has mystical powers.' He laughed weakly, adding, 'Forget it, I'm beginning to sound like an idiot.'

'Well, it appears to have ended happily enough.' Sky spoke gently — a false sound which made Daniel feel uneasy. He was fairly certain that although she was putting on a polite front, she didn't really want to make the effort of liking him.

'We don't make a habit of taking in domestic pets.' Sky sipped her coffee and continued, 'But the greyhound was found on our doorstep, and she did have nasty puncture wounds in her left shoulder.'

Daniel shuddered. 'Any idea of the cause?'

'I'm not sure, but if I had to guess I'd say she'd been lanced with a pitchfork. The holes were about eighteen centimetres apart, quite deep, and needed four stitches. Her deltoid muscle will be bruised for a week or two.'

As they talked Shack Skinner came round from the back of the house. Sky made the necessary introductions and Shack helped Daniel lift his luggage from the Volvo.

Daniel wanted to be friendly with his new manager, but she seemed determined to make things difficult for him. It was almost as if she resented his arrival at the shelter. He felt a coldness, a flatness in her voice, and she avoided all but the most essential eye contact. Her full lips told him she had a great smile — but he didn't hold out much hope of seeing it.

'I'll have to call the vet.' Sky walked towards the house with long, purposeful strides. 'Dogs aren't really my territory so it's best if he checks her over. He's bound to give Degsey a shot of antibiotics.'

'Oh, right . . . ' Daniel called out, fishing around for something kind to say. 'Thanks for fixing up the greyhound. I'm sure Seamus is very grateful.'

Shack watched her disappear through the front door, then grinned as he turned to Daniel. 'Don't let her manner put you off. She's a bit anti-men at the moment. Her last assistant manager was female so I expect you'll take a bit of getting used to.'

Shack and Daniel each carried a suitcase through to the kitchen. The large room gave Daniel a pleasant feeling of cosiness. The old coal range and a huge pine dresser sparkling with crockery brought back magical memories. It made him think of his grandmother's kitchen during his childhood.

'Shack's an unusual name,' Daniel said, helping himself to coffee and giving Scooter a friendly pat.

'It's a nickname.' Shack lowered his voice to a whisper and added, 'When I was a kid I helped my dad run a hire business on Swiftly beach. It was called the Surf Shack . . . and I guess the name sort of stuck. I was christened Cedric, but don't you dare tell anyone . . . especially Jonathan . . . or you'll ruin my street image.'

'Who's Jonathan?'

'Sky's twelve-year-old brother. They're

from Sussex. He and Spring are down for two weeks of the school holidays.'

'Do you live in?'

'No, I live at Yelland with my dad. My parents split up a couple of years ago. Mum re-married and lives in Yorkshire, but it's no big deal. I usually see her and my new stepfather at least once a year. They've got a camper van and spend holidays touring the West Country.'

'Are you permanent staff?'

'No, part-time Job Skills . . . which reminds me . . . ' He glanced at the kitchen clock. 'I should have phoned Bideford College about three hours ago. A course I'm attending. I'll have to catch up next week. I got rather carried away watching Sky stitch up the greyhound.'

'I'm very glad for Seamus's sake she's alright,' Daniel admitted, warming to Shack's thoughtful and easy-going manner. 'He dotes on Degsey.'

'Seamus being the old tinker?'

'Yes. His caravan's back at Westleigh. He's lost Mister Rafferty, his horse, so I promised I'd think of a way of getting the van back here. He won't live anywhere else.'

Shack's jaw tensed. 'Are you sure the horse wasn't stolen? We've had a load of thefts in the West Country lately.'

'That's possible. It makes a lot of sense.' Daniel tugged at a longish lock of hair as things began to crystallise. 'Perhaps Degsey disturbed the horse thieves . . . You know, tried to stop them and — '

'Got wounded for her efforts,' Shack put in angrily, grinding the words.

Daniel's face darkened at the thought of it and he moved his head in a series of slow, deliberating nods. It certainly fitted the facts as he knew them. Seamus had described the animals as his 'family' so Degsey would be protecting her pups and probably Mister Rafferty as well.

'Any ideas on how we can shift the caravan?' Daniel posed the question. 'My Volvo car's fitted with a tow-bar.'

'Parts of Westleigh moorland can be boggy. I wouldn't like to chance it.'

'The caravan's cumbersome too. It'll be awkward to manoeuvre.'

'We'll use Napoleon and Josephine.' Shack snapped his fingers. 'They're knocking on a bit — fourteen I think Sky said — but she's used them to raise funds for the shelter in the past. She had a load of special harness made up so they could pull carnival floats and suchlike.'

'Horses?'

'No, donkeys! They got dumped on us

when they got a bit too doddery for beach-rides.'

Daniel grinned, relieved. 'Sounds perfect. Can I see them?'

Shack led Daniel through the back door, and across a small yard which passed the office. It was a purpose-built structure, with red bricks to match the house and large roof windows. Pots of petunias and fuchsias stood neatly around the base and one side was covered in trellis-work where creeping plants were encouraged to grow.

Daniel looked past the office to a variety of animal pens, some open air, some not. There was a large concrete yard, several open-sided sheds with their own strip of pasture, a wooden feed outbuilding, storehouse, and numerous fully enclosed breeze-block buildings. Finally, another concrete yard led to some stables and a large paddock. Beyond this was the beach and the far-off foamy sparkle of the sea.

A large external telephone bell shrilled loudly just as Shack turned the handle on the office door. Jonathan was sitting at a computer work-station playing a space adventure game. Coloured images darted across the monitor before being obliterated by a click from a joystick. Shack ushered Daniel inside, and reached for the telephone.

Jonathan beat him to it, snatching up the receiver.

'Good morning, Oyster Gables,' he announced chirpily.

'You shouldn't be playing games on the works' computer ... ' Shack glared at Jonathan and made a throat-slitting gesture.

'Yes, he's here. Who's calling? Hold on.' Jonathan covered the mouthpiece with his hand. 'And you shouldn't be getting calls at work from girlfriends.'

'Who is it?'

'Somebody called Claire.'

Shack flushed angrily and took the receiver from Jonathan's now outstretched hand. He pressed himself into a corner and began a whispered conversation.

Daniel introduced himself to Jonathan, glancing round at the office furnishings. There was a roll-top desk with maps of the area above it, three filing cabinets, a typewriter on a workbench and a small stove with a kettle and two electric rings. A ceiling fan whirred soothingly overhead and one wall was totally dominated by a huge bookcase. A quick scan of the titles revealed veterinary and care-problem volumes dealing with every conceivable wild animal.

'Would you like an Oyster Gables window sticker?' Jonathan was asking, opening a drawer and pulling out various coloured strips of printed vinyl. 'I can fix it to your car's rear window.'

Daniel nodded agreement, pointing to a blue one.

'Sky did a terrific job on the greyhound,' Jonathan went on, his lips parting in a toothy grin. 'If you ever want a button sewn on your shirt she's an expert with a needle.'

'I'll remember that.' Daniel returned the smile, thinking that he seemed very young, very confident.

'Strange about the tooth, though,' Jonathan added matter-of-factly.

'What tooth?'

'Haven't you seen the greyhound?'

'Not yet.'

'W-e-l-l ... ' he dragged out the word, playing Managing Director, swivelling back and forth in a squeaky chair behind the desk and fiddling with the numbers on a cube desk calendar. 'I was assisting with the anaesthetic, positioning the tube in the dog's mouth ... and there it was ... a lower canine ... '

'Jonathan,' Daniel said, a trifle harsher than he'd meant, 'I don't know what on earth you're talking about.'

'A solid gold fang.' He did an impression of a werewolf. It wasn't a very good impression. It reminded Daniel of a tame sea-lion wanting to be thrown a fish.

Uncertainty flickered in Daniel's eyes. He was about to ask Jonathan to explain more fully when Shack cradled the phone.

'The evil swines!' Shack inhaled and exhaled deeply, to defuse his emotions. 'Four livery horses were stolen from Marshwood last night. That was Claire Morgan, a stable girl who works there . . . an old girlfriend. She says they just busted the padlocks and helped themselves.'

Daniel's face darkened as he began to consider various aspects of the situation. 'So Mister Rafferty . . . '

'Was probably stolen by the same outfit,' Shack put in, opening the office door. 'Better not say anything to Seamus — not yet. Old horses can sometimes end up as dog meat.'

They talked over the implications of this fresh development as Shack steered Daniel towards the donkey pen. Most of the outbuildings had auxiliary heat — the small mammal casualties having the comfort of a heated pad under their bedding, the larger mammals an infra-red lamp above the holding cages. In one building Daniel was shown mice, voles and shrews who were housed in small plastic fish tanks with top opening lids, and in another he saw squirrels, weasels, rabbits and hares who were kept either in wooden cages or hutches with small mesh aviaries.

'All casualties,' Shack informed him as they walked. 'Either attacks from predators or victims of road traffic accidents. As soon as they're well enough they'll be released back into the wild.'

They passed deer who had fresh hay as bedding and were kept in a small outside paddock, then entered a breeze-block building housing badgers, foxes and stoats. Here, the cages were built with far more strength. Daniel noted the thick vertical bars as Shack explained that the construction was designed to securely hold even the most cantankerous animal.

Next, Daniel was shown the isolation shed. It was a small structure, but you couldn't enter unless you'd washed your wellington boots in a tray of antiseptic fluid. New admissions were quarantined for 72 hours, Shack explained, so as to prevent the possibility of cross-infection.

Daniel was suitably impressed. At the safari park he'd been used to large compounds with far fewer animals which, apart from the occasional zoo-swap were never released. Here at Oyster Gables, animals came and animals went. With such a large turnover of different species kept in close proximity, space was at a premium so cleanliness and hygiene was obviously of great importance. Every concrete floor and walkway, Daniel noticed, had been hosed clean and there was the sharp tang of disinfectant in the air.

'Napoleon and Josephine,' Shack announced, as they crossed to the donkey pen. He leaned on the securing rail. 'This old pair will shift Seamus's caravan — no problem.'

Daniel fondled the donkey's huge ears, feeling little puffs of vapour pump rhythmically from their nostrils as they sniffed his hand, their velvet lips touching his palm and curling up. He grinned as their tongues rasped against his fingers. They were bright-eyed, alert, and looked in excellent condition for their 14 years.

'Leave it to me,' Shack continued. 'I'll harness them up, then walk them to Westleigh. Should be fun driving the caravan back to Oyster Gables.'

'Will you need help?'

'Nope. I've finished for the day . . . you haven't. And as this isn't strictly shelter business then the boss-lady can't moan.'

'It's appreciated.'

'It's nothing. You go and unpack.'

Daniel lifted a hand in thanks and made to

move off. He paused as a question nibbled at the periphery of his mind.

'Jonathan mentioned something odd.' He turned back to Shack. 'Something about Degsey having a gold tooth . . . ?'

'Oh, that.' Shack shrugged. 'Mmm, I noticed it during surgery.'

'So what did you think?'

'Not a lot. Sky thought it was probably some sort of dental implant. Gypsies can have funny ways . . . they use gold and stuff because of superstitions. Do you think it's important?'

'Not really. Just curious, I suppose.'

Shack gave a lopsided grin. 'Sky said it was a blasted nuisance because it was glinting in her eyes under the surgery lights. Powerful stuff, gypsy gold.'

★ ★ ★

'Degsey's not havin' any antibiological injections, so there's an end to it! The dog 'twas raised wi' the fruits and remedies o' the forest; herbs, plants and roots all provided by the good lord above. Chemicals be no good for her. I'll make the wee dog better meself. You'll not be lettin' no veterinary touch her with no hypo-thingamy needles. Ah sure no, no, never. Never!'

Seamus was in full vocal flow as Sky listened to him in white-lipped silence. Daniel also remained quiet, not wishing to voice an opinion and probably put his foot in it on his very first day. He stroked Degsey's silky ears as her moist nose nuzzled his legs, seeing for the first time the greyhound bitch which had dominated most of the morning's conversation. Her mouth was closed, so he couldn't see the tooth, but she had a very beautiful face, he decided, admiring her body markings and the solid thickness of her muscular physique. She had a deep chest with plenty of lung-room, strong neck, powerful hindquarters and she stood high on her feet. All excellent qualities, Daniel thought, remembering a lecture he'd attended at college on animals that were purpose-built for speed. She had a surgical dressing on her left shoulder and walked with a slight limp, but this didn't appear to be causing distress.

Scooter was lying on the kitchen floor, flicking the odd glance at his basket and wrinkling his forehead even more than usual to portray his most wounded expression. Spring had put Degsey's three pups in his personal wicker retreat, and his big brown eyes were expressing disapproval.

'Mr Horrigan,' Sky peaked her nostrils and spoke coldly, defensively. 'Earlier I cleaned

Degsey's wounds and surgically stitched them. Now I'm advising, most strongly, that she has an intramuscular antibiotic injection to fight any remaining bacterial infection. I could do it myself, but I'm not too familiar with greyhounds. Therefore, the ratio of drug to body weight should be administered by a qualified vet.'

'Have you ever seen creatures find wellness by seeking out a cure for themselves?' Seamus posed the question.

'Of course.' Sky shifted her weight from one foot to the other, looking slightly angry as she absently inspected the palm of her hand.

'Then you'll be knowin' that when a dog grazes on grass 'tis most certain it has a stomach ache.'

'I've seen that.' Spring's blue eyes, bright as a squirrels, swerved to Sky. 'Scooter sometimes eats grass.'

''Tis nature's way.' Seamus pulled a pipe from the pocket of his old corduroy jacket and sucked on the stem. 'Oh ay, animals know about these tings.'

'No smoking, Mr Horrigan, please!' Sky tut-tutted disapprovingly.

'It's not lit.' Daniel came to Seamus's defence, then wished he hadn't as Sky glared at him, her eyebrows moving in annoyance.

'You may smoke in the office,' she said to

61

Seamus, trying to sound benevolent.

Seamus nodded, put the pipe away and moved to the back door. He fingered his earring thoughtfully, then turned. 'Degsey has mystical powers and wi' me help she could have healed her own wounds, but . . . ' He raised his hands in submission before Sky could jump in. 'I'll not let you be tinkin' I'm an ungrateful old man, because full of gratitude I am. You did a fine job . . . very fine, 'tis true. But me wish now is that you leave poor Degsey to me own healin' ways.'

'She's your dog, Mr Horrigan,' Sky's words trickled out reluctantly. 'I've told you the facts, but the decision in the end is your own.'

Seamus looked comfortable with the compromise. He exited the back door and Degsey limped outside with her master.

Daniel watched Sky's every feature as he explained about Shack, the donkeys, and the caravan. She smiled at him, but it wasn't very reassuring.

'So Shack's bringing the caravan back here?'

'If that's okay with you?'

'Of course. It can stay on the forecourt till Mr Horrigan's ready to leave us.'

Daniel looked pleased and slightly confused. Sky's tone seemed pleasant enough and she was actually agreeing with something he hadn't asked permission to do.

'Sorry to plunge you in the deep end, Daniel,' she went on, not sounding sorry at all. 'But we have a badger who's due for release today. Do you feel confident enough to handle it?'

'His name's Beethoven,' Spring said amiably. 'He's always getting into scrapes and he seems to spend more time at Oyster Gables than he does in the wild.'

'Yes . . . I'll take him . . . You're the shelter's manager,' Daniel agreed, nodding to Sky. 'I'm here to learn.'

'Good,' she replied curtly. 'Remember that fact and we'll all get along famously.'

'What were your favourite animals at the safari park?' Spring asked.

'I liked the monkeys, chimps and gorillas. I worked a lot with the orang-utans . . . so they'd have to be pretty high on my list of favourites.'

'No exotic animals from far-away lands at Oyster Gables,' Sky put in quickly, pressing her lips together. 'I'm afraid we're far more basic . . . much more down to earth.'

'I'm looking forward to the challenge.'

'We're all very pleased you're here.' Spring smiled, glancing quickly at Sky from under long lashes.

'Yes . . . yes, of course we are.' Sky didn't

sound particularly convincing. She turned the conversation back to business. 'So use the Escort van and take Beethoven to Scamper-buck Ring at Fremington. You'll find it clearly marked on the map in the office. That's where he was rescued — he was in a male supremacy fight and came off worst. We always try to release badgers exactly where they're found, and there's an established sett in that part of the woodland.'

'Shouldn't I wait until dusk?' Daniel queried.

'Normally, yes . . . but Beethoven knows the release routine backwards. Daylight won't worry him. He's a regular casualty at Oyster Gables . . . an easy going old boar who won't give you any aggravation.'

'I'll take you to the sett.' Spring crinkled her nose at Daniel.

'I'm afraid not,' Sky tried to sound reasonable. 'I'll need you and Jonathan to help me with the midday feeds.'

'What about Hannah and Megan, can't they help you?'

'You know they're only volunteers who assist during the school holidays. Besides, they're not due in until later.'

'Will you be going to Scamperbuck Ring?'

'No, just Daniel.'

'Oh, mosh! You said earlier . . . ' Spring

frowned at her sister and fidgeted awkwardly. 'You said that Beethoven had a powerful bite and it needed two adults to — '

'Yes, I know what I said, but I've reconsidered. I'm sure that someone who has safari park experience won't have a smidgen of trouble with a plain, old badger.'

3

Beethoven decided to make life difficult for Daniel. The lid of the transporting cage had been unlocked and was now hinged down flatly on a piece of mossy turf awaiting the badger to make a dignified exit.

A dash for freedom, Daniel assumed.

No such luck.

Daniel had positioned himself in a clearing, well inside Scamperbuck Ring. He'd carefully studied the office map and knew that his location was within a 100 metre radius of the badger sett where Beethoven had been found. Spring had made him a few written notes and he double-checked these as he stood at the rear of the cage. All okay, he was in the right spot . . . brook to the left, broken stile to the right, and a far-off fringe of silver birch trees straight ahead. He began stamping his feet and making shooing noises in an effort to encourage the badger to exit the steel-barred container.

Sky had equipped him with a short wooden rod, and this was meant to be used as a prodding tool in times of difficulty. Daniel crouched and tried rasping it across the top of the cage, then when this had no effect he resorted to a metallic banging which was loud enough to wake the dead.

The dead maybe, but not Beethoven.

The badger looked inquisitively out of the escape aperture, but seemed in no hurry to go anywhere. He weaved his long snout back and forth, twitching his whiskers at the warm smell of sun-kissed leaves and forest grasses. His dark, tiny eyes were barely visible, blending in with the facial black stripes which ran sleekly up from his nose to the bristles of his ears.

Daniel peered through the top bars of the cage and eyed the badger cautiously. Beethoven looked back at him with a 'I'll-leave-in-my-own-good-time' expression . . . but time wasn't on Daniel's side. This was the first real duty he'd been given at Oyster Gables, and he wanted to make a good impression on Sky. Arriving back late at the shelter would only give her cause to complain and prompt her to ask awkward questions.

Beethoven's rump was now towards the rear of the transporting cage, so Daniel took the stick and gave a hefty prod into the badger's fleshy fur. He didn't expect such a violent reaction, and wasn't really aware that he'd let his fingers stray briefly between the bars. The badger's coat immediately bushed out and he turned with lightning speed, the great power in his jaws making an audible clacking sound as his teeth snapped high up on the stick, catching the tip of Daniel's thumb.

'Grief!' Daniel cursed as pain lanced up his arm to his elbow. He felt the sudden stickiness of blood. It was seeping into the right thumb-piece of the stout, protective gloves loaned to him by Spring.

He instinctively jumped back, pulling off the damaged glove, and temporarily staunching the blood flow as best he could with the tail-piece of his shirt. The crimson redness blossomed out on the white cotton material . . . making it look far worse than it was. A brief examination of the injured thumb showed a small piece of flesh missing from under the nail. No more than a bad nick, Daniel consoled himself, deciding to make things easier by tearing a portion of cloth from his shirt-tail and winding it round his thumb.

Beethoven still remained obstinately in the cage. Daniel watched as, with a flick of the animal's neck, the stick was tossed disparagingly out of the escape hatch.

What now? Daniel was turning a few options over in his mind when, much to his amazement, the answer presented itself in the form of a big sow with three members of her family. The female badger and her four-month-old youngsters emerged from a large burrow and stood tentatively in front of the fringe of birch trees.

Daniel stood stock still, knowing that the big sow was granting him a very rare privilege. Badgers were nocturnal creatures and seldom, if ever, did they venture out in daylight hours. Daniel watched as the group were illuminated by a shaft of sunlight which coiled down through the branches and glistened in shimmering tints off their sleek, stripy faces.

Beethoven spotted his family immediately. The sow called to him with a soft whickering sound and he stretched out his thick neck to respond in kind. He carefully edged his way out of the escape opening, shook himself, and gouged wavy little furrows of earth in the mossy grass as he lazily extended his powerful front claws. Daniel felt a glow of excitement course through his body as he watched the badger's greeting ritual. He momentarily forgot the throbbing in his thumb, just grinned and breathed a sigh of relief as Beethoven finally lolloped away to join his family group. He saw them exchange playful nudges, scooting round in affectionate circles before disappearing into the shadowy depths of Scamperbuck Ring.

Daniel lifted the empty cage and closed it. The torn shirt hanging raggedly out of the waistband of his trousers jerked him back to reality. He looked and felt a total mess as he tucked the shirt in the best way he could before tying the ripped piece of material more firmly around his thumb. He pulled the glove back on and made his way to the Escort van, trying to ignore thoughts of Sky's reaction when she saw his dishevelled state.

It was Shack Skinner who spotted Daniel first. Seamus's caravan dominated the forecourt of Oyster Gables, and Shack was leading Napoleon and Josephine across to the shelter's large double gates. He waited as Daniel parked the Escort van. He held a donkey by a halter in each hand, and had numerous pieces of harness and leather tack slung across his chest and over his broad shoulders.

'I got a load of dodgy looks from motorists, but the donkeys were well up to the job,' he called out as Daniel crossed to meet him. 'Seamus, Degsey, and the pups are inside the caravan. You wanted to see the old boy's face when we rolled up. He could hardly believe it.'

'Great stuff. Well done.' Daniel pulled off

his right glove and displayed his bloody thumb.

'Beethoven?'

'Beethoven,' Daniel affirmed and explained briefly what had happened at Scamperbuck Ring.

'You look in a state.' Shack eyed his tangled shirt.

'I need a shower.'

'Have you had a tetanus shot?'

'I had a booster just before I left the safari park.'

'The boss-lady will clean up the bite. You know, antiseptic and stuff. She's in the office.'

Daniel nodded listlessly.

'Unless you're into alternative medicine.' Shack displayed a wicked grin. 'Seamus has got all these herbs and potions in the caravan. He's mixing some up for Degsey. I bet he'd love to play doctors with your thumb.'

Daniel grinned back. 'I'll take my chances with Sky,' he said.

They went their separate ways. On his walk to the bathroom Daniel stopped at his bedroom to pick up a clean denim shirt. It was a large, low-ceilinged room, neat and clean, with a freshly vacuumed smell to it. There were three china geese flying across the pale blue emulsion paint of one wall and covering the floor was a faded carpet patterned with huge swirls. An over-stuffed chintzy arm-chair dominated one corner of the room and a big old-fashioned wardrobe rested against a wall which creaked as he trod on a loose board beneath the carpet. A single bed sat under the window and, lying there at night, you could hear the sea hissing and thundering in.

Daniel had a hot shower and changed into his fresh denim shirt before grabbing a cola from the kitchen fridge. He made his way to the office, and on pushing open the door, wondered faintly who or what would be colder, Sky or the fizzy drink.

On this occasion it was the drink.

'Hi, Daniel,' Sky smiled, deciding to be nice. 'Everything go alright?'

'Beethoven's back with his family,' Daniel said.

Sky gave a relaxed nod, stretching her legs against the work-station's footrest. She was transferring handwritten information from a box of record cards onto the computer database. Each mammal or bird casualty was initially issued with a card stating where and when it had been found, what injuries it had sustained, the treatment it had received, plus notes on drugs and diet. Finally, it was given a pet name and a release date.

'So Beethoven was released at Scamper-buck Ring on . . . ' She checked the desk cube calender, and tapped in the date using the computer keys. 'Oh, heavens!' She glimpsed the makeshift dressing on Daniel's thumb. 'You've hurt yourself.'

Daniel wasn't sure whether she was genuinely concerned or just putting on a practised caring voice. She had this strange way of saying one thing, whilst her eyes expressed either nothing, or faint amusement.

She crossed to the first aid box hanging on the wall by the bookshelf and picked out some items. 'Sit,' she ordered, pointing to the work-station chair.

Daniel sat.

He could smell a faint trace of a tantalising perfume as she leaned over him, expertly working with scissors to cut free the shirt bandage from his thumb. In no time at all she'd cleaned the bite, swabbed it with iodine, applied some antiseptic cream and dressed it.

'You'll live,' she said brightly, her long fingers plucking at the collar of his shirt, straightening it . . . then she looked quickly away, almost embarrassed by the familiarity of her actions.

'There are two portions of shepherd's pie in the oven,' she announced, now using her

73

flat professional voice. 'Plenty for you and Seamus. Jonathan and Spring have both eaten and I've fed Degsey and the pups.'

Daniel murmured a thank you and stood up. He was certainly getting used to her mood swings and wasn't going to say anything to jeopardise his lunch. Sky smoothed a wandering lock of hair back behind her ear, trying to appear unperturbed.

'See you for a ride later,' she said as he reached the door. 'We usually exercise the livery horses on the beach at weekends.'

'Fine.'

'You *can* ride?' The question was asked with a tinge of sarcasm.

Daniel was an excellent horseman, but he said, 'I expect I'll get the hang of it.'

He left Sky staring unblinkingly at the computer monitor, her fingers busily rat-tatting at the keyboard.

★ ★ ★

Seamus Horrigan's caravan was lavishly carved and gilded both inside and out. It was a sight to behold and sat on the forecourt of Oyster Gables with all the splendour of an ancient galleon in harbour.

The oak spokes of its huge wheels were painted in the brightest of bright yellow:

twelve spokes on the front wheel, fourteen on the rear. These supported thick iron tyres and were secured to the fore-carriage and hind-carriage by hubs with gleaming brass ends.

Its roof was pure white lead which dazzled when caught by the sun; its body a hot maroon colour decorated with gold, red and green. Two brass lamps, a candle in each, were fixed either side of the door.

There was a mass of exterior carving, punctuated with tiny cut-glass mirrors; and the shafts, once carried proudly by Mister Rafferty, were embellished with lines of colour varying in thickness to emphasise their perfect form.

The caravan's porch-brackets were carved in wych-elm in a three dimensional design of flowers, leaves and entwined stems. The shutters were bright yellow with sunflower decorations, and the door panel exhibited a St George-killing-the-Dragon theme against a background of spade-shaped leaves.

For Jonathan and Spring it was a magical, breath-taking world. A true cave of delights.

They sat on a locker seat beside a chest of drawers opposite the stove. Both listened wide-eyed as the old gypsy recounted travelling stories. He talked of the old times as he used a pestle and mortar to grind up herbs, tree bark and other substances into a thick paste. Degsey and her pups were curled asleep on a skin rug at his feet.

'Ah to be sure, Mister Rafferty could pull me wagon for eighteen mile a day,' Seamus reminisced. ''Tis a nomadic life at that, and I've crossed and re-crossed the Irish Sea many times.'

'Will you ever find Mister Rafferty?' Jonathan asked.

'Who can say, Jonathan boy.' He lifted his shoulders in a despairing gesture. ''Tis for sure I miss the old devil. To grip the reins in yer hands and hear the rumble o' the wagon beneath you, listening to the clink and rattle o' the bit and harness links . . . 'tis the most beautifullest o' feelings.'

'You have a lovely home.' Spring began talking in rapid little bursts. 'Can I live here? Can I tour the country with you and Degsey? Oh, please say, yes.'

'So you want t'be a traveller?' Seamus added a few drops of coloured oil to the mixture. 'A traveller, a tinker and a gypsy.'

'Can I be all three?'

'T'be sure you can. Is Seamus Horrigan not all three himself?'

'And can she drive your caravan?' Jonathan asked.

'Wagon, boy, wagon! A true traveller never says caravan.'

76

'How big is the wagon?' Jonathan corrected himself. 'You know, size and weight and stuff?'

''Tis called a Reading and she be about twelve feet includin' the front porch, and about thirteen-and-a-half feet includin' the back porch.'

'What's that in metres?'

'Don't know metres.' He lifted grey wisps of eyebrows. ''Tis seventy year since I went to school.'

'How about weight?' Jonathan pressed on relentlessly.

'Lordy, lordy, boy, you ask enough questions to vex a saint! She be thirty hundredweight . . . and before y'be askin' her age, she be older than your da' and his da' before him. Built in the early nineteen-hundreds so she was.'

Seamus had finished his grinding and mixing. He replaced pieces of twig, bark, herbs, and vials of oil into different drawers of a tiny, veneered tabletop cabinet, then turned his attention to Degsey.

'Up, me wee darlin'.' He smiled easily, coaxing Degsey to her feet. The greyhound yawned, showing a glint of gold, looking up at her master with expressive, trusting eyes.

'When will you tell us how she got her tooth?' Jonathan asked anxiously.

Seamus stroked the edge of his jaw. 'You be curious to know o'Degsey's mystical powers?'

'Bursting,' Spring admitted.

'Well, we don't want you to burst, wee Spring,' he said, after a moment's reflection. ''Tis a long story. 'Tis the most magicallest story you'll ever hear . . .'

'So you will tell us?' Jonathan ran a tongue over dry lips.

'Ay, tonight, after dark. 'Bout ten o'clock. Ask permission to stay up and we'll drink tea round the wagon. Bring Sky, the donkey man and Danny boy.'

Spring and Jonathan exchanged grins of delight.

'I'll ask Sky to make some Cornish pasties,' Jonathan said.

'I be likin' the pasties.' Seamus nodded approval. 'Will y'sister be mindin' the task?'

'Of course not,' Jonathan told him. 'She makes the best pastry in Swiftly.'

'Jus' so long as she pricks it t'let the wee spirits out.'

'She always pricks it,' Spring put in, 'but I'll remind her if you like.'

'Good, good, then pasties it be. I'll be cleanin' Mister Rafferty's harness tonight. 'Tis a weekly chore, but must be done . . . even though the ole fella not be wi' us.'

'Can we help?' Spring and Jonathan asked in unison.

'T'be sure you can. It will be hard work, mind.'

Both nodded eagerly.

Seamus got on with the task in hand asking them to hold Degsey still. He carefully peeled Sky's dressing from the greyhound's shoulder noting that the wound was weeping slightly under the stitches. Degsey didn't flinch as he replaced it with a fresh dressing smeared with the sticky substance he'd been preparing. He spoke of the healing properties of the balm, telling Spring and Jonathan that the dog's limp would be cured within 24 hours.

'Hello, all!' Daniel stuck his head through the top half of the front porch door. He held up some slices of bread and two steaming plates of shepherd's pie. 'Grub up, Seamus.'

'By Jaminee 'tis me pal, Danny.' The old Irishman sniffed the air as a delicious aroma wafted into the caravan. 'I can smell me favourite . . . Meat and p'tetters.'

Seamus ushered him in, clearing the pestle and mortar from the table to make room for the food. He produced two sets of knives and forks from a drawer and stuffed a napkin into the front of his shirt.

'Place 'em down, Danny me boy.' He

smiled gleefully, rubbing his hands. 'And let's be tuckin' in.'

Daniel sat on the locker seat beside the stove, opposite Spring and Jonathan.

'Any news o' Mister Rafferty?' Seamus asked.

Daniel gave his head a mournful shake. 'None as yet.'

The puppies were still fast asleep but Degsey stretched her neck forward and sniffed at Daniel's shoes. Her tail slashed at the air like a whip as she moved her firm-muscled body under his hands, craving love, begging for approval.

'So what have you been doing to her?' Daniel asked, noticing the fresh dressing as he stretched a hand to caress Degsey's ears. 'What magic potion have you been brewing?'

'Crushing bits of old leaves and trees and stuff,' Jonathan put in, 'with a club-shaped thing in a bowl.'

'Fruits o' the forest,' Seamus said, taking a forkful of shepherd's pie.

'Which are?' Daniel showed genuine interest.

Seamus spoke between heaped mouthfuls of pie, explaining how he'd used the herb comfrey to promote healing of the skin wound, creosote bush to help Degsey's body fight infection, calendula oil to reduce fever and relieve pain, and the bark of an elderberry tree for its mystic properties.

''Tis good to plant an elderberry near your house,' Seamus added, his eyes flickering with amusement as he glanced at Spring. 'It'll bring you good luck and protect against disease.'

'Sounds tosh to me,' Jonathan declared positively. 'When I'm ill I go to the doctor.'

'Ay, very wise, Jonathan,' Seamus agreed. 'But don't you be forgettin' that folklore and plant medicines have been wi' us since the beginnin' o' time.'

As if to reinforce Seamus's point, Degsey crossed to her water bowl and began lapping gently at the contents.

'And does the wee dog not agree wi' me words?' Seamus's flinty eyes beamed with self-congratulation as he nudged Daniel to look. 'The water contains essence o' white willow bark, so it does. A gypsy cure t'help bring fever down and quell pain.'

Daniel couldn't resist smiling as he finished his meal. He wiped his plate clean with a slice of bread . . . then wished he hadn't. Seamus glimpsed the bandage on his thumb.

'Hurt y'self, boy?'

'A nick. It's nothing.'

'Will you not be lettin' old Seamus treat it? It should have been bathed in garlic . . . 'Tis the bestest ting to disinfect a wound.'

'Sky sorted me out.'

'Antibiologicals?'

'No, iodine, and antiseptic cream. It's healing nicely.'

'And you be sure you wouldn't like me to take a wee gander?'

'Very sure . . . thanks.'

Seamus nodded slowly, accepting the verdict. Daniel watched the old gypsy savour the last few forkfuls of his pie, then let his gaze wander over the sumptuous fittings of the caravan's interior. He hadn't noticed much on the last occasion due to the panic over Degsey's disappearance.

The cabinet work was of dark-red polished mahogany with the glazed cupboard shelves. trimmed with bobble-fringe and held in place by brass-headed studs. To the right side of him was the old Colchester stove with its mirror-polished brass front, curved mantel shelf, and floor rail guard which housed a brass shovel, tongs and poker. Both front corners of the caravan had a small bow-fronted cupboard displaying china, and immediately opposite him was a chest of drawers. His eyes were drawn to a splendid brass lamp, fixed to one side of the window, and Seamus followed his gaze calling it, 'Me Angel lamp.'

At the back of the caravan were the two-berth sleeping quarters. These comprised bunk beds; the top bunk just below the rear window.

Daniel was immediately impressed by the quality of the fine linen sheets and pillow cases fringed with crochet work. The upper bed, for guests, had a satin-covered eiderdown; the lower, which Daniel presumed was Seamus's berth, a patchwork quilt. The curtains were lace-edged velvet, looped as drapes, and tied back to the bedposts with gold-tasselled cord.

Daniel was suitably impressed. Everything sparkled with long hours of cleaning, and the rich colours of the woods could only have been acquired with decades of polishing. The furnishings, Daniel mused, would certainly have done a large country house proud.

'Me belly be full.' Seamus broke into Daniel's thoughts, rubbing his moustache with his napkin and reaching for his pipe. 'God bless the kitchen and all belongin' to it.'

'Sky cooked your pie,' Spring told him. 'I had cabbage and mushroom hotpot.'

'Do you not be likin' the pie o' the shepherds?'

'She's a veggie freak.' Jonathan sniffed disapprovingly.

Seamus tapped out his pipe with a slow,

questioning deliberation. He frowned at Daniel, not understanding the words.

'Spring only eats vegetables,' he explained. 'No meat.'

'What do you do when you're travelling?' quizzed Jonathan. 'Do you hunt and trap things? Have you got a gun?'

'No gun,' Seamus said, noticing that Spring was glancing uneasily at him. He pondered before saying, ''Tis vegetables I eat, given t'me by farmers in trade for a few hours work.'

Spring smiled, giving a nod of approval.

He exchanged a sideways glance with Daniel and began filling his pipe. He could have told Jonathan how he relied on Degsey to catch him a rabbit or hare — or even the odd pheasant or grouse, but he decided on discretion in front of Spring.

'You must eat meat ... sometimes.' Jonathan pressed Seamus for an answer.

'Oh ay, I have a bit on occasion ... like today,' he hedged. 'I be admittin' I'm not a true veggie freak like y'sister.'

'Thought not.' Jonathan gave a grunt of satisfaction.

All heads turned towards the front porch as steps rattled on the footboard. Seamus stood up, looking relieved at having escaped any further quizzing on his eating habits.

'Mr Rusk?' A girl's head peered over the top half of the porch doors. 'Mr Daniel Rusk?'

Her face was delicately shaped and framed with short, fair hair. She had a fine forehead, ears with almost no lobes, and lips that were sardonic and lively. Daniel guessed her to be around fifteen.

He rose to greet her and she introduced herself as Megan Fairchild, one of Oyster Gables' volunteer helpers.

'Sky says to tell you the horses are tacked up and ready for your ride,' Megan said.

Daniel had virtually forgotten about exercising the livery horses. As he said his goodbyes to Seamus, Jonathan and Spring, he pondered on whether Sky's mood would be sociable, or whether he would be met with her more common arrogant self-confidence.

They picked their way across the concrete yard and past the storehouse. Megan spoke knowledgeably about the various cases of injured animals and birds she'd encountered at Oyster Gables then guided Daniel towards the breeze-block outbuilding which housed the small mammals. There, he briefly exchanged smiles with Hannah Fullerton, another of the shelter's young volunteers. She had springy, red-gold hair, a freckled complexion, and wore a waxed jacket and green wellington boots about four sizes too large. He left them hosing down a flagstone path and pressed onto the stables.

Sky was sitting astride a grey mare which pranced around the curve of the building, tail up, neck arched, the nerves in its flanks twitching as it halted snortingly to face him.

'You're not dressed!' She looked down at his jeans and shoes and made an indistinct sound that conveyed annoyance. 'I expected as much. You'll find a pair of riding boots and a hard hat in Sir Galahad's box . . . I had to guess at the size.'

Daniel glanced at her pale cream jodhpurs, having presumed she'd be wearing them, and admiring the way they suited her. He also liked the wild way her tawny cascade of hair spilled from under her hat. She looked scrubbed, shining and radiant and wore only a hint of make-up.

'The mare's called Excalibur.' Sky made some effort at politeness, assuming Daniel was admiring the horse rather than her. She slipped her feet from the stirrup irons, stretching her legs. 'Whenever you're ready, Daniel.' She smiled tolerantly. 'Take your time.'

Daniel made his way to Sir Galahad's box. The horse was a showy chestnut gelding with a lot of Arab in him. He sported a white blaze and three white socks and stood around sixteen hands. His ribs were well sprung, giving way to broad, muscular hindquarters. Daniel found himself being nuzzled playfully as he pulled on the boots and fastened the hard hat.

Compared to the rest of the animal units, the stable area appeared run down and impoverished-looking; comprising three loose boxes which had seen far better days. They weren't really needed, Daniel thought logically, knowing that the shelter didn't deal with horses apart from the extra funds generated by the livery money. He gazed round at the cracked mangers, the lopsided doors badly in need of re-hanging, and the powdery moss-covered brickwork which had probably been standing for hundreds of years. There was fresh hay in the hay-nets, and uncontaminated straw on the floors. Everywhere was clean and tidy — he couldn't fault it — but unless the Oyster Gables Trust were prepared to spend money upgrading the structure, then the natural elements would force the stables into total disrepair.

Sky was waiting for him by the paddock. She leaned forward in the saddle, her fingers working loose the metal keeper that held the five-barred gate. Daniel coaxed Sir Galahad to move at a fluid, collected trot just as the gate swung inwards. He held the reins almost loose, his manner implying security and confidence.

'See you on the beach!' Daniel fortified himself with a deep breath and grinned wryly. Suddenly he was enjoying himself.

A mountain of chestnut haunch swung past Sky's face as Sir Galahad responded immediately to the pressure of Daniel's heels, springing straight into a gallop. The big horse was literally flying as he ate up the turf, crossing the paddock at full stretch with Daniel coaxing him towards a gate on the far side. Through the wisps of streaming mane Daniel could see the beach and the sea beyond. Terns, herring gulls and guillemots bobbed on the creamy foam of the breakers.

Sky's pulses were racing wildly as she sent Excalibur forward into a faster pace, encouraging the mare with soft, supportive words. She began closing on Sir Galahad's rump, preparing to rein in as Daniel pulled up at the gate . . .

Only he didn't.

Daniel's blistering gallop continued.

He was perfectly balanced and his hands were moving with extraordinary force and rhythm as he concentrated on Sir Galahad's pacing, correcting the horse's leg action slightly before pushing forward and effort-lessly spanning the gate . . .

It was a glorious jump, with the chestnut's heels showing the wooden framework plenty of daylight. Sky felt an angry flush run up her cheeks as she reined in, watching the big gelding's hooves dig into the soft sand as Daniel cruised smoothly to a halt. Sir Galahad was quivering and steaming as Daniel swung the horse round jubilantly to face her.

Sky bubbled with anger as she unhooked the gate and gently walked Excalibur through to the beach. Her hazel eyes contracted their irises as she met Daniel's gaze.

'Of all the stupid, irresponsible, hare-brained . . . ' She broke off huffily. 'You could easily have injured that horse.'

'Nonsense, he loved it.'

'T-that gate's never been jumped before. You were just showing off.'

'I felt Galahad wanted to do it.' He fingered the damp hair off his brow. 'Is it against the rules?'

'No, of course not.'

'Then no harm done.'

Sky looked away and smoothed imaginary wrinkles from her jodhpurs. 'Peggy would have never behaved like that.'

'Who's Peggy?'

'My previous assistant manager.'

'Well Peggy's not here, and I am . . . only in a temporary capacity, I know. So you'll just have to put up with my impulsive little ways until Peggy returns.'

She flushed defensively, her chin uptilted. This was the first time she'd seen a tinge of annoyance in his expression and she didn't like it. She wanted to reply . . . to perhaps apologise for her anger. Certainly a small voice inside her wanted to tell him it had been a brilliant jump — a well-judged piece of riding — and that he was obviously a good horseman . . . but common sense dictated that she hold a strong line and say nothing.

'Relax, Sky, it's a beautiful day so enjoy it.' Daniel remained cool and unruffled as he jogged Sir Galahad on.

It wasn't easy to shake off her aloofness but as her face softened she managed to portray a ghost of a smile. For the first time in a long while, she found herself appreciating some male company, so she relinquished her tracking position and eased Excalibur along-side to join Daniel. They trotted forward in the sheltered bay, reaching the sea and then skirting it, letting the lacy foam of salt water gurgle around the horses' fetlocks. Small waves combed the sleek silvery beach, sucking back and shifting pebbles and tiny marine creatures into nearby rock pools.

'What's this place called?' Daniel was very impressed.

'Delight Cove.'

'Delight Cove.' He repeated the words, squinting into the sun and puckering his lips into a silent whistle. 'It certainly lives up to its name.'

Sky indicated a strip of breakwater which ran from the far side of the paddock to the sea. 'Oyster Gables own this section of the beach. We're very lucky. It came with the house.'

The promenade was alive with people. All wore T-shirts, or delicate summer dresses, or swimming costumes. Sun cream was liberally applied as temperatures nudged 30°C. The public beaches were rapidly filling with glistening, oily bodies. Hotels and guest houses along the seafront wavered in the heat haze.

Sky and Daniel went from trot to canter, doing various fun manoeuvres with Excalibur and Sir Galahad as they caught the spray from the breakers, experiencing an exhilarating sense of freedom. They were totally unaware that their every move was being intently watched by two men from the quayside.

'Two little beauties. One chestnut, one grey.' Tony Ryker lowered his binoculars.

'They're nice lookers. They'll fetch good money at auction.'

Ryker had returned to the area with the aim of capturing Degsey. On finding Seamus and the caravan gone, he'd dragged a reluctant Martin Griggs onto Swiftly for some sun and sea air.

Griggs flicked an indifferent eyebrow and sucked ketchup off the drooping end of a sausage wrapped tightly in a long, soggy roll. 'You don't know where they're stabled,' he murmured, biting into a third of the bread, his words puffing around the load in his mouth. 'They could've come from anywhere . . . might even have been brought by trailer.'

'Wrong, my little ferret. It's a private beach.'

'So?'

'So the beach belongs to an animal rescue place called Oyster something or other. They keep a couple of livery horses to make a bit of money on the side. I've passed it many times in the car. It's just up the road.'

Griggs said, almost inaudibly, 'So you plan to steal 'em?'

He nodded. 'Sir Galahad and Excalibur.'

'You know their names . . . ?'

'I have my contacts.' He fiddled with his diamond-studded signet ring, twisting it. 'I listen and learn, Griggsy. I never turn a deaf ear when there's dishonest money to be made.'

Ryker put the binoculars back to his eyes and indicated the various ways of gaining rear entry to Oyster Gables. His tattooed forearm made a sweep as he pointed out the breakwater and the beach gate which led to the paddock, informing Griggs that the stable area was obscured by the roofs of other buildings.

'Are you barkin' mad?' Griggs made a sound of disgust in his throat and looked uncomfortable. 'I'm not climbing over breakwaters and crossing beaches just to get two horses. The sea can be unpredictable. What about tides and stuff?'

'Are you frightened of the water?'

'You know I can't swim.'

'You don't wash much either. Are you allergic to the liquid that comes out of taps?'

Griggs bridled. 'I shower once a week — and sometimes I use your deodorant. So don't try and be funny.'

Ryker ignored him, deep in thought as he tapped a fingernail against his teeth. 'The beach method is less dangerous,' he mused. 'You're well away from the house. I'll get a local timetable that lists the tides.'

'I'm still not doing it,' Griggs rasped. 'I'm liable to get a nosebleed, so you'll have to think of something else.'

Ryker's eyes roamed over the roof of Oyster Gables, restlessly seeking focus. He fingered his lips uncertainly. 'Okay, we'll use our normal routine . . . front entry. With two horses on the premises there has to be easy access.'

Griggs rolled the empty mustard-stained hot-dog wrapper between his palms and tossed it into the sea. 'When do you plan to get 'em?'

'Soon. I've had a tip off that three livery horses are being kept temporarily at a farm at Penhill. That's just down the road from Swiftly, so we'll make a night of it.'

Griggs's bony shoulders lifted moodily. 'Thought we were supposed to be looking for the gypsies?'

Ryker set his jaw. 'Well we couldn't find them, could we? No caravan at Westleigh . . . nothing.'

'I'm glad they're gone — especially that blasted devil dog.'

'Luckily we haven't had a wasted journey.' Ryker gave a muted chuckle and lit a cheroot with a book-match. He watched Sir Galahad and Excalibur trot back to the paddock gate, before adding, 'Two more for our collection, my little ferret. And they're ours for the taking.'

4

It was a clear, warm night, and for the past hour Seamus, Spring and Jonathan had been carefully cleaning every section of Mister Rafferty's strap harness.

There was a mountain of it.

They'd used a bucket of water with sponges, some bars of saddle-soap, and a can of silver polish with cloths. Spring and Jonathan had sat beside Seamus on the footboard, listening as he explained the purpose of each piece of tack. Spring had cleaned the bridle fitted with blinkers and snaffle bit, while Jonathan had struggled with the huge collar and thick leather traces which connected onto a back-strap in order to hold up the shafts. Seamus finished saddle-soaping the crupper strap, which went around the base of the tail, then all three had got to grips with the mass of leather reins.

They were four-and-a-half metres long, hand-stitched and decorated with glorious silver mountings. When the leather had been thoroughly cleaned, three pairs of hands had worked briskly away with the polish, buffing and brightening every little silver crest and motif. It was a painstaking business but both Spring and Jonathan had thrown themselves energetically into the job and eventually the reins glittered and twinkled as Seamus lit the candles in the two carriage lamps which flanked the front door.

The cleaning now complete, Seamus had stowed the gleaming harness in the pan-box at the caravan's rear end, and sent Jonathan and Spring off to wash and change at the house.

Seamus did likewise, putting on a clean white shirt with stiffened collar, beige corduroy trousers and suede waist-coat. The black belt of his trousers was punctuated with silver diamond and heart motifs, similar to those on Mister Rafferty's harness. He changed by the light from two candles, fixed in brass mounts attached to the bed posts. He carefully combed his long thinning wisps of grey hair, fastening them back in a pony-tail with a bright strip of cloth, then he consulted his pocket watch. Almost ten o'clock . . . time for him to go through his nightly ritual of lighting the paraffin Angel lamp.

It was a tradition of travellers that the quality of the Angel lamp reflected the personal pride taken in owning a caravan. Seamus Horrigan's lamp was particularly splendid — having been cast in solid brass, and displaying a flying cherub holding Pan-pipes to its mouth. The oil reservoir was made from ruby red cut-glass, and the globe had been hand-painted with forest scenes.

Seamus carefully removed the globe and the chimney and put a match to the wick. As the flame licked at the air he replaced the glass pieces and adjusted the burner so that a warm, flickering glow illuminated the caravan's interior, spilling out through the porch doors.

Degsey was curled on the skin rug with her pups, but when her eyes sensed the light from the Angel lamp she stretched, turned her head, and stared unblinkingly into the globe. She'd watched her master do this nightly since the day she'd been born, and this evening was no exception. Seamus looked at the lamp with almost hypnotic reverence and took a few seconds to thank the Almighty for giving him another day.

Two of the pups remained sleeping, but the third, whose markings matched her mother's so closely, stretched her head into the soft hollow of Degsey's throat and followed her gaze to the Angel lamp. This pup, the only bitch in the litter, had been fittingly named 'Little Degsey' by Spring.

Seamus gathered some clean, but old, woollen rugs from inside a locker seat and exited the caravan. The light from the Angel lamp bloomed out of the nearside window illuminating the grass verge alongside the parking area. Seamus placed rugs down at strategic points along the verge so that wherever his guests sat the caravan's footboard would be in full view.

Earlier, Spring and Jonathan had taken the still-limping Degsey for a short walk and gathered driftwood from Delight Cove for the fire. Now, freshly washed and changed they were back erecting a metal tripod which Seamus called a 'chittie' to support the large copper kettle. It held four and a half litres of water and Jonathan had struggled to fill it.

Seamus built a nest with tightly twisted strips of newspaper and tented some pieces of driftwood in a close-knit pattern around it.

'Plenty o' air,' he advised Jonathan and Spring, his aged, craggy face seamed with wrinkles as he carefully added more sticks to the arrangement. 'Build it right and the old kettle'll boil faster than usin' any modern gas ring.'

Earlier, Daniel had placed a large piece of aluminium sheeting in front of the caravan to stop any scorch marks penetrating the forecourt's tarmac. It had last been used on Guy Fawkes night and it was now serving a dual purpose as Seamus put a match to the wigwam structure of driftwood. The fire caught immediately, popping and crackling as it sent up a spiral of sparks which danced like silvery spirits in the warm night air.

The noise of a motorcycle heralded the arrival of Shack and his girlfriend Sophie. They removed their crash helmets and crossed the forecourt like two wavering silhouettes, haloed against the camp-fire's brightness.

''Tis the donkey man and his wee girl,' Seamus announced, extending a leathery hand as Shack introduced Sophie.

She was seventeen, dark and plumpish, with green eyes that held a glow of intelligence and a sparkle of fun. She asked to look inside the caravan and Spring gave her a guided tour, taking the opportunity to load up a tray with seven mugs, a huge teapot, tea caddy, sugar, milk and tea-spoons. Shack's biceps bulged beneath the short sleeves of his tightly stretched black shirt as he carried the tray down the wooden steps. He placed it beside Seamus, then he and Sophie sat with knees clasped on a rug on the grass verge.

The fire was blazing nicely and the water in the kettle was already beginning to hiss. The caravan loomed majestically behind Spring and Jonathan, its bright colours picked out by the flames as they sat around the chittie, replenishing the fire with pieces of driftwood.

Shack and Sophie asked countless questions about Seamus's lifestyle, and the old gypsy recounted many interesting episodes from his travelling past. He made enough money to feed himself, Degsey and Mister Rafferty, he told them, by stopping here and there and doing odd jobs. If really pushed for some odd pennies, then he would rely on his ancient craft of making baskets from willow and strips of split hazel, and sell them by the roadside. Shack replied jokingly that Seamus had better teach him the art, so that he could save enough cash to rebuild the stables.

'This looks cosy.' Daniel emerged from the blackness and joined the fireside group. He was wearing a short-sleeved cotton shirt, worn outside lightweight trousers.

'Hello, everyone.' Sky was a few paces behind him with Scooter at her heels. She held a mobile phone in one hand and a carrier bag in the other and smiled easily at Seamus as she stood by the chittie. 'Freshly cooked Cornish pasties,' she told him, taking foil-wrapped little parcels from the bag and distributing them to all. 'They're piping hot, so be careful.'

''Tis more than kind.' Seamus's face creased with delight as he juggled the heated silver wrapper between his fingers. 'I be

100

admittin' I'm a poor cook when it comes t'pastry.'

Spring was eyeing Sky speculatively. Sky turned to meet her gaze.

'And before you ask,' she said, moving her head in a series of slow, thoughtful nods. 'Yes, your pasty contains soya and vegetables, and yes I did prick them as instructed.'

Spring bobbed her head approvingly and looked at Seamus. His lips, under the ragged moustache, pursed into a smile.

The lid of the large copper kettle was beginning to rattle under the pressure of steam. Seamus lifted it from the chittie, thoroughly warming the teapot before adding tea from the caddy. It was now Jonathan's turn to fill the pot and following Seamus's instructions he placed it close to the fire to infuse.

'Do you need any help?' Sophie called out, wrapping an arm tightly around Shack's waist.

Seamus signalled that all was well, but Sophie's actions prompted a question from Spring to Daniel.

'I expect you have tons and tons of girlfriends,' she said, her eyes mischievous. 'But is there a special one somewhere?'

Daniel gave a small, disconsolate grin. 'There was one . . . an administrative assistant at the safari park. She emigrated to New Zealand about three months ago. Her parents were going to live there, so she went too.'

'Don't embarrass, Daniel,' Sky said, quietly pleased with the answer. 'You shouldn't ask personal questions . . . It's very rude.'

A smile played around the corners of Jonathan's lips. 'You could say girls travel to the other side of the world to avoid Mr Rusk.'

Daniel grinned at that and Sky wanted to smile too, but for the sake of correctness she tut-tutted and gave Jonathan a fierce look, keeping her amusement under control.

She, Daniel and Scooter crossed to a rug on the grass verge, Sky curling her legs under her as she sat. She was wearing thonged sandals which looped behind her heels, jeans and a white, lace blouse buttoned high on her throat. Her hair had been pulled upwards and secured by a small beaded band.

Seamus checked the fire and then carefully stirred the tea leaves in the pot. He counted five revolutions with a long-handled spoon one way, and then five revolutions the other way before asking Spring to fill and distribute the mugs. He stood upright, wincing slightly as he stretched his old bones. Cleaning the harness and the general bustle of the day had prompted some rheumatic aches in his joints and he walked stiffly to the caravan, resting against one of the shafts before making his way up the steps.

Degsey, as if on cue, padded out onto the porch and lay on the footboard beside her master. Seamus sat with her head resting on his thigh, fondling her ears, silhouetted by the feathery shadows cast by the light from the Angel lamp. She gazed up at him with nothing less than worship in her dark, intelligent eyes.

'Any news of the lost horse?' Sophie asked, genuinely concerned as she took a bite of her pasty. Shack gave her a reproving nudge, remembering the call from Marshwood Stables and wishing she hadn't asked the question.

'Ahh! Nothin'.' Seamus's gentle face clouded over as he stared at the empty shafts. 'And miss him so I do. Mister Rafferty be pullin' me wagon for the last seventeen year, and he be hard t'replace.'

'Can't you buy a new one?' Jonathan asked, peeling the foil from his pasty. 'A younger horse would pull your cara ... I mean ... wagon much faster.'

''Tis true, but 'tis not youth I be wantin', 'tis knowledge,' he said, blowing out his moustache with a sigh. 'A 'sperienced horse knows how t'get a heavy wagon rollin' by usin' his own weight. Gentle, y'see, young 'un . . . Gentler than a summer breeze in the glens of Antrim. Mister Rafferty would lean slowly forward in his harness 'til he felt the traces tighten . . . then off . . . smooth as moleskin. No jerkin' old Seamus, Mister Rafferty be tinkin' . . . no rattlin' his master's weary bones . . . ' He paused, toying with his unlit pipe, his eyes fixed on a distant point in time. When he spoke again it was almost if he was talking to himself: 'Oh ay, the old devil were even too clever t'let Seamus use the brake . . . might strain the old boy's back, he be tinkin'. So, on a steep hill he'd use his muscles by sittin' back in the shafts, takin' the full weight o' the wagon on himself.'

There was a few seconds' awkward silence. Glances were exchanged as nobody knew exactly how to respond.

Eventually Daniel forced a hopeful note into his voice and said, 'We'll do everything to get him back for you, Seamus. That's a promise.'

''Tis faith in you I have, Danny boy. Forgi' me for gassin' on . . . Me brain be fair twizzled wi' the loss.' He crinkled some life into his flinty blue eyes and took a huge mouthful of his pasty.

'Tell us about Degsey,' Jonathan piped up.

'Me wee dog?' Seamus feigned ignorance

as his hand caressed Degsey's long, athletic neck. 'So what do you want t'be knowin'?'

'The tooth! The tooth!' Spring's blue eyes were fixed pleadingly upon Seamus.

'We . . . ll,' he began, 'then I shall have to be startin' at the beginnin'.'

He finished his pasty, took a gulp of his tea and launched into the story of Degsey's birth. He explained that Degsey's mother was a retired racing greyhound called Deggoran Odyssey whom he'd adopted when she was just three years old.

'She be a kind, faithful bitch,' he went on, 'but she not be wanted by her owners 'cause her racing days be over. So I took her and loved her as me own.'

'What about Degsey's father?' quizzed Shack, leaning forward with interest.

'An Irish Derby winner. One o' the finest racing dogs in the land . . . They romanced each other whenever they met; while I be doin' a few odd jobs at Shelbourne Park race-track in Dublin. The little devils must've canoodled because the result be me darlin' Degsey.'

Every time her name was mentioned, Degsey nestled her chin more firmly against Seamus's thigh, watching the sparks burst from the fire and blinking sleepily at her master.

'So how many pups did Deggoran Odyssey have?' Sky asked.

'	'Twas only the one.' Seamus's eyes were misty, faraway. 'Me wagon be stopped for the night near Knockgrafton at the foot o' the Galtee mountains . . . 'tis the beautifullest o' places and me wee girl went to sleep outside. As the sun went down she lay on a rich green carpet o' four-leaf clovers stretching as far as the eye could see . . . It be a sight to behold. 'Twas magical. Then — ' He paused, swallowed hard, tears pricking his eyes as he relived the memory. 'Then . . . me wee girl had trouble givin' birth. It be hard for her . . . Somethin' be wrong. There be more than one pup, but she hem . . . hemor . . . '

'Haemorrhaged,' Sky said softly.

'Ay, 'twas terrible.' He drew a ragged breath. 'She managed just the one . . . Degsey . . . then, god-love-her she died wi' me fingers strokin' her face . . . In me arms she be when the Almighty finally called her name and took her up to heaven.'

The words held everyone spellbound. Shack and Daniel both swallowed large lumps in their throats, Sophie's small white teeth worked on her lower lip and Jonathan noisily gulped down his tea trying not to show his inner feelings. Tears came so suddenly to Spring that she couldn't stop them. She felt the wetness on her cheeks and made no effort to conceal the emotion that Seamus's words had aroused. She ran to the old gypsy and buried her face in his lap, feeling Degsey's soft breath against her face.

'Now, now, me wee Spring.' Seamus touched a finger to the dusting of freckles on one cheek, catching a shining wet drop. ' 'Tis not me wish t'be upsettin' you with me stories.'

She looked up at him, then turned her head to meet Degsey's soothing gaze. The dog's huge brown eyes were entrancing. She felt the tremor in her shoulders gradually subside and the tears begin to dry as an almost over-whelmingly calming inner contentment swept through her body.

There was a momentary silence. Everyone seemed puzzled as to what to do next.

'I think I've worked out how she came to be called Degsey,' Sky eventually said, trying to lighten the highly-charged atmosphere. 'You took the 'DEG' from Deggoran and the 'SEY' from Odyssey to make an unusual first name.'

'That's the one!' Seamus nodded. 'Me darlin' girl be named after her mammy so she is.'

'How did you wean her?' Shack asked.

'By hand usin' a dolly's bottle. She be on

solid food after 'bout three week.'

'Have you ever raced her on a track? She looks as if she could run a blinding race.'

'I not be believin' in it. 'Tisn't nat'ral. Racin' dogs spend their lives in kennels . . . so 'tis no life at all. As long as old Seamus has his health from the good Lord then Degsey will run free t'chase the wind.'

'And the pups?'

'Ay, them too.'

Jonathan had put on a manly front. He topped up his mug from the teapot and coughed a couple of times to clear the thickness in his throat before saying, 'Please go on. Don't leave the story about the tooth half told.'

Seamus carefully filled his pipe with herbal tobacco from an old leather pouch and tilted his head to Spring. She met his scrutinising gaze with slightly bloodshot eyes which begged him to continue. His brow creased as he exchanged a quick glance with Sky who nodded approval.

He struggled on, a little painfully. 'I buried Deggoran Odyssey under some wild daffodils, where the sun peeps over the Galtee mountains . . . but 'twas strange. As I lifted her from the carpet o' four-leaf clovers they be pale . . . not dark green . . . and the paleness exactly matched where she lay.

'Twas like a pattern o' her body. Says I to meself, she must've sapped and drawed all the power from the clovers whilst bearin' wee Degsey. All the god-given Irish serendipity had been passed to me new wee babbie girl.'

Everyone looked at everyone else. Spring was wide-eyed, staring at Degsey, Sophie's jaw hung slightly open as she gazed at Shack, Daniel blinked in astonishment at Seamus, and Sky's mouth had gone dry as she fixed Daniel with a perplexed look.

Daniel said tentatively, 'So is that why you think Degsey has special powers?'

'Be sure, 'tis one reason . . .'

'And the other?' Daniel pressed.

Seamus put a match to his pipe and puffed out a cloud of fragrant smoke. Slowly, his hand moved down Degsey's neck to her muzzle. He lifted the spittle-wet pouch of pink flesh to expose her sharp, bottom left canine tooth. All, apart from Daniel and Sophie had seen it before, but now in the shadows thrown up by the firelight; in the eerie tautness that still pervaded the air, the soft glint of gold made everyone stare.

Seamus said, 'A cluricaun knocked out me wee girl's tooth when me wagon pulled in near Donegal on the banks o' Lough Swilly. 'Twas a spiteful, evil little devil . . . screechin' curses. 'Twas jealous o' Degsey's good fortune.'

'Who or what is a cluricaun?' Sky asked, intrigued.

'A banished relative o' the leprechauns,' he told her, his voice liltingly soft. 'A lazy cousin or twin. Oh ay, I see him clear as I'm seeing you. A slouchin', jeerin' little person in a green jacket and red cap. He saw Degsey be sleepin' so he swung his wee hammer. Crack it went on her tooth . . . breakin' it clean. Planned so it was, 'cause it not be her milk tooth. The mischievous cluricaun had bided his time . . . waited five month 'til her permanent teeth be fully growed.'

Spring shifted her position, snuggling closer to Degsey so that she was cushioned against the softness of the greyhound's warm body. Degsey sniffed Spring's hair and swallowed contentedly.

'Why would the little man want the tooth?' she queried, gazing up at Seamus.

'To steal some o' the luck. To make a talisman or charm to hang in his den, m'be . . . 'Tis fact they be corrupt and sinful little varmints.'

'So you had an implant made of gold?' Sky ventured the question, giving a drooling Scooter the last piece of her pasty.

'Ach no!' Seamus stroked the edge of his

jaw and permitted himself a smile as he sucked on his pipe. 'Not that I know what an implant be . . . but the tooth be Fin's doin'.'

'Fin?'

'Fin the leprechaun. He be an elder, and seen the cluricaun's antics so he had. He'd been watchin' over little Degsey since we left Knockgrafton, guessin' that the cluricaun be up t'mischief. He knew about the luck from the clovers and he knew Degsey be special.'

'We've read about leprechauns at school.' Jonathan pressed his lips together thoughtfully. 'They're not real. They're sprites or elves or something. They look a bit like those plastic gnomes you buy for the garden.'

Shack grinned and even Daniel had difficulty suppressing a smile. Sky glanced from Scooter to Seamus, flicking a doubting eyebrow.

'So y'not be believin' in leprechauns at all at all?' Seamus looked at Jonathan, tapping the bridge of his nose with his pipe stem. 'You be tinkin' old Seamus be imaginin' Fin's visits t'be sure?'

'Well I . . . ' Jonathan hesitated, then smiled warily. 'No, I'm not sure . . . I suppose if you say you saw him, then you must have.'

'What was Fin wearing?' Spring broke in, fascinated by the story, her eyes huge and bright and quizzical.

'Well, let me tink . . . ' Seamus puffed meditatively on his pipe as he collected his memories. 'He be all in red so he was . . . Ay, leprechauns always wear red, 'cause that be the colour o' wizardry. His coat had seven rows o' buttons, with seven buttons in each row, and his hat be three-cornered and sewed with gold lace. Leprechauns be shoe-makers so Fin's shoes were grand t'be sure . . . soft scarlet leather sewn t'gether with huge silver buckles. 'Twas the splendidest wee fellow you could wish t'see, he was.'

'How tall was he?' Sky asked with a dubious but polite smile.

'He be about a span and a quarter tall.'

'Span?' Sophie looked inquiringly at Shack, who shrugged.

Seamus demonstrated by spreading the fingers of a calloused hand. He explained that a span was the distance between the tip of his thumb and little finger.

'Fin was a very little man,' Spring said with assertive innocence.

'T'be sure there, leprechauns be the littlest people who have fallen from heaven and landed on earth.'

'Have you seen them making shoes?'

'Not seen, little Spring, but often heard 'em. When me and Mister Rafferty be pulled up for the night, I be laid in bed many a time listenin' t'leprechauns playing music on pipes, flutes or fiddles . . . and hearin' the tap, tap, tap of the elfin hammer as they be busily makin' shoes.'

A grin momentarily disturbed Sky's impassive features. She turned to Daniel, asking softly, 'Are we supposed to be taking this seriously?'

Daniel glanced from Spring to Jonathan, then from Shack to Sophie. Nobody appeared to be taking it as a joke, or the lunatic ramblings of a senile old man . . . and certainly no-one looked bored.

'I think we should just enjoy the story,' Daniel said, with emphatic assurance, pulling his legs tight to his chest and linking fingers around knees. 'Everyone else seems to be.'

'But it is *only* a story?'

'Is it?' Daniel threw the question back at her.

'Oh, I don't know what to think.' Sky shifted uneasily, shrugging her narrow shoulders.

'Fin spoke to me in the Gaelic,' Seamus continued briskly, watching Jonathan place the remaining pieces of driftwood on the fire. 'Ah yes, the wee man promised t'make Degsey's tooth as good as new by usin' leprechaun gold.'

'It *is* very shiny,' Spring remarked.

'Leprechaun gold be the most enchantedest and powerfullest gold in the world. 'Tis precious. It be mined a tiny speck at a time and the tooth be built up wi' wee slivers, day after day, week after week.'

'It must have taken ages,' Jonathan suggested.

'Oh ay, two month o' work. Fin added the golden fragments each evenin' while Degsey be asleep. He would arrive at me wagon wearin' his little leather apron and carryin' the littlest of hammers and a file. He'd work until the early hours, bangin', filin', and shapin' so he would.'

'Where did the gold come from?' Sophie asked, intrigued.

'Secret wee mines, missie . . . well hidden from us mortals. 'Tis not meant for us t'be findin' 'em that is. Fin and his siblings would work all day extractin' the concealed particles o' gold. T'be sure his family be very industr'ous little people.'

'And when the tooth was complete,' Spring added glowingly, 'Degsey became a greyhound with mystical powers.'

'That's so, she got her luck from the clovers and her special strengths from the leprechaun gold. She leads a charmed life t'be sure.'

Seamus banged the remnants out from his

pipe by tapping it against the footboard. Grey layers of fragrant, herbal smoke hung in the luminescent firelight.

Sophie, was unsure whether Seamus was about to continue. On impulse, shyly, she found herself asking, 'How exactly do Degsey's powers work?'

Both Spring and Jonathan seemed to visibly grow a few extra centimetres as they held their breaths, gazing unflinchingly up at the old gypsy's weather-beaten face, waiting for him to answer.

' 'Tis an energy or force . . . but I not be rightly knowin' how it works,' Seamus admitted mildly. 'I do know that Degsey uses her serendipity to take care o' her old master, and it's got me out o' a scrape many a time. 'Tis an unpr'dictable ting . . . but it occurs sure enough it does. Ay, there have been some strange happenings . . . and most times she has t'be smilin' so the sunshine or a bright light can glint off her tooth.'

'But dogs don't smile,' Jonathan put in.

Seamus's pouched eyes regarded him with amusement from under the shaggy brows. 'T'be sure they do, young 'un. Have you never seen wee Scooter smile an' all?'

'I've seen him pant when he's hot, or curl up his lip in a growl.'

115

'And when he pants can you see his tongue?'

'Yes.'

'His bottom teeth?'

'Of course.'

'Then 'tis most likely you be confusin' some o' his pants wi' some o' his smiles.'

'Hmph.' He frowned and thought it over. 'I — I suppose it's possible he might have smiled . . . sometimes.'

'O' course he has. Does me darlin' Degsey not be givin' old Seamus lots o' smiles?'

'So when she was injured,' Spring gulped as a thought flashed in her mind, 'she used her special powers to bring you to Oyster Gables. I remember that her tooth was glinting under the surgery lights . . . Sky was stitching her shoulder and she complained that it was spoiling her concentration. That must have been the energy working.'

Sky exchanged a knowing glance with Shack. Both remembered the incident well.

Spring raised herself on an elbow and gave the greyhound an affectionate hug. The dog turned to gaze at her, her lower jaw dropping and quivering with excited curiosity as the scent of a rabbit wafted in on the night air. 'She's doing it now,' Spring announced glowingly. 'Look everyone, she's smiling!'

Sky's mobile phone was resting on the rug

116

next to Scooter. It suddenly trilled for attention.

'Oyster Gables Animal Shelter,' Sky said putting the instrument to her ear, listening, then adding, 'Yes, all right. We can be there in ten minutes.'

'Problems?' Daniel asked.

'That was Roy, a petrol attendant from the garage we use at Muddlebridge.' She stood up and stretched. 'A fox has been hit by a vehicle and taken refuge in a gap along-side the forecourt.'

'So we're needed?'

'Very definitely.' Sky turned to Seamus and made apologies for leaving early, then she asked Sophie to take care of Spring, Jonathan and Scooter until she returned. 'Shouldn't be much more than half-an-hour,' she added with her usual brisk efficiency.

Shack was already on his feet. 'Do you need my help?' he asked cheerfully.

'Daniel and I can cope . . . besides you're not supposed to be working this time of night. You'll get me in trouble with the Job Skills people.'

He ran ahead, pulling keys from his pocket as he reached the shelter's padlocked front entrance gates that led to the yard. 'As it's a fox then you'll need a holding cage, the Grasper and the protection of some trapper's mitts,' he called back. 'I'll get them.'

As used by dog-catchers, but equally effective for wild animals, the Grasper was a simple device consisting of a flexible noose which protruded from the end of a hollow pole. Slid around the neck of a potential biter it enabled the user to bring the animal under control from a safe distance and therefore minimised the risk of injury.

Sky and Daniel wove their way past the Escort van to the side-door of the house. They kicked off their shoes and quickly changed into wellingtons. Sky collected her first aid case from the hall table, and within seconds they were both back outside.

Shack had loaded the holding cage and the Grasper and was closing the van's rear doors. 'You're ready to go,' he said, giving a couple of taps on the roof as he handed two pairs of protective trapper's mitts to Daniel.

Sky was already at the wheel as Daniel slipped into the passenger seat. She signalled her thanks to Shack as the van's engine coughed noisily into life.

Seamus, Sophie, Jonathan and Spring all waved as the Escort's headlights arced past the caravan. Daniel turned to see Little Degsey put in her first appearance of the evening. The pup was illuminated by the porch carriage lamps as she squeezed her wiry body between Seamus and Spring, stretching out her long forelegs and dipping her back as she yawned hugely before edging down cosily beside her mother. Daniel had to admit that seeing the pair side-by-side, in the half light, that the resemblance between mother and daughter was remarkable. Both sets of brindle splashes on white were identical — three irregular patches at exactly the same point on each body, with the brindle and white mix on the head and tail. Give Little Degsey another nine months, Daniel thought, and the pair would be impossible to separate.

The van had left Swiftly village and was now heading north-east to Muddlebridge. Sky's slim fingers made economical turns of the wheel as, barely within the speed restrictions, she covered the three-mile journey with ease. She swung right into the garage forecourt, and halted the van by an attendant who was leaning against one of the pumps. He was early twenties, swarthy and thick-set. He looked fit and hard.

'Hello, Roy.' Sky removed a flashlight from the glove box and was out of the door before Daniel had even released his seat-belt. 'Is the fox badly injured?'

'Reckon it's busted a rear leg,' Roy said, turning to indicate a gap between the workshop and toilets where the creature had sought sanctuary. 'It seemed to be dragging it after it got hit. Clobbered by a council truck, I think.'

Sky nodded, looking towards the hiding place. 'Is there an exit the other end?'

'No, it's blocked off. It can't get out at the rear.'

'Did you notice which direction it came from . . . before it got hit?'

'Horseshoe Coppice, I think.'

Daniel lifted the holding cage and Grasper from the back of the van and put on a pair of trapper's mitts. Sky did likewise as a couple of cars pulled in for petrol.

'Must get on, Ms Patakin,' Roy said keenly, lifting an acknowledging hand to a waiting motorist. 'I'll leave you both to it.'

Sky switched on the flashlight and followed Daniel to the space between the two buildings. The gap was about a metre wide; certainly room enough for a person to manoeuvre quickly if the need arose.

'You or me?' Sky asked.

'You or me what?'

'To use the Grasper.' Sky's face couldn't conceal a hint of exasperation. 'Have you handled one before?'

The early easy manner around the campfire had gone and her voice had switched back to its condescending tone. Daniel had hoped that the general chumminess of the evening would have spilled over to thaw out her superior front, but she stood before him with a haughty aloofness, lips compressed.

Daniel showed her what he hoped was a disarming smile and confirmed that he had used a Grasper, many times. He added with deliberate smugness that he'd noosed the young of most safari park big cats with a similar, though more industrial type of device.

'Then you shouldn't have a problem,' Sky spoke briskly in an attempt to assert her dominance. The flashlight raked the gap, illuminating dead leaves, an old tyre and various pieces of litter.

'I see the fox.' Daniel edged forward, holding the Grasper two-handedly, the noose dangling at the ready.

'Vixen,' Sky corrected, unable to resist a smile which Daniel couldn't see. 'I can see swollen teats on her belly. She must have cubs somewhere.'

'All right; *vixen* then.' Daniel briefly raised his eyes, then concentrated on the job in hand.

There was a flurry of movement as the vixen spun round in disoriented circles when she realised that there was no rear escape.

She eventually settled, crouching to face Daniel, a small growl forming in her throat as she showed him her tiny, but very white needle-sharp teeth.

Daniel could feel a prickle of perspiration on his upper lip as he gently teased the noose around the animal's neck.

She was stock still. Unmoving.

In one fluid wrist movement, he gave a sharp tug on the loop below the Grasper's handle and the noose closed sweetly. The vixen was trapped. A high-pitched squealing bombarded Daniel's ears as she twisted, turned, fought and scratched at the pole with her paws. He exhaled gratefully, backing out of the gap, keeping the pole fully extended as he dragged (rather than cause further damage by lifting) the vixen's supple body towards Sky.

'Well done.' She nodded approvingly and bent to apply a mittened hand to the animal's scruff.

Daniel was pleased with the simplicity of the capture and although inwardly his nerves jangled he looked cool and kempt as he opened the sprung door of the holding cage.

'Okay to release the Grasper?' he asked.

Sky nodded.

There was plenty of high, penetrating squealing, but the vixen stilled as Sky took a tight grip on her scruff. The noose was now disengaged and Sky ran a practised eye over the long, dangling body looking for signs of concussion, head and jaw damage and abdominal injuries. As Daniel removed his mitts she held the vixen at arms length, mouth towards her, and asked him to do a quick, on-the-spot examination.

'Now?' A frown cut deep just above the bridge of his nose. He knew she was testing him.

'Have you a problem with that?' Sky spoke patiently, as to a tiresome child. 'If you think there's a fracture then I have a temporary splint in my case.'

Daniel ran quick, deft fingers over the vixen's body, pinching the toes for a reflex action, and carefully folding and manipulating each joint to check for mobility.

'I can't tell positively without an X-ray,' he informed her, 'but I don't think there's a fracture.'

Sky was quietly impressed, but her voice was still a little starched as she asked, 'Any further thoughts?'

At this point the vixen decided to empty her bladder over Daniel's shirt. The urine was warm and slightly sticky but he deliberately didn't flinch, knowing this was the natural reaction of a frightened animal.

Daniel fought down a smile as he glanced at Sky. Her eyes were uncommonly large and held a look of faintly mocking amusement which bewitched him. He cleared his throat, considered, then said, 'In my opinion she has muscle or nerve damage in her right rear leg. There's no external bleeding and she seems reasonably healthy.' He looked closely at some bald patches of fur. 'There's a touch of ringworm, but that can be easily rectified.'

'Good.' Sky sounded somewhat irritated at Daniel's thorough analysis. She placed the vixen without difficulty in the holding cage and shut the sprung door. 'I suggest we keep her at Oyster Gables overnight, and if she's mobile and fit in the morning then we release her back into Horseshoe Coppice. If we hang onto her for too long then her cubs will be at risk.'

Daniel nodded agreement and bent to retrieve the Grasper. He ignored the strong smell of uric acid caused by the wetness on his shirt which was now clinging patchily, uncomfortably, to his body.

'Are you all right?' Sky asked.

'I expect I'll pong a bit in the Escort.'

'Occupational hazard. You can clean up back at the shelter.'

'I'm actually quite pleased. I feel as if I've been through some sort of Oyster Gables initiation ceremony.'

'It could have been avoided.'

'Avoided?'

'Mm, we needn't have used the Grasper at all.'

Daniel looked at her blankly. His forehead creased as he raked his dark hair back with a hand. 'No Grasper. I don't follow?'

A small grin tensed at the corners of Sky's mouth as they walked to the van. 'All you had to do was borrow Degsey from Seamus Horrigan,' she said, unable to resist a final poke of fun at the gypsy's story. 'I'm sure she would have given you one of her golden smiles and charmed the vixen into the cage.'

There was no answer to that, and Daniel didn't even try to invent one.

5

Martin Griggs was 24 hours overdue, and Tony Ryker was not best pleased.

Ryker was a creature of habit. A man who liked routine. A man who always worked to a well-tried system, where delays didn't happen and excuses wouldn't be tolerated. The trip to sell ten horses at the Southall horse auction had been planned to take three days — it always took Griggs three days — one day to cover the journey to Greater London, one day to attend the auction, and one day to return to Hele. But this time it had taken four. Griggs had phoned to explain the situation, but excuses would not pacify Ryker. As far as he was concerned time was money. Griggs should have been back, and what was left of the week devoted to stealing new stock.

He paced, snatching a look at his watch every now and then. Two p.m. and no sign. He ambled past his gleaming red BMW car, polishing a mud mark from its wing with his tattooed forearm. As he walked he cast a critical eye over the six old horses that would journey from Harwich to a continental slaughter house. He lit a cheroot with a bookmatch as one by one the animals sauntered over to a rusted gate to greet him.

If they were hoping for a sugar lump or a mint sweet or even a kind word — then they were knocking at the wrong door. To Ryker they were just cash on legs, perishable livestock which were burning a hole in his pocket the longer they stayed.

At least, during the time Griggs had been away, Ryker had tossed down some hay and given them a meagre daily portion of oats.

Not that Ryker was playing stableman out of the kindness of his heart — far from it. He didn't expect prime meat on the hoof, but business sense dictated that the horses needed to look reasonably fit by keeping on a bit of bodyweight. Dull coats, tangled manes, body sores, lethargic movements, and ribs which showed through flesh like the spars of a ship, would not be appreciated by Ryker's foreign buyers.

One horse looked okay, he reassured himself — the chestnut gypsy cob. He watched it prance arrogantly past him, tossing its neck, bright-eyed and still full of spirit. He actually allowed himself the luxury of a smile as he observed the old cob's antics. There was a few years work left in the horse and the thought fleetingly crossed his mind that he could possibly sell it on for a bit extra . . . but he dismissed the idea as being more trouble than it was worth. Mister Rafferty would join Saturday's abattoir shipment, and that was an end to it.

With Griggs away, Ryker had been occupied in his usual clandestine pursuit of scouring the Devon countryside for yet more horses to fill the now empty Hele warehouse. He'd spotted three at an Okehampton smallholding and two at a Tiverton riding school. These, coupled with the three short-stay livery horses being kept at Penhill, and Sir Galahad and Excalibur at Oyster Gables, rounded up nicely to his magic figure of ten. The sooner Griggs returned, he reflected, the sooner they could continue their rustling exploits.

An ever-deepening throb of a noisy engine heralded the arrival of the travelling horse-box. Ryker strode purposefully from the paddock to meet it. He watched it exit a fork in the track by the warehouse and rattle over a couple of acres of lumpy terrain. He avoided the clouds of dust as Griggs stamped on the brakes, narrowly missing the BMW. Griggs reversed the vehicle into a shabby corrugated iron structure concealing it from prying eyes, and jumped from the cab.

'About flippin' time.' Ryker gave him a level, unsmiling look. 'Thought you'd decided to take a London vacation.'

'Don't start, Tony.' Griggs's brown eyes flared. 'I've had a lousy time of it . . . delays all round. The Southall guest house kicked me out 'cause you only booked two days. I had a terrible nosebleed and spent last night sleeping in the cab.'

'Good. I'm all for saving money. You're pampered too much as it is.'

Griggs reached inside his leather jacket and pulled out a zipped-up money pouch. He slapped it into Ryker's outstretched open hand. 'Nine thousand, seven hundred pounds,' he said, lifting and sniffing at his underarm. 'I'm smelly and I need a shower. Shall I wait while you count the money,' he added with a touch of sarcasm, 'or have I your permission to use the bathroom?'

'I'd reckoned on £10,000.' Ryker strode ahead of him, making a line for the mobile home. 'How come there's a shortfall?'

'I told you on the phone that the market was heaving with horses. I think I did well, considering.'

'So give me the auction breakdown?'

'Seven went for nine-hundred each, two fetched a thousand each, and the piebald made fourteen-hundred.'

Ryker swung on him as he reached the home's frosted glass-panelled kitchen door.

His eyes were probing. 'Haven't stuffed a few hundred pounds in your back pocket, have you?'

'There's an auctioneer's receipt in the pouch.' Griggs rubbed a grimy palm over his face and met his gaze scornfully. 'I don't know why I bother. I work my darned fingers to the bone, go without sleep, drive the two-hundred miles back without even stopping for the lavatory, then get accused of stealing.'

'You were a thief when I first met you, Griggsy, and you'll always be a thief. Leopards don't change their spots.'

Griggs pushed past Ryker and headed moodily for the bathroom, grabbing a can of beer from the fridge. 'Pity we're not dealing in leopards,' he grunted. 'I would have got a heck of a lot more for 'em.'

He stumped off along the corridor, irritation in every line of his body. Ryker suppressed a chuckle as the bathroom door slammed . . . hard.

'And don't forget to pull the chain,' he called out, unable to resist another stab of ridicule. 'You keep blocking up the U-bend with toilet paper!'

Ryker sat at the kitchen table, his stubby fingers drawing back the zip on the money pouch. There were nine banded packs of a

£1,000 each, plus £700 in loose notes.

Griggs received 20% of the auction money, less expenses. Ryker left one pack of a £1,000 on the table plus the odd £700. He struggled to hold back a lopsided grin as he replaced the bulk of the money in the pouch.

'Your wages are on the table,' he announced, looking towards the bathroom door. 'Your share comes to one thousand nine-hundred and forty-pounds, but I've deducted expenses plus the cost of the hot dog I bought you at Swiftly.'

'You're a prince.' Griggs's thick, muffled voice was barely audible above the flush of the cistern. 'Pretty soon my expenses are going to be more than my earnings!'

'You've been skimping on food for the old nags,' Ryker retorted loudly. 'I allow you two pounds a day for each horse, but I'm not blind. It's obvious you haven't been giving them any extra feed. I reckon you've been squandering the money on beer. Some of the horses are downright skinny. I've seen more fat on a butcher's pencil!'

Minutes ran by. Griggs was taking a shower as Ryker crossed to a wall safe in the lounge. He clicked it open and placed the pouch inside.

Griggs thrived on a bit of mockery, he convinced himself, closing the door and spinning the combination. That's what made their partnership work. The occasional putdown kept Griggs in line, kept him from straying, stopped him getting ideas above his station. Derision came naturally to Ryker. He'd been a bully at school and never lost the habit.

He thought of that, and he liked the memories.

'What you cooking for lunch?' Ryker collided with Griggs as he re-entered the kitchen. He was jamming the money into the back pockets of his leather jeans with one hand and pulling a clean T-shirt awkwardly over his head with the other.

'I thought *you* might offer to do the cooking for a change.' Griggs gave him a blistering look and added stiffly, 'I've just spent five hours on the road and I'm dead beat.'

'Now don't start doing your whining old crone act on me. Have I not just paid your wages? Am I not just about to start plotting our route for tonight's haul?'

Ryker pulled a map from a kitchen drawer and made a big, theatrical performance of unfolding it. He then reached up to a cupboard for a pen and paper before sitting at the table and jotting down some road directions.

'I've been busy, my little ferret . . . no let

up at all. I've found two horses which are kept in a paddock at Tiverton, and three which are boxed at Okehampton.'

'Tiverton's a fair journey,' Griggs said.

'I'll be driving,' Ryker murmured soothingly, laying on some phoney charm, 'but the actual stealing should be a doddle for someone with your expertise.'

'Oh, yeah . . . right.' Griggs liked the sudden flattery. He snatched a glance over Ryker's shoulder as he began jotting down places and journey times.

'Five tonight,' Ryker said, fiddling with his diamond-studded signet ring. 'And five tomorrow night. How does that suit?'

'Alright.' Griggs heaved a sigh. 'So can't we do the short run tonight? The three at Penhill and the two at that Oyster place?'

'Of course, Griggsy. However you want to play it.' He displayed an unnatural smile that curled up like a frosted leaf. It wasn't very convincing but it had the desired effect on his partner.

Griggs acquiesced. 'Chicken and chips okay?'

★　★　★

Sky, Shack and Daniel were busily engaged on a rescue mission.

A dog walker had alerted Oyster Gables that a deer had been caught in a snare at Knightacott Woods, so the hunt was on to find it, free it, and check out any injuries.

It was a short journey, less than five miles from Swiftly, and Sky had taken the van as far as she dare along a narrow rutted track leading past an old paper mill with its now dilapidated water-wheel. The track ended abruptly at a series of marshy pools with spear grass growing around the edges.

The sun was gaining in strength and the sky a wash of flat blue as all three climbed out of the vehicle and collected their pieces of equipment from the rear of the van. Sky clutched her first aid case, Shack jammed a rolled canvas stretcher under his arm and an empty bran sack into his belt, and Daniel carefully slipped a rifle out of its soft leather case.

Daniel had loaded the rifle with a tranquilliser dart, checked that the safety-catch was on, and slung it over his shoulder. He'd received training and been granted a firearms certificate whilst working at the safari park, so he was no stranger to handling weapons. He'd earned the enviable reputation of being a crack shot and the last animal he'd tranquillised with a dart had been a leopard which had contracted feline influenza.

Since the setting up of Oyster Gables the rifle had only been used twice. Peggy, Daniel's predecessor, was the only one licensed for the weapon, and on each occasion it had been fired at deer who were injured and who would have been impossible to catch without 'darting'.

Today was slightly different. If the deer had been snared then it wouldn't be in a position to run anywhere, and Sky hoped to be able to tranquillise the animal by hand.

'We've brought the rifle along as a safeguard.' Sky was parading her efficient, controlled air which was becoming her habitual expression whenever she was in Daniel's company. 'If we're prudent we won't need it.'

Daniel nodded, perfectly aware of the situation.

A pair of jays screeched their displeasure at human intrusion as the three followed a winding path through the heather, bracken and furze. They passed an earthen bank riddled with rabbit holes and followed a stream that led to a small waterfall. Ahead of them, in the soft dewy brightness, lay a clump of pewter-coloured willow trees. They had been uprooted by a long-ago storm, and their lifeless branches now straddled the stream.

'I see it.' Shack raised a halting hand. 'It's a

male — I can see its antlers. It's lying by the broken willows.'

Sky and Daniel both looked, their eyes spotting the buff-brown head and dappled neck of a large fallow buck hanging over the bank, moving restlessly to keep its face clear of the stream.

'The trappers must know deer drink here,' Daniel remarked, 'so it makes them an easy target.'

'It's lying down through exhaustion,' Sky said, gesturing everyone forward. 'I can't see the snare but be careful of the hind legs. If they lash about then you'll get badly kicked.'

'Can you quieten it without a tranquilliser dart?' Shack asked softly.

'I intend to try.' Sky removed a syringe from her first aid case and withdrew a measured amount of sedative from a small vial. 'Right, I'm relying on you two to hold it as still as possible. Its antlers might be flat rather than branched, but they're powerful. Be very careful.'

Daniel placed his rifle against a tree stump and looked at Shack who nodded his readiness.

The deer was now fully aware of their presence and was flicking its brown ears from side to side as it made an awkward attempt to clamber to its feet. The snare was now visible, glinting malevolently from a bloodied hind leg. The sight wasn't pretty, but at least it was restricting the very tired animal's leverage as it tried desperately to stand up.

Shack thrashed forward and was on the buck in seconds. He'd approached it via the stream, slopping through knee-high water to reach it. Daniel followed in his wake, and as Shack got to grips with the antlers, pinning them to the bank, Daniel let most of his upper bodyweight slide across the buck's spotted shoulders, clamping his hands around the front hooves.

The teamwork functioned well. Apart from one hind leg the buck was pinned. Shack's teeth were gritted, and his breath was coming in hot little pants of exertion as he held onto the antlers, pressing them into the turf. The sinews in his forearms bulked out like rope and his hands were shaking with effort from the strength in the deer's neck, but his expression was one of determination.

Sky skidded to the ground on her knees beside the fallow buck, leaning safely against Daniel's extended arms as she judged the distance in order to avoid being hit by the free flailing hind hoof. She found the large muscle mass on the animal's white-spotted rump and deftly punctured the skin with the needle. She pushed on the hypodermic's plunger, watching the plastic syringe empty as the fluid entered the deer.

She was sweating slightly and this heightened the effect of her perfume as she briefly glanced in Daniel's direction. He'd caught the fragrance and was holding her sultry good looks unblinkingly. Sky was also drawn to his gaze. She found the darkness behind Daniel's eyes to be strangely, compulsively magnetic. A flush threatened to betray her feelings so she forced herself to break his gaze, clearing her mind, concentrating her thoughts on the fallow deer and the job in hand.

The buck's beautiful but frightened eyes showed huge circles of white, staring up at her as she extracted the needle. Slowly they began to flicker, wanting to close.

'Good boy,' she comforted, letting out a relieved breath. 'You're going to be fine.'

The buck's strength was waning and the tension began to ease on Shack's arms. He released one hand, grinning at the milky blueness of his palm and the tiny indentations left by the antlers. He shook life back into his fingers, showing Sky a mock pained expression.

Daniel could also feel the animal's muscles relaxing under the weight of his body. He watched the motion in the unfettered hind leg gradually slacken to a soft paddle as the drug

138

found its way round the nervous system.

'He's sedated,' Sky announced, relaxing slightly. She turned to Shack. 'Must weigh around a hundred kilos. Can you cover his head?'

Shack pulled the bran sack from his belt. He lifted the head of the now calm fallow buck with one hand, and slid the hessian covering over the antlers and down to the shoulders with the other.

Sky unclipped a pair of strong fencing pliers from inside the lid of her first aid case. She ran a gentle hand down the deer's trapped hind leg and examined the harsh metal loop which had severed the flesh to the bone. 'It's a locking snare.' Sky's eyebrows were down, her face taut with deliberation. 'Once I've snipped it off I'll cut it into pieces and leave them on the bank. At least that way the trappers will know we're aware of their activities.'

'Bloodthirsty swines!' Shack's breath hissed as he flexed his jaw. He began to empty the water from his wellingtons.

Daniel watched as the pliers bit into the loop and the snare pinged and lashed away. That was the third trapped animal this week, he reflected, as Sky snipped the wire into harmless little bits. A rabbit, a fox, and now a deer. The rabbit and fox had both been caught with legal free-running snares, but the locking snare was illegal and had to be reported to the local police.

'I'll treat the wounds back at Oyster Gables.' Sky unrolled the stretcher and laid it flat on the bank alongside the buck. 'Okay, let's get the patient on board.'

Everyone pulled, heaved and lifted. There were a lot of sweaty brows and a fair bit of cursing, but eventually the fallow buck was eased onto the canvas. Daniel gripped the two metal poles by the animal's sack-covered head, while Shack gripped the two at the rump. The hooves dangled over the stretcher as they lifted; but apart from the odd twitch, movement from the animal was minimal.

'Let's go.' Sky closed her first aid case and retrieved the rifle from the tree stump. She gave a slight, breathy laugh as she added, 'It's only a few hundred metres back to the Escort.'

Shack and Daniel took the strain as Sky led the way, retracing her footsteps. There were a couple of pauses enroute for extra air to be sucked into lungs, then weak with relief they arrived at the van. Sky opened the rear doors and the stretcher was manhandled inside.

Shack jumped into the back, sitting on the floor as he supported the buck's head. He looked a dishevelled mess. His jeans were soaked up to his thighs, and his face and arms were splattered with mud. He wiped his forehead with the back of his hand as perspiration stung into his eyes.

Sky and Daniel looked the worse for wear too. Both knees of Sky's jeans were grass-stained; one was torn, and she was picking little pieces of moss and forest debris from her hair.

Daniel's jeans were sodden up to the back pockets, his sweatshirt was streaked with leaf-mould and he had sustained a grazed elbow. All three were in need of an urgent shower, plus a reviving cup of tea or coffee.

'Well done everyone.' Sky started the van, and reversed back down the narrow track. 'The buck will have to be kept sedated and housed in a confinement pen. I'll immediately put him on an intravenous drip and treat the bruises we can see, but some will take a few days before they fully erupt.'

'How long will we keep him at the shelter?' Shack asked.

'Minimum of a week . . . ' Sky paused, and a trace of amusement looked out from her eyes. 'You won't be getting much sleep tonight, Daniel.'

'Post-capture myopathy,' he murmured, surprising her slightly.

'Post . . . what?' Shack wiped a limp strand

141

of hair from his forehead.

'You've dealt with deer before?' Sky shot Daniel an inquiring glance.

'We had a kiddies corner at the safari park — various tame animals which children could get close to — so I do know that an injured deer is the world's worst creature for dying on you.' He looked at Shack. 'In the early stages of confinement the slightest stress or trauma will kill them.'

'So you'll see the buck through the night?' Sky squared her shoulders, turning the van towards Swiftly.

'Definitely the assistant manager's job,' Daniel agreed. 'I wouldn't expect the boss-lady to lose her beauty sleep.'

Sky said nothing, just gave a small cough and concentrated on the road ahead. Shack grinned wryly.

'Not that she needs any.' Daniel abandoned all pretence and risked the stroke of a forefinger down the back of Sky's hand. He expected her to shift her position on the wheel, or at the very least to fix him with a cold, measuring look.

She didn't do either. 'Check on the buck about two a.m., and then again about five,' she said smiling, she hoped, reassuringly.

'I can do that job,' Shack interjected quickly. 'I was going to ask if I could spend the night at Oyster Gables. My mum and stepfather have driven down to Lynmouth for a short break. They're bound to pop over to Yelland to see me.'

'Perhaps you should make the effort to see them,' Sky said.

'I will . . . sometime. At the moment I'm alright with dad . . . I'm settled.'

'Okay.'

'Okay, you'll let me stay and look after the buck?'

'No, okay you can stay the night.' Her voice took on a teasing note. 'If you stay, then you go to bed. Daniel's the one who will be losing sleep.'

Daniel found himself smiling. He really didn't mind. A fallow deer for company during the night? No problem. Suddenly everything was okay between him and Sky . . . and for the moment that was all that mattered.

★   ★   ★

Tony Ryker's features were thrown into stark relief in the spluttering flare of a book-match.

'Stop worrying,' he told Griggs, breathing on a cheroot. 'I have it on good authority that this place is run by kids.'

It was 1.50 a.m. and they were both sitting

in the cab of the travelling horse-box. Ryker had reversed the vehicle clear of the road and parked just short of the two huge conifer trees which flanked the driveway to Oyster Gables.

'I just feel uneasy, that's all,' Griggs said, dipping into a large holdall and handing Ryker a ski-mask. 'I can't help it if I get these strange feelings.'

'We've got three horses in the back from Penhill,' Ryker reminded him in a light, casual tone. 'Did they cause us a problem? No. So now we're collecting two more. Trust Tony, it'll be easy.'

Griggs pulled on his ski-mask and gloves then rummaged around in the holdall checking the contents. Flashlight, bolt-cutters, head-collar with halter and two sets of four bootees. They were elasticated stretch nylon, with chamois leather soles, which fitted snugly around the hooves of a horse to the fetlocks. When attached they completely dampened the clacking sound of horseshoes, and with the house being in such close proximity to the shelter's front entrance gates Ryker had decided to use them.

'Easy money,' Ryker grunted positively to himself, pulling on a pair of gloves and the ski-mask. He slid from the cab and made his way leisurely round to the ramp.

He watched Griggs scoot off into the

darkness carrying the holdall, then paused briefly looking up at the house windows for any light, listening for any noise.

Nothing. All asleep.

He plumed smoke through both nostrils of the mask, leaning back against the ramp, waiting for the signal from Griggs's flashlight. Should only be a matter of seconds, he told himself. Commonsense dictated that a wild animal shelter wouldn't bother with heavy-duty padlocks.

Time passed.

He held the glow of the cheroot against his wristwatch then tossed the butt away. He began to fidget. There was a quirk of unease in his eyes as he realised that something must be wrong. No sign of a signal. Griggs was taking too long . . . far too long.

He cursed inwardly and decided to investigate. He hadn't taken more than a couple of steps before he saw the wavering shape of Griggs's gangly, light-framed body running towards him.

'Tony . . . Tony . . . ' Griggs panted as he slithered and swayed to a halt, almost colliding with Ryker. He held the flashlight in his right hand and blood was pulsing in his temples. 'I've just seen . . . hellfire . . . It's here . . . the thing's here . . . '

'Speak properly!' Ryker grabbed his

shoulders with a touch of impatience. 'What have you seen? Make sense!'

'The gypsy caravan.' Griggs worked hard at letting his voice out evenly. 'It's parked up by the gates. Y-you can't see it from here 'cause it's lying back on the forecourt.'

Ryker looked at Griggs, his top lip drawn upwards in a small, nervous spasm.

'The caravan,' Griggs, said again. 'The one you've been trying to track down.'

'Did you see the dog?'

'No . . . and I don't want to.'

Griggs went to walk back to the cab, but Ryker's thick fingers snared his arm. 'Where the heck are you going?'

'Home. I'm getting stressed-out and I can feel a nose-bleed coming on. I'm not stealing horses from here.'

'Forget the horses. I want that greyhound.'

'Then you find it . . . but don't count on me.' Griggs paused to fortify himself with a deep breath. 'We haven't got the gear for dog-napping. Let's get out while we can.'

'Not before I've got the full picture,' he muttered, his jaw muscles fluttering. 'So maybe we can't get it tonight, but I need to take a close look. Are you wearing a belt?'

'Do what?'

Ryker repeated the question, adding, 'I'm wearing braces. Take it off.'

Griggs grumbled under his breath, surly and unwilling as he fumbled to free the belt from the waist of his leather jeans.

Ryker coiled it through the buckle and slipped his free hand through the loop. 'Collar and lead in one,' he said, demonstrating — jerking the end hard, so it snapped tight across his forearm.

'You're barking mad.' Griggs's voice cracked. 'You'll never outsmart that greyhound . . . *never!*'

'Just being prepared, my little ferret. The dog might fancy an early morning stroll. So who better than you and me to take it for one?'

Ryker nudged Griggs towards the house. The big man moved forward with deliberate dead-silent slowness. Griggs followed reluctantly, still muttering curses, one hand gripping the waistband of his jeans to stop them from slipping. Ryker was oblivious to Griggs's inarticulate complaints. An opportunity had presented itself — and now, more than anything, he was obsessed with stealing Degsey.

Daniel didn't see the shadowy outlines as they furtively passed the kitchen window. He hadn't bothered to switch on the light, preferring to make coffee by the cosy glow from the old coal cooking range. He yawned and knuckled tiredness from his eyes, stirring hot water into a mug.

Scooter had left the confines of his basket and was generally being a nuisance. He had heard movement outside and was padding up and down the hall to the side door — a process he repeated several times.

'Scooter, behave!' Daniel added milk and sugar to his coffee. 'I'll let you out in a minute . . . when I check on the deer.'

The dog suddenly stopped pacing, his eyes looking upwards and beyond Daniel. The coffee mug hovered half way to Daniel's mouth as a flicker of motion caught his eye.

He turned to face Shack Skinner as he stumbled into the kitchen. His face was still misty with sleep and his curly hair tousled. He was pulling a Scottish rugby shirt over his head with one hand and hooking moccasins over the back of bare heels with the other. A pulse was pounding in his throat and Daniel could hear the rasp of his breath as Shack looked at him with panicky eyes, placing a finger to his lips.

'Intruders.' Shack's voice was barely more than a tremulous whisper. 'Outside on the forecourt.'

Daniel gulped. 'How many?'

'Two, I think. I was coming to give you a hand with the buck, when I spotted them from the bedroom window.' Shack unhooked Scooter's collar and lead from the wall peg and found the boxer immediately at his heels. 'Get the rifle,' he said, fastening the collar. 'They look as if they mean business, so we'd better go prepared.'

'Shouldn't we ring the police?'

'No time . . . Hurry.'

Daniel dug the key to the gun cabinet from his pocket. He crossed quickly to the cupboard under the stairs and released the padlock on the heavy-gauge upright metal box. The tranquilliser darts were in sealed containers on a shelf above. He left them, slung the rifle over his shoulder, and made his way back to the kitchen.

Shack was waiting by the side-door. He held Scooter in one hand and a heavy rubber torch in the other.

'I haven't loaded the rifle,' Daniel told him.

'Didn't expect you would.' Shack's mouth quirked grimly. 'Just so long as they don't know it. Are you ready?'

'Ready.'

A finger of fear crept down Daniel's back, icing his kidneys as Shack gently turned the door handle.

Tony Ryker had made an inspection by circling the caravan and was now standing on the grass verge contemplating his next move.

Griggs was deliberately hanging back, not wishing to play any major part in any plan that Ryker had in mind.

Suddenly both men had an instant of paralysis.

The hinged flap-like aperture in the caravan's front door creaked and slowly lifted. Degsey exited the wagon, one carefully placed paw at a time. She moved fluently and there was no sign of the pitchfork injury. She looked from Ryker to Griggs, crouching on her haunches as she lay guard across the footboard. A tangle of smells sharpened by the warm night air pricked at her nostrils, tugged at her memory. Horses . . . the scent of horses was overpowering, rekindling memories of Mister Rafferty. Faintly, imperceptibly, she knew she could smell the old cob, and she was also fully aware that she was now face-to-face with the evil men who had stolen him. Her muzzle lifted as a resonant growl began to build.

'Flashlight,' Ryker mouthed the word, stabbing an impatient finger towards Griggs.

'N-no.' He shook his head violently. His mind was numb and his actions stiff as he backed away.

Ryker took some hurried steps towards him and wrenched the lamp from his fingers. 'What the heck's wrong with you?' he grated.

'D-don't turn on the flashlight,' Griggs managed to choke out. 'I-I'm warning you, Tony. Don't let it glint off the dog's tooth.'

Ryker gave a grunt of irritation and was about to thumb the switch when Daniel stepped out of the shadows. Griggs felt his insides tighten like a fist as the rifle was levelled at his body.

'Stand still!' Daniel said, deliberately throwing a harsh note into his voice. He swept the barrel of the rifle towards Ryker. 'Move closer together!'

Ryker didn't flinch. He said, with relish, 'Grow up, sonny. You haven't got the nerve to use that.'

Shack appeared at Daniel's shoulder. He held a now-growling Scooter who was straining at his leash. He clicked on the heavy rubber torch, illuminating both men in the flared radius of the beam.

'Take off those masks,' he commanded. 'Let's get a good look at you.'

Griggs, shielding his eyes, had shuffled nearer to Ryker. He hooked his thumbs under the ski-mask, preparing to peel it over his face.

Ryker knocked his hands away. 'No kid gives me orders.' He spoke to Daniel in a dangerously tight, over-controlled voice. 'We're going to walk out of here . . . and there's not a thing you can do about it.'

Scooter looked at them and gave three half-hearted barks.

'And as for that overweight lapdog,' Ryker continued, 'he looks about as dangerous as a ping-pong ball against a tank.'

Daniel exchanged a quick glance with Shack. The words rang true because Scooter was a pet, not a guard dog. Like the majority of his breed he was all bluster and very little action.

Ryker's gaze shifted to the upstairs windows of the house. A light had come on. Sky's bedroom. She'd been woken by Scooter's barking and the curtains were moving.

Several things happened next but they were just an indistinguishable blur.

Ryker suddenly pitched himself at Daniel and, with a manic burst of strength, brought both hands down in a clubbing action against the rifle. It sent the gun cartwheeling away, and the sheer weight and force of the move took Daniel to his knees.

Griggs reacted instantly by aiming a kick at the now free Scooter. It was not karate or kung fu, just crude — vicious. His toecap struck the dog's ribcage with a jarring thud sending a painful squeal to Scooter's throat. He rolled over a couple of times, then limped under the caravan, whimpering slightly, seeking refuge.

Shack held the heavy torch at arm's length, swinging it in front of him and threatening to use it as a weapon unless Ryker backed off. The big man laughed and dodged sideways, sending Shack off balance as he tried to catch Ryker with a mistimed and rather inexpert lunge. His own momentum carried him towards the caravan's hind-carriage and his legs tangled as he reached it. He fell awkwardly, tumbling head first into the nearside wheel, his mouth bouncing painfully against the hard edge of the heavy iron tyre. There was a hollow click from his teeth as his jaw snapped shut and a blemish of blood issued from between his lips. He scrabbled for balance and righted himself by gripping the wheel's thick, brightly coloured spokes.

Ryker bore down on him instantly, allowing no time for senses to be recovered.

Shack felt the torch being prised from his fingers as the big man used his ample weight to pin him against the wheel. A scorpion tattoo floated in front of his eyes and he held onto the image, knowing it was desperately important to store it in the depths of his memory.

One by one his fingers were being peeled forcibly back from the indented rubber grip of the torch as Ryker wrestled it from his hand. The big man grated a contemptuous laugh as he retrieved it and tossed it up and away.

It went high, spinning almost in slow motion, lighting up fragments of greenery, spilling its glow over segments of the forecourt before it began its whirling descent.

Griggs looked stricken as the heavy rubber torch struck the caravan's white lead roof, then rolled slowly past the chimney stack before bouncing down and settling on the footboard.

A yellow hoop of light stencilled itself across Degsey's face. She was still lying with her muzzle drawn back as she turned her head to look at Daniel.

'No!' Griggs saw the bright glint of gold and let out a shrill scream.

Daniel crawled towards the rifle and retrieved it.

Griggs began to run.

Ryker now had his solid bulk on top of Shack. He was gripped in a head hold and he felt the big man's thumbs worming their way towards his eyes. He struggled and squirmed but he was hopelessly outmatched in both weight and strength.

Daniel was now on his feet. Somewhere in a tiny pocket of his awareness he knew that his priorities lay with stopping Ryker — helping Shack — but he couldn't hold or concentrate on that thought.

Get the other one . . . the other one . . . a small voice in his head kept saying.

He looked at the rifle balanced in his hands, stock pressed firmly against his shoulder. It was no good to him, he reasoned. He hadn't loaded it. So why was he holding it in a firing position?

Degsey imprisoned Daniel with her gaze and he blinked rapidly, trying to blot out the shimmer of gold that was blurring his vision. No use. His thoughts began to swirl and dissolve, his actions became numb and uncoordinated. Under his arms pores popped moisture, and the skin between his shoulder blades tweaked and prickled as he was gripped by the radar-like strength of Degsey's stare.

His tongue seemed to be held fast against the roof of his mouth as he lifted the rifle's telescopic sight to his eye, framing Griggs in the centre of the crossed-hairs. He heard a metallic click as, without his touching it, the safety-catch disengaged. Sweat began to puddle in his eyebrows as his finger involuntarily eased back on the trigger, taking up the slack.

Griggs was fleeing, snatching the odd

glance over his shoulder, varying his gait and direction, running in a weaving path to make himself a harder target. Without a belt around his waist he was losing control of his leather jeans — and his pace now slowed to an awkward stumble as they dropped to his thighs, exposing tight, bright red underpants.

As if giving a signal, Degsey blinked.

Daniel fired.

Griggs screamed.

Instead of an empty '*phutt*', there was a harder sound as Daniel felt the pressure of a tranquilliser dart leaving the barrel. He saw Griggs grip his left buttock then stagger forward in a clumsy jumble of limbs as he hit the ground.

Ryker had heard the noise of the rifle and he immediately released his grip on Shack. He got unsteadily to his feet, raising submissive hands to Daniel, looking towards the prostrate body of Griggs.

'Y-you crazy kid. I-I never thought . . . '

'Go help your friend,' Daniel said bluntly.

As Ryker fled, Shack looked up at Daniel and smiled, stretching his bruised mouth with a painful wince. 'I thought you said you hadn't loaded that thing,' he murmured.

'I must have forgotten to *unload* it.' Sky's voice came from behind them. She was wrapped in a white towelling robe, her hair mussed, her face pink and showing sleepy bewilderment. 'I picked up the weapon at Knightacott Woods, and I locked it in the gun cupboard. I didn't check it, so it's my fault. Daniel's not to blame.'

Suddenly all eyes were on Degsey. She stood up and shook herself, stretching her long legs. A paw caught the heavy rubber torch that had settled on the footboard and it rolled forward, falling between the caravan's shafts and hitting the tarmac. There was a tinkling sound as the lens fractured, extinguishing the light, sending shards of glass in all directions. It was as if she had completed her task and was no longer needed. She looked from Daniel to Shack to Sky before nosing open the caravan's hinged aperture and disappearing back inside.

'That's one heck of a weird dog.' Shack got to his feet, eyeing Daniel. He coughed and spat, leaving slimy streamers of blood down his chin. 'Did she do anything to help us — apart from just lying there?'

Daniel cleared his throat, a prominent Adam's apple jerking, 'She more than lived up to Seamus's expectations,' he said.

'I don't follow ... ?' Shack's brow puckered.

'Tell you later.'

Ryker had reached Griggs. He helped him

partially to his feet then decided to carry him in a fireman's lift past the two huge conifer trees. He opened the cab's passenger door and pitched him face first onto the seat.

'W-where did he get me? Is there much blood?' Griggs burbled.

From the glow of the cab's interior light Ryker could see the tranquilliser dart sticking into Griggs's left buttock. He gripped the plastic shaft and yanked out the needle.

'He got you in the backside with a dart,' he said. 'The kind used to knock out animals. The drug's discharged itself, but I dare say you'll live.'

Griggs didn't reply. Dizziness and nausea were already undermining him.

Ryker climbed into the driving seat, pulled off his mask, and started the engine. He gave a shaky sigh of relief as he said mockingly, 'Has anyone ever told you that you've got a shocking taste in underpants, Griggsy?'

Spring and Jonathan had joined the gathering round the caravan. Both were walking about in bare feet and pyjamas.

'I've found some clues,' Jonathan announced after doing a recce of the area. 'A holdall with stuff in it, and a leather belt.'

'Give them to Daniel.' Sky's voice sharpened. 'And both of you put some slippers on at once!'

'Scooter's hurt.' Spring appeared from underneath the caravan. 'He's licking his ribs.'

'I'll see to him in a moment.' Sky was holding a tissue to Shack's mouth, trying to stem the blood which trickled with alarming insistency onto his rugby shirt.

'What were those men after?' she asked Daniel.

He rummaged through the holdall and pulled out a bootee. 'By the look of this gear . . . Horses.'

'Rustlers?'

He nodded.

'Grief.' She shuddered slightly.

There was a rattle as the caravan's porch doors opened and Seamus appeared holding an oil lamp, his bowed shoulders draped in a quilt. He blinked in bafflement as the lamplight flickered across his craggy features.

'Blood and blunderbushes!' he exclaimed, looking at the mixture of emotions on the various faces. 'Is somethin' amiss? Me brain be fair twizzled wi' all the noise.'

Just his nonplussed presence helped lighten the atmosphere. In the clamour of what had happened, everyone had forgotten about Seamus.

Grins were exchanged, followed by a few giggles, and pretty soon the whole forecourt rang with uncontrollable laughter.

6

Very little sleep had been had since Ryker's and Griggs's unsuccessful visit. Only a confused Seamus had considered it worth going back to bed. Sky had busied herself between tending to Shack's bruises and the wounded Scooter, Daniel had sat up keeping a close eye on the fallow buck, and Spring and Jonathan were far too excited by the morning's happenings to consider doing anything apart from bombarding everyone with questions.

'I think you should lend a hand getting breakfast,' Daniel suggested, entering the kitchen from the yard and washing his hands at the large butler sink. He was talking to Spring and Jonathan who were tagging his every move.

'It's Sky's turn to cook breakfast,' Jonathan said breezily.

'Sky's busy with the vet. She's worried about Scooter.'

'I couldn't cook bacon,' Spring set her jaw stubbornly, 'the smell would make me sick.'

Daniel dried his hands and reached into a cupboard for a box of cornflakes. 'This morning we'll all have juice and cereal,' he announced without compromise, setting each of them various kitchen duties. 'And don't forget Seamus,' he added. 'Top of the milk on his cornflakes, and tea without sugar.'

There was a slight roughness in Daniel's throat and redness round his eyes to remind him of the excesses of the previous 24 hours. He yawned and stretched and joined Shack at the scrubbed pine table. Normally, he and Sky would take turns to cook breakfast, but this morning he was determined that Spring and Jonathan should pull their weight.

'Toast as well for me, please,' Daniel requested loudly. He let his left eyelid droop in a barely perceptible wink to Shack.

'Two sugars for me, kids,' Shack said, playing along.

'None for Sky.' Daniel turned his back and sat down, trying hard to stifle a quirky smile. 'She has a sweetener from a little clicky container . . . if you can find it.'

'I know what she has.' Jonathan's blue eyes flashed with irritation as he lowered the kettle onto a hotplate. 'She is *my* sister.'

Shack was studying the leather belt left behind by Griggs. It was fairly ordinary and had Size 32 stamped near the buckle. He placed it to one side and emptied the contents from the recovered holdall onto the kitchen table. Bolt-cutters, head-collar and halter, two sets of hoof bootees and a half-empty packet of book-matches.

There was a sickly blueness about his mouth, and as he examined each of the objects in turn, his face showed an unforgiving intensity, with none of the easy self-confidence that was usually so much part of him.

'We've got to stop this pair of rustlers,' he said, after a moment's reflection. 'If we don't do something, then no horse in the West Country is safe.'

'Owners should have their animals marked,' Spring announced emphatically.

'Electronic micro-chipping, hoof-branding, or the freeze-marking of a serial number on the horse's coat,' Shack agreed. 'Trouble is, people just won't spend the extra money.'

Daniel began fiddling with the book-matches.

'Silver Seagull Public House at Ilfracombe.' He read the printed words from the gold-embossed cover aloud. 'If they use this place on a regular basis then we might be able to track them down.'

'We didn't see their faces. They were wearing masks.'

'True, but we have descriptions of sorts.'

'Like one being big, and one being skinny?'

'Did you notice anything else?'

'One was wearing red knickers,' Jonathan interjected, as he crossed to the fridge for a jug of orange juice.

'He also had evil eyes,' Spring put in, distributing cornflakes into six bowls.

'I'm surprised you could see his eyes,' Shack said, folding his arms on the table and leaning forward. 'It was very dark.'

'She couldn't,' Jonathan stated. 'We were watching from an upstairs window.'

'Well . . . er . . . ' Spring was struggling. She fidgeted and flounced her fair hair before adding, 'Anybody who would deliberately kick Scooter must have evil eyes.'

'Son-of-a-pig!' Jonathan said with feeling.

Daniel decided to swing the conversation back to where it mattered. 'Did you notice anything unusual about the man you were fighting?' he asked Shack. 'Anything at all?'

Shack fingered his swollen lip and shook his head despondently.

'Shack was too busy punching him,' Jonathan interjected, nearly overfilling the teapot as he shaped like a boxer. 'A left hook to the jaw . . . a right jab to the body . . . '

'Too busy *not* punching him,' Shack amended significantly, 'he was far too powerful. When he went for a head-hold I thought I was going to black — ' he broke off, slapping the back of his neck with his palm. He stared a little oddly at Daniel as a vital section of memory slipped into place. 'Of course, the tattoo . . . how the heck could I forget that!'

'Tattoo?'

'Yes. He had gloves on but as he prised the torch from my fingers so the sleeves of his jacket rode up his arms. I saw it clearly. A birth-sign tattoo. On his right . . . ' he paused, considered. 'Yes, definitely his right forearm.'

Daniel arched an eyebrow. 'Which birth-sign?'

'Scorpio. It was a large yellow and blue scorpion.'

'Excellent clue!' Jonathan exclaimed, dropping slices of bread into the toaster. 'If we can find the tattooed man then we should find Mister Rafferty, eh, Daniel?'

Daniel nodded, deep in thought. He was quietly pleased. The tattoo was a major breakthrough, and now, at least, they had something to follow up. A plan began to form in his mind as Spring placed mugs of tea and bowls brimming with milky cornflakes on the table.

'Odd behaviour,' Shack murmured to Daniel, picking up Griggs's belt. 'Why would anyone risk losing their trousers?'

'To steal a greyhound?' Daniel suggested.

'Degsey? You're joking.'

'It's the only logical explanation. They were both standing by Degsey when we confronted them.'

'And a fat lot of use she turned out to be.' He sniffed his disapproval. 'It was all she could do to barely manage a growl.'

Daniel dug into his cornflakes, and between spoonfuls told Shack the full story about the torch, the tooth and the rifle.

'She held my gaze, her tooth shimmering . . . almost blinding me,' he went on. 'I lost all sense of reality . . . cocooned in her spell. It sounds crazy, I know, but things happened that were beyond my control. Degsey's inner energy, or whatever you want to call it, disengaged the gun's safety-catch and her mental powers forced me to pull the trigger. I didn't do anything voluntarily . . . I fought against it . . . But if she hadn't influenced me to fire, then the tattooed man might have killed you.'

Shack let his breath trickle out slowly. He sat back in his chair looking totally confounded. 'I had no idea,' he said quietly. 'Thank you, Degsey.'

'It was the leprechaun gold.' Spring had returned to the table holding Seamus's filled breakfast tray. She'd caught most of Daniel's words and was glowing with immediate pleasure.

''Tis the most enchantedest and power-fullest gold in the world,' Jonathan piped up, doing a bad impression of Seamus's Irish accent.

'I guess it is,' Shack said, standing up and stretching before taking the tray from Spring's hands.

Sky entered from the back door, nearly colliding with Shack as he made his way outside. She kicked off her wellingtons and hung her white coat on a peg. Her hair was ruffled against her forehead and her eyes were gritty through lack of sleep. She pulled up a chair and sank into it, giving a breathy sigh of exhaustion.

'The vet's just left,' she told Daniel. 'He's very pleased with the way you nursed the buck through the night. The animal's had an injection and seems settled. I'll be treating the wounds caused by the snare so we'll just have to keep our fingers crossed. Scooter's okay too — just bruising — no cracked ribs.'

'Where is he?' Jonathan asked, bringing hot, buttered toast to the table. Spring followed behind with Sky's cornflakes, juice and tea.

'Sitting on the caravan footboard with Degsey. Seems the two of them have forged an inseparable friendship . . . ' Sky paused, suddenly aware that she was being waited on. 'What have I done to deserve this VIP treatment?' she asked, sipping her orange juice and smiling appreciatively. 'Little brother and sister getting breakfast? Are you both feeling unwell?'

'We thought we'd do our bit . . . All pull together and that kind of stuff.' Jonathan avoided Daniel's eyes and looked a bit sheepish as he jerked out the words. 'You've been up all night . . . working very hard and that . . . ' He ventured an engaging grin. 'Just trying to help in a time of crisis.'

Sky shot Daniel a questioning look. He raked a hand through his thick hair and shrugged innocently.

'Well thank you — both of you.' Although weary she managed an impish grin. 'As you're obviously in a benevolent mood, can I ask one more favour?'

'Not the washing up?' Jonathan responded with a groan.

'No, something far more exciting.'

'Like what?'

'Three hedgehogs are due for release today. Can you manage that?'

'Oh, yes please!' Spring's eyes flung open to their very limit.

Sky went on to explain that she intended to send Shack home early so that he could rest and recover from his injuries. Megan and Hannah would take over Shack's normal duties, while she and Daniel released two foxes at Scamperbuck Ring.

'When I released the vixen we captured at the garage,' Daniel murmured reflectively, draining his mug of tea, 'I got a fair bit of abuse from a passing farmer at Horseshoe Coppice.'

'There's always been a conflict of interests,' Sky explained. 'Farmers don't like foxes, sometimes with good reason — so we're caught in the middle. It's Oyster Gables' policy to treat all wild animals equally. In our eyes they're all God's creatures.'

Shack returned with Seamus's breakfast tray. Both the cereal and the tea were untouched.

'Isn't the old boy hungry?' Daniel queried.

'Nope.' Shack's eyes appeared heavy and troubled as he shook his head. 'It's a bit worrying really. He says his rheumatics are playing him up, but I think there's more to it than that. He looks sort of grey . . . washed out.'

'Shall I call a doctor?'

'Seamus see a doctor, are you kidding?' Shack smiled, stretching his bruised mouth with a painful wince. 'I left him mixing up some herbs. He seems convinced he can cure himself.'

'There's only one real cure . . . ' Spring began hesitantly.

'Mister Rafferty,' Jonathan interrupted. 'He wants to get back on the road and he's pining for the old horse. Whenever I talk to him he asks if there's any news.'

Shack crunched toast and exchanged a knowing glance with Daniel.

'The vet told me that three horses were stolen in the early hours from Penhill,' Sky murmured bitterly. 'It must have been the same men. We were very lucky not to lose Excalibur and Sir Galahad.'

'It's becoming an epidemic,' Shack said.

'They're hateful people. Can't we . . . Can't we do something . . . ?' Spring broke off with a shudder.

Daniel saw the exchange of looks pass between them, the eyes expressing anger, a hint of dismay, of helplessness. He nibbled on a slice of darkly-browned toast as a plan began to form in his mind. If a carrot was dangled in front of the rustlers' noses — something they couldn't resist — then he reckoned they could be flushed out and caught. He had half an idea which, given a bit more time, and some luck, could be brought together to form a cohesive whole.

His expression tightened as he said, 'Don't worry, Spring. We'll catch them — and soon.'

Griggs was far from happy.

He'd been drugged for around six hours and had woken suffering dizziness, nausea, delirium and vomiting.

Ryker had put him to bed and was now holding a plastic bucket propped against his partner's chin as once again his face reddened, his chest heaved and he spewed out a mouthful of phlegmy sickness.

'Mind what you're doing!' Ryker flared, clicking his tongue against his teeth as his shirt cuff was suddenly stippled with a yellowish slime.

'I'm about to croak, T-Tony,' Griggs spluttered, gripping the bucket and wiping spittle from his mouth with the corner of the duvet. 'T-that dart must have contained enough poison to put down an elephant.'

'They don't contain poison, they contain a tranquilliser.'

'B-but I'm dying.'

'You're not dying. Your body's reacted badly to the drug, that's all.'

He heaved again, retched, and managed a large burp. He pushed the bucket away and sank back onto the pillow. His eyes were hazy and bloodshot and he was sweating slightly.

'Anyway, you deserve to be feeling lousy,'

Ryker informed him. 'Running away like that — leaving the holdall behind.'

'Did I?' Griggs looked confused.

'Of all the stupid things . . . All because of that blasted dog.'

'The greyhound at Swiftly . . . ' He groaned as an image of Degsey suddenly registered. 'I remember now! You were obsessed with capturing it, and I paid the price. In all the kerfuffle it's no wonder I forgot to pick up the bag.'

'I'll dock the price of the tools from your next pay-packet.'

'Ta, you're all heart.'

'Luckily nothing can be traced. It was all old gear, bought years ago.'

Griggs cringed slightly as he shifted the position of his buttocks in the bed. 'My backside's throbbing like hell,' he complained.

'Good,' Ryker countered smoothly. 'You wouldn't have been shot if you hadn't panicked. Now, because you're laid up, everything will have to be delayed for a couple of days. I'd scheduled three horses at Okehampton and the two at Tiverton for tonight's haul . . . Now all my plans are totally messed up.'

'Oh, I am sorry!' A thick vein bulged and jumped in Griggs's temple as he lifted his head from the pillow. 'I'm ill, don't you understand? I'm lying here suffering agonies. All I'm short of is one of my nosebleeds to crown the whole thing off.'

'Don't you dare bleed over the duvet. A bloodstain won't wash out.'

Griggs glared at him.

'What about the old nags?' Ryker continued. 'Our Belgium contact is expecting the shipment on Saturday. You're supposed to be driving them to Harwich.'

'No chance. You'll have to postpone it.'

'Until when?'

'Until I'm fully recovered! Now leave me alone to get some rest.'

Ryker made for the door. He turned as he reached it. 'I suppose you're expecting me to muck out the horses and feed them?'

'Well, someone's got to do it.'

Ryker cursed under his breath.

'The sooner you start,' Griggs added, 'the sooner you'll get finished.'

'And the cooking? What about that?'

'Don't worry on my account. I couldn't eat a thing.'

Ryker's mouth bunched in anger. 'I'm not asking if you'd like anything, I'm asking *you* if *you'll* be doing it!'

Griggs shook his head with a deliberate slowness and once again reached for the bucket. 'Food's in the fridge,' he said, belching twice — loudly — and managing a small dribble of vomit. 'You never could get the hang of the microwave. All those timing gadgets and touch-controls. Now's your chance to learn.'

★ ★ ★

'A trap?' Sky said, glancing at Daniel after a moment's reflection. 'So who or what is the cheese?'

'Either of the livery horses,' Daniel responded. 'We'll let them steal one — but we'll be a step ahead of their every move.'

They had left Swiftly village and were driving towards Scamperbuck Ring in Daniel's estate car. Degsey and Scooter had come along for the ride and were lying in the rear behind the dog-guard. Spring and Jonathan occupied the back seats, holding three transporting cages. Two contained foxes, the other held three hedgehogs.

They would all be released where they had been found. The foxes at Scamperbuck Ring, which was non-hunting land, and the hedgehogs in the nearby grounds of a large country house.

The injuries suffered were fairly common-place and Sky had dealt with similar

173

casualties in the past. One fox had lost an eye in a fight, whilst the other had dislocated its pelvis when in collision with a car. All three hedgehogs had been found in a compost heap where they had sustained unintentional wounds caused by a garden fork. The creatures had been sleeping when the accident had happened, and a very concerned gardener had immediately brought them to Oyster Gables for treatment.

'Here are the keys, kids.' Sky turned in her seat and handed a leather pouch to Jonathan. 'Mr and Mrs Blake are away on holiday so use the large brass key to open the garden gate. Walk past the lawns to the summer-house and release the hedgehogs close to the rose arbour. They'll be fine.'

Daniel slowed the Volvo and indicated left as he turned the vehicle into a huge tree-lined driveway. The roof of an elegant Georgian house was just visible above neatly trimmed blocks of tall hedging. Daniel rolled to a halt on crunching gravel and parked just short of the garden gate where a wrought-iron sign had been scrolled to form the house name: 'Greenacres'.

'Half-an-hour,' Sky informed her brother and sister, glancing at her watch. 'We'll be back by then. Take Scooter and when you've finished walk back down the driveway and wait carefully by the road entrance for us to pick you up.'

Jonathan and Spring leapt from the estate car anxious to complete their mission of rehabilitation. They lifted out the cage holding the hedgehogs and opened the hatchback door to collect an eagerly panting Scooter. Sky waved and Degsey pressed her wet nose against the rear window, watching keenly as Daniel reversed the Volvo into the turning circle and backtracked the vehicle down the drive to the main road.

'Are you sure we can catch the horse thieves?' Sky asked, picking up the earlier conversation as she leaned over her seat to check the transporting cages protecting the two foxes were positioned securely. 'I couldn't risk endangering a livery horse — not unless the plan was completely foolproof.'

'Cast iron,' Daniel told her. 'We'll need a small Rice trailer to tow the horse. Can you borrow one?'

'Shouldn't be a problem.' She nibbled on her lower lip and eyed Daniel suspiciously.

'I hope you're a good actress,' he said.

'Actress?' Sky's eyes sparkled with curiosity. 'Just what are you planning Daniel Rusk?'

'Shack's checking something out for me. I'll talk it over properly with you if all the pieces drop into place.'

'But Shack's supposed to be at home resting.'

'The checking will be done tonight. It's Friday, so he'll be visiting Sophie at Ilfracombe as usual.'

Sky said nothing, just frowned.

'There's a public house in the town called the Silver Seagull,' Daniel told her.

Sky looked vague. 'I know. What about it?'

'I'm pretty sure it's used by the rustlers. What I need to know — and what Shack will try and find out — is whether they have a routine for calling there. For my scheme to work the timing has to be perfect.'

Daniel eased the Volvo clear of the driveway and into the ribbon of traffic threading its way towards Fremington. Immediately adjacent to Greenacres was a huge expanse of Ministry of Defence training land whose advertising hoarding announced: FOR SALE. 130 ACRES. The location, encompassed by a high wire-mesh fence, had once been used by the Royal Marines for military exercises but had long since been evacuated and left to the ravages of the weather.

As Daniel adjusted his rear-view mirror he noticed that Degsey was taking more than a passing interest in the abandoned site. She was standing stiffly behind the dog-guard, her muscles quivering, her brilliant brown eyes full of hidden secrets as she stared fixedly at a large, partly demolished building. It had originally been constructed to resemble an enemy fortification which could be stormed during military manoeuvres. The windows had been blown out and the now crumbling brickwork had been studded with gunfire during mock battles. For some reason it fascinated Degsey. She began to growl . . . a deep growl which suddenly erupted into persistent barking.

'Shhh, Degsey.' Sky turned, following the dog's gaze to the tumbledown building behind the wire. Her eyes flicked curiously to Daniel. 'What on earth's the matter with her?'

Daniel shrugged, confused by Degsey's actions. He knew that greyhounds rarely barked unless keyed up for a racing or chasing event — and he'd never heard Degsey bark before — so her present behaviour seemed totally out of character.

'Maybe she's seen a rabbit,' he offered without much conviction.

Degsey continued to bark until the Volvo had sped past the perimeter fence and the view of the derelict building was replaced by thick leafy woodland. Daniel glanced in the mirror as she settled herself behind the dog-guard, long legs stretched forward, chin resting on the lower securing bar. The irises of her eyes were like huge droplets of cut-glass and Daniel could see his own miniature reflection mirrored many times. He blinked, slightly unnerved, and forced his attention back to the job in hand.

Scamperbuck Ring lay ahead.

Daniel glanced briefly at Sky. Her profile was silhouetted against the sweltering sunshine streaming through the car window. He left the main road via a side cutaway and steered the Volvo over some rough terrain and towards a clearing. All around there was birdsong and above them shafts of summer sunlight punched feathery holes in the branches causing patches of brightness and shadow to slick across the rich green foliage. The Ring's atmosphere was stickily hot and Daniel felt his polo shirt tugging damply at his shoulder blades as he negotiated a left turn and then a right, before nosing the Volvo into a hollow of shade.

'I love this place.' Sky was relaxed and smiling as she swung her legs clear of the car's bulkhead. A wave of warm air assailed her, a quickening of summer, a mixture of humid earth and dry wood, of leaves and grasses, broken only by a faint scent of the wild creatures which had made Scamperbuck Ring their home. She stretched sleepily, letting fragments of dappled sunlight play across her bare arms.

Daniel opened the hatchback and couldn't resist a grin as he spotted the blue Oyster Gables advertising sticker fixed by Jonathan to the Volvo's rear window. He attached a lead to Degsey's collar and watched Sky reach into the vehicle for the two transporting cages which contained the foxes. She smiled at him as she stretched forward; her hair was teased into its usual wildness — a kind of tawny froth which accentuated the line of her cheekbones. He smiled back, knowing he'd earned her friendship, her affection, but now he hoped for an extra special kind of closeness. He knew only too well that just being near to her made him feel giddy and light-headed . . . He also knew that given the slightest bit of encouragement it would only be too easy to fall head-over-heels in love with her.

'Here we are, boys.' Sky knelt and spoke to the foxes as she positioned the transporting cages on a carpet of grass well inside the Ring. 'I don't want to see either of you back at Oyster Gables,' she added positively, 'so stay out of trouble.'

Degsey lay by Daniel's feet, her expressive ears twitching as she waited for the foxes' moment of release. They sensed freedom

179

— smelled it — spinning around in the cages like whirling dervishes. Daniel took a firmer grip on Degsey's lead in case she decided to give chase.

Sky nodded to Daniel then slipped both catches on the hinged doors.

The foxes flew out. They were just a reddish-brown blur as they separated and made the 50-metre dash across open ground for cover. Foxes were well-known for their hurdling abilities and Sky laughed, Daniel grinned, and Degsey gave a tug on the lead as they showed off their athleticism by jumping a high bank of gorse and bracken before disappearing into a dense thicket of hazel.

'They'll soon go to ground.' Sky's eyes sparkled with satisfaction as she cupped a hand to her forehead, shielding her face from the sun. 'There are several resident families in this part of the Ring.'

Daniel noticed a pause as she compressed her lips and sighed. The foxes had gone and now she began to look a little distant. Various cheerless expressions darted across her face as she re-fastened the doors on the transporting cages and climbed to her feet.

'You okay?' he asked.

She allowed him to take her fingers into his grasp. Her nails were well-tended but innocent of polish, cut shortish but

180

smoothly manicured in a business-like, practical manner.

'Releasing casualties is supposed to be the most rewarding part of the job,' she murmured, making a valiant attempt at a smile, 'but it still leaves me with a large lump in my throat. I suppose I shouldn't get so attached to them.'

'You care deeply for the animals,' he said softly, pressing her fingers. 'It's only natural to feel sad when they go.'

'The foxes have their freedom but I'm being selfish.' She drew a long breath and tilted her head on one side so her tawny mass of hair swung free across her face. 'So you see Daniel, I'm not such a toughie after all.'

He began to play with her unresisting fingers. 'I'm seeing the real Sky Patakin, and I wouldn't have you any other way.'

'I was pretty awful to you when you first arrived.'

'I know.'

'I'd requested another female for the assistant manager's job.'

'Sexist.'

'I'm sorry.

'You're forgiven.'

They stood motionless, just looking at each other as they inhaled the pleasant scent of fir and cedar. Daniel's throat felt dry and he knew he desperately wanted to hold Sky close and kiss her. But would she accept such a move? Was his timing completely wrong — as it had been in the past? The questions tumbled over in his mind and he could feel his neck muscles nervously tighten as he searched unsuccessfully for answers.

Degsey was still lying at Daniel's feet, long white legs stretched in front of her as she panted in the heat. Daniel's gaze shifted momentarily from Sky to the greyhound as he remembered how Seamus had lectured Jonathan on the subtleties of Degsey's smile. Was it possible that he was witnessing it now? Certainly her open mouth curled up at the corners, lifting long folds of flesh in a curious, quirky way that complimented the dark mysterious twinkle in her eyes. They seemed to be reading his every expression, every gesture, every move.

He watched the rich pinkness of her tongue form a valley between her two sharp lower canines, wetting the gold tooth which now winked at him as it was caught by a ray of sunlight. Instantly everything became beautifully simple — and he knew, in some way, his thoughts and actions were being intensified by Degsey's presence.

Almost subconsciously he moved his hands to Sky's hips and then gently traced a finger over her neck, her lips, her nose. She bent her forehead to his shoulder, her hands clutching at his waist. She wanted to stay there forever, lost in his tenderness as he cradled her in the warmth of his arms.

Daniel kissed her closed eyes and the tiny pulse that beat at her temple.

Sky's heartbeat quickened. She gave an involuntary gasp of pleasure.

'I'm very glad I came to Swiftly,' Daniel murmured, his lips on her cheek.

'Me too.' Her eyes were bright with a vague sense of her own desirability. She rested her hand on the nape of his neck where his damp hair had curled in the warmth of the sun.

Daniel kissed her more demandingly and Sky responded by clinging tightly to him for slightly longer than she intended.

'Wow!' Daniel broke the kiss and laughed suddenly, his gaze dropping to Degsey. 'When you do things girl, you certainly do them properly.'

Sky's cool dark eyes lingered on him. 'Me?'

'No, Degsey.'

'You were talking to Degsey?'

'Mmm. When I first held you I was hesitating whether to — '

'Daniel Rusk, are you saying a dog made you kiss me?'

'Well, yes . . . I mean no . . . It wasn't like that. I wanted to kiss you — desperately. Her tooth helped things along, I suppose.'

'Her tooth!' she exclaimed with some resentment. 'You don't still believe in Seamus's magical hocus-pocus, do you?'

'I'd be a liar if I told you I didn't,' he said with mild humour.

'So the kiss wasn't spontaneous?'

'Of course it was. I think I'm falling in love with you.'

'But you needed a nudge.' Her face flushed hot at the thought as she folded her arms and looked down at Degsey. She stared at the greyhound challengingly, her eyebrows raised. 'Apparently Daniel needs your approval before he can be guided by his heart. I don't believe you have special powers, Degsey, but if you're trying to be clever, then stop it!'

Degsey inched herself closer to Daniel then looked up at Sky with her huge brown riveting eyes.

Sky picked up the transporting cages and turned smartly on her heel. 'We'd better collect Jonathan and Spring,' she said brusquely.

★　★　★

184

There was no sign of the children waiting at the bottom of the slip-road that led from 'Greenacres'. Sky tut-tutted and checked her wristwatch as Daniel swung the Volvo clear of the main road and cruised gently to a halt alongside a grass verge.

Degsey had her nose pressed firmly against the rear window and was making distraught, nervy little movements with her head. She could see the adjacent Ministry of Defence training area and once again the dynamo of energy which normally hummed quietly inside her body had started to race wildly. She began to bark loudly and with a continuous urgency.

'Oh no, not again . . . ' Sky began, then blinked, went pale, swallowed hard. She'd turned her head to chastise the greyhound but stopped short on glimpsing an empty transporting cage propped against the base of the high wire mesh fence.

'Spring and Jonathan were definitely here,' she said, touching dry lips with a dry tongue. She pointed. 'T-that's the cage that held the hedgehogs.'

Daniel immediately flung open the car door, jumped out of the driving seat and sprinted across to the fence. He could see that a section of wire mesh had been cut and bent back, leaving just enough room for a body to squeeze through. A quickly suppressed flash of panic came and went from his eyes as he took in the warning words of a notice pinned to a metal post. It read: M.o.D. PROPERTY. KEEP OUT. BUILDINGS UNSAFE & DANGEROUS.

Degsey's muffled barking was still beating at Daniel's ears and he knew he desperately wanted the dog with him. The greyhound had a sixth sense — of that he was sure — and now he intended to put her talent to its full use.

Sky had got out of the Volvo and was shielding the sun from her eyes as she frantically scanned the length of the perimeter fence. Daniel shouted to her, indicating the gap in the mesh. 'I reckon they've gone through here,' he said, his breathing suddenly jerky and clogged. 'Bring Degsey!'

The greyhound responded to Daniel's voice and dived clear of the hatchback the moment it was opened. She ducked past the leather lead held in Sky's outstretched hand and made an immediate bee-line for the fence. Daniel felt her soft, supple body streak past his legs as she powered herself through the gap, setting a blistering pace towards the partly demolished hangar-sized building that resembled an enemy fortification.

'This fence has been deliberately cut,' Sky

said breathlessly, easing herself through the gap. 'Spring and Jonathan would never do that.'

'Vandals would,' Daniel responded, following her. 'The clipped ends of the mesh have gone rusty. It's been like this for some time.'

Degsey had settled on all fours beside a tumbledown wall which at one time had served as a bombardment barrier during military exercises. She could hear sounds and noises inaudible to the human ear and her muscles quivered in anticipation of what she must do. She now had a clear view of the rickety, bullet-scarred building which had prompted her earlier unease and triggered her uncompromising barking. She'd felt odd sensations prickle the hairs along her backbone when Daniel had first driven past it in the car — a premature warning of foreboding which teased at her razor-sharp senses and spelled imminent danger. Now, as she threaded her way forward, avoiding obstacles and sharp pieces of debris, her acute perception stirred up images of Spring, Jonathan and Scooter.

She knew they were inside the building and she also knew they were in desperate trouble.

7

'Degsey's disappeared into that building!' There was a note of desperation in Daniel's voice as he dodged across a concrete compound pitted with shell craters. He'd taken Sky's hand and they were weaving their way past old tyres, rusty oil drums, huge wooden spools which had once held cables, and the chewed-up remains of a training area now hindering their progress.

'Perhaps Degsey's found — ' Sky began, then stopped in her tracks as the letters of a large worn and battered notice-board came into view. It was nailed to what was left of the hanger-sized building's front door and the message made her gasp, her features tightening as if in pain. Stencilled boldly in red paint it stated: KEEP CLEAR. THIS STRUCTURE IS IN DANGER OF COLLAPSE.

Sky uttered a faint moan. 'Oh, no, please tell me they haven't . . . '

'Take it easy,' Daniel said, steadying Sky's arm and squeezing it reassuringly. 'We can't be sure that Jonathan and Spring are inside.'

A couple of throaty barks — unmistakably Scooter — ended all further speculation. Sky and Daniel exchanged worried glances.

'Stay behind me, stay close, and watch your footing,' Daniel said cautiously, cursing as he knocked his ankle against a boulder. He kicked some loose rubble aside in order to reach the door. It was already half-open and hanging at a precarious angle by one hinge — easy enough for small bodies and dogs to get through but not wide enough for him or Sky.

He pushed it stiffly, hearing a groan of resistance before it opened fully under the pressure from his shoulder. A cascade of powdery brick-dust billowed downwards, covering Sky's hair like a veil and clinging uncomfortably to her eyelashes. Daniel heaved a cough as the dust caught in his throat and stuck grittily to the filmy sweat on his forehead. A few seconds passed as both waited for the air to become breathable before they made their way cautiously inside.

At eye-level there wasn't much to see — just a huge expanse of vacant space and Scooter panting fretfully and running round in circles on the rubble-strewn floor. The air was fusty and smelled of damp concrete and rotting wood. Daniel blinked to clear his vision and knuckled his eyes as he focussed on Degsey.

Through a haze of dust he saw the

greyhound had used the springy power of her thighs to leap onto an old metal-framed canteen table still occupying the centre of the room. The building's roof had caved inwards leaving a gaping hole where a few slates still hung dangerously suspended.

Degsey lay perfectly still under the broken roof, her head and body bathed in a fragmented pattern of sunlight. Her eyes were gleaming and alert as they systematically recorded the hazards around her.

'Up there!' Sky's voice rose shrilly. She went rigid, clutching at Daniel's arm as the creaky movement of an old metal staircase flickered at the corner of her eye. 'Something's moving. Is it . . . ?'

Daniel squinted towards the roof, his eyes scanning the broken rafters to where an observation balcony was linked to the staircase and ran the full length of one wall. There, huddled in a corner, looking down at him with feverish eyes, were Spring and Jonathan.

'It's them.' Daniel swallowed, the saliva thickening in his throat.

Sky just stared, a hectic flush suffusing her face.

'W . . . we can't get down!' Jonathan shouted the words, shifting his position slightly on the balcony. He'd taken off his shirt and was holding it in a tight little bundle on his lap. There was a circular bruise on his forearm and his fingernails were ingrained with dirt. 'We came up here to rescue a barn owl. I . . . It was hit by a lorry as it dived for small mammals at the roadside. W . . . we watched it while we were waiting for you to pick us up . . . and it flew into this old building.' He pointed to his torn shirt, adding, 'I've got it here . . . wrapped up. I think it's broken a wing.'

Daniel was becoming increasingly aware that every time Jonathan drew a breath his shoulders would flex against the wall and cause the whole balcony structure to move. Little puffs of red brick-dust pattered downwards as the anchor points for the metal staircase moved alarmingly.

'Don't talk and don't move,' Daniel instructed, edging forward, his feet crunching over broken glass. 'I'll come up and get you.'

'But it's not safe,' Sky whispered the words, her teeth biting into her bottom lip. 'If you put your weight on those stair treads then the balcony could collapse.'

'I've no choice. Cross your fingers that the structure holds.'

'I'll go . . . I'm just as capable,' Sky said quickly. 'I'm also much lighter.'

'Not a chance. There's no way I'm risking

you getting injured.'

'Then we have to get help.'

'No time.'

'There must be some other — '

Sky paused with her mouth open on hearing the ugly graunch of metal rasping against metal, followed by a loud crack. One end of the balcony dropped ten precious centimetres nearer to the ground. Scooter let out a distressed bark as brick chippings rained down on him. Spring screamed in terror as both she and Jonathan were now tilted at an angle where gravity threatened to take them on a roller-coaster ride to certain injury.

'Grab hold of the rails!' Daniel reacted immediately. 'Don't slip! Hang on tightly!'

Daniel's palms were sweating and he could feel a vein pulsing beneath his ear as he wrapped his fingers around the iron bannister. His knuckles showed chalky white as, in one bound, he spanned the staircase to the third tread, praying inwardly that the structure would withstand his bodyweight.

No such luck. The metal treads rasped a noisy warning and shuddered violently against the balcony.

Spring and Jonathan bounced slightly as the whole structure tilted perilously lower. There was a noise like sporadic gunfire as bolts pinged out of their sockets. Dust billowed and loose roof tiles clattered to the floor as a huge gash opened up in the wall behind Daniel just as he jumped clear of the staircase. He watched the large crack rip through the plaster as it spidered upwards. It was like a can-opener splitting a tin and it ran from floor to ceiling, its progress dislodging one of the roof rafters.

Sky felt herself being pulled to one side by Daniel as the rafter crashed with ear-stunning force to the ground. Sharp wooden splinters scattered in all directions narrowly missing her face but she was barely aware of the danger. Her thoughts were with her brother and sister as she stood, her hands twisting her hair, damp with fright, the mask of her composure askew, tears brimming in eyes focussed upwards in a unblinking stare.

'We're slipping! Please, please help us!' Jonathan's breath came in harsh gasps between his dry lips. He was clinging to an upright rail with one hand, while the other hand stopped Spring from falling as it clutched at the belt of her jeans.

It wasn't fear that blanched Daniel's face; it was the realisation that in his own hands lay the decision of how to initiate a rescue. His mind zigzagged wildly as he looked up at the two helpless figures suspended high above him. How long would they be able to hang on? Would the whole building collapse? Would he and Sky be engulfed in falling debris?

There was a deep rumbling noise which shook the very foundations of the construction. Sky clung to Daniel as the sound of shifting walls and crumbling masonry crashed around her ears. She knew she was trapped in the middle of a nightmare that was only seconds from reaching its climax . . .

'Degsey! Degsey!' Spring's shrill voice cut through the destructive clamour. Tears smarted under her eyelids as swept by sudden vertigo her head lolled sideways and she glimpsed the unmoving greyhound. 'Use your special powers, Degsey . . . Some of Seamus's se . . . serendipity! Oh, smile for us, please!'

Degsey's soft eyes lifted towards Spring and blinked sleepily against the shafts of sunlight which angled in through the gash in the roof. Slowly, very slowly, her lower jaw dropped and her muzzle quivered, forming deep little crevices and crinkles in the supple skin. The outside edge of her bottom lip was black and shiny, contrasting starkly against the tiny globules of saliva which glistened on her pink tongue as she displayed her sharp, gold canine tooth. She could have been panting, but she wasn't. Spring and Jonathan both knew that she was showing them her huge, wonderful smile.

Suddenly, unbelievingly, there was a tomb-like silence.

No more rumbles, crashes or tremors. No more falling masonry. Nothing. The only sounds were the ticking of Daniel's wrist-watch and Jonathan's laboured breathing.

'W . . . what's happening?' Sky swallowed rapidly, her throat pulsing.

She turned to look at Degsey, lifting a hand to shield her eyes from the laser-bright glint of the tooth. It was irradiating a blinding gold halo which seemed to expand and brush against the walls of the building.

'No time to waste.' Daniel knew exactly what was happening and immediately launched himself up the staircase.

He was conscious of his lungs rhythmically filling and emptying as he powered over the treads — each one now easily accepting his weight and holding firm.

The balcony loomed ahead of him. It was hanging at a lopsided angle where the metal had buckled, distorted, and tilted downwards like some hideous fairground slide.

'She . . . she's slipping . . . ' Jonathan's mouth was twisted in a grimace as he strained to keep hold of Spring's belt. His arm and fingers had gone numb under the pressure and he could feel his sister begin to slither from his grasp.

'Daniel . . . ' Spring shrieked the name as Jonathan involuntarily released his grip.

'Stay on your back!' Daniel yelled hoarsely, dropping to his knees and spreading out his arms. 'Don't be frightened. I'll catch you!'

She lost a shoe as she spiralled towards him.

Twenty metres . . . ten . . .

The balcony uprights flashed madly past her eyes but there was no time for fear. She held her breath as she bounced a couple of times, then felt a gush of relief as Daniel's strong hands halted her progress, sweeping her upwards and cushioning her against his chest. He held her there for a comforting moment, marvelling at the fact that although weary she could still manage a bright, dancing smile.

'Make your way carefully down the staircase,' he instructed, lowering her feet to the treads. 'Sky's waiting for you.'

Degsey watched Spring's progress with her all-seeing gaze. Nothing escaped her attention. Neither her smile nor the halo of light faltered as she charted Spring's journey to the safety of Sky's arms. Scooter darted around gleefully and there were lots of hugs as sister was reunited with sister.

Jonathan was now standing upright and gingerly testing the balcony for strength. The laser-bright halo from Degsey's tooth danced across his legs as he shifted his bodyweight this way and that. Nothing moved. The structure was as steady as a rock.

Sweat beaded his forehead as he edged his way down the balcony incline towards the staircase. He was still clutching the barn owl in his torn shirt and despite barely managing to remain upright he refused Daniel's offer of help and remained stubbornly independent of making it on his own.

Sky, Spring and Scooter watched anxiously from floor level.

Degsey remained on the table, bathed in sunlight.

'There ... did it!' Jonathan almost collapsed with exhaustion as he finally reached the staircase. He grabbed Daniel convulsively, shaking and giddy with effort.

'Let's join Sky and get away from here,' Daniel said hurriedly. 'Degsey can't keep smiling for ever.'

Jonathan accepted a steadying hand as he carefully made his way down the treads. He had his eyes fixed on Sky and Spring, showing them both a shaky but relieved grin, whereas Daniel kept snatching sideways glances at the greyhound.

Degsey had come unexpectedly into his life.

And now she had saved his life . . . All of their lives.

Not forgetting Seamus and Fin and a gold tooth.

The series of events tumbled over one another in Daniel's mind. He knew that had it not been for Degsey's intervention the staircase and balcony would now be just a tangled mass on the floor. He reflected grimly that the wall behind him was defying gravity by remaining staunchly vertical. By rights it should have collapsed and brought the building crashing down around them.

The whole episode defied all logic. It couldn't be explained rationally and would only be believed if witnessed first hand. Any interested party, listening when the story was later recounted, would find it about as real as a hologram.

'Sweetheart!' Sky's smile was a mockery of its usual brilliance as she gathered Jonathan in her arms, planting tiny kisses on his forehead. 'Are you sure you're alright? No broken bones — just bruises?'

'I'm fine.' Jonathan exhaled a short fervent sigh of relief to keep his nerves in check. His bare body was gleaming like moist putty and he displayed the purplish knock on his forearm with pride. 'I got the bruise rescuing the barn owl,' he said, handing the little body still wrapped in his shirt to Sky. 'It *will* be okay, won't it?'

Sky's lips were pressed together regretfully as she looked down at the owl's beautiful, winsome, heart-shaped face. The eyes were closed and as she felt inside the shirt, caressing the soft, mottled brown wings, the lack of warmth confirmed the worst.

'Is he dead?' asked Spring in a half-whisper.

Sky nodded uncomfortably.

Jonathan looked away, distressed. 'H . . . he was alright when I picked him up from the balcony. H . . . he was dazed, but he was moving. That's why I wrapped him up in the shirt.'

'My guess is he broke his neck when the lorry hit him,' Sky said, applying gentle pressure to the skeletal conformation at the base of the bird's head. She nodded to herself, confirming her diagnosis. 'What you witnessed was probably just a series of nervous spasms. It happens. I'm very sorry.'

Jonathan nodded and let out a long, slow breath. 'I'll take him back to Oyster Gables and bury him.'

Degsey was getting restless. Daniel threw an anxious glance at her, watching as she shifted her haunches into a more comfortable position on the table. He was overwhelmed by the strength of her spirit but he could see that she was suddenly looking exhausted, panting now as she tried to muster more energy.

'We really ought to be moving,' he said, throwing a note of urgency into his voice. 'I know Degsey can work miracles, but we're pushing her special powers to the limits.'

Spring, Jonathan and Sky turned to look at the greyhound. In the heat of all the bizarre happenings they had been too self-absorbed to notice that Degsey was tiring dramatically as she constantly monitored and took stock of everything happening around her. The reassuring gold light which had seared at their eyes with such intensity had lost its bright edge and was now gradually beginning to soften and wane.

Scooter let out a yelp and jumped backwards as a piece of crumbling masonry plummeted down from the roof. It narrowly missed his front paws, shattering into fragments.

'Something's happening to Degsey!' Spring exclaimed with nervous loudness. 'Her tooth . . . It's losing — '

'Its strength,' Jonathan put in, swallowing hard.

Daniel immediately saw the danger. He could feel a rumble beneath his feet as the crack in the wall began to widen. Little puffs of plaster heralded another tremor. 'Everyone outside!' he urged, grasping Scooter's collar. 'Degsey's powers are weakening so go now . . . Hurry!'

Feet trampled over floor debris in the rush for the door. Sky wrapped protective arms around Jonathan and Spring as she shepherded them outside. Daniel followed, manhandling Scooter in order to get him clear of any danger. The boxer didn't want to leave Degsey and he was making his feelings firmly felt by sitting on his rump and stubbornly resisting. Daniel heaved and strained on the thick leather collar before physically dragging Scooter away.

Outside, everyone stood looking at everyone else. All faces were creased with the exhaustion of the ordeal and all looked sweaty and dishevelled. Matted hair, faces smeared with brick dust, torn clothing and tiny cuts and scraped knuckles became apparent when scrutinised in the bright sunshine.

The building shuddered once more. Daniel looked up as tiles shook loose and began to slide into the roof's gaping hole. They seemed to fall in slow motion — as if some mad magician was performing a grotesque trick with a gigantic pack of playing cards.

'Wait over there.' Daniel indicated a safe area about ten metres away. 'We're all standing too close. This building could collapse at any moment.'

They all felt unutterably weary and their eyes reflected their physical exhaustion as they began to trek to the point of safety — everyone that is, except Spring. She stood her ground, her lower lip jutting out stubbornly as she grabbed Daniel's arm to voice an urgent question.

'Why isn't Degsey with us? Why hasn't she followed us?'

'She's probably waiting for us to get clear,' Daniel responded. 'She's still using her powers to prop up the structure . . . giving us time to find safety.'

'B . . . but you said her powers were weakening. She'll be killed if she doesn't come out.'

Daniel shifted uneasily. There was a tight pause.

The taste of salt fell on Spring's lip as she glared at him. 'We can't leave her . . . we just can't!'

'She'll be alright. She's a very clever dog who can take care of herself.'

Spring opened her mouth to argue but no words came. She was staring at the red, stencilled warning sign attached to the building's door. Only it wasn't — not any more. Pressure from the loose bricks above had forced out the nails, splitting the wood, and sending it crashing to the ground. A main supporting girder followed, dropping with such force that Daniel had only a split second to react. He threw both arms around Spring's waist and using almost a judo throw, lifted her, spun his body, and dived to safety. He landed heavily on his side with Spring cushioned protectively against his ribcage.

'Are you alright, Daniel? Are you hurt?' Jonathan was behind him, trying desperately to pull him well clear of the building.

'I'm okay.' He mumbled the answer and winced from the pain in his side as he tried to sit upright.

Sky helped Spring to her feet and they all managed to stagger the few extra metres to complete safety.

Then the inevitable happened.

The fallen girder released a chain reaction of ruthless demolition. In a tidal wave of naked force each of the four walls folded like cardboard and tumbled inwards sending bricks thundering earthwards to be reduced to rubble.

Spring's head was bent, her fair fall of hair obscuring her features as she clasped her hands to her ears. Sky and Jonathan had both covered their eyes and turned away, leaving only Daniel to witness the scene of destruction. His mouth drooped as he watched the tumbling masonry. All animation left his face, leaving it slack and drained of expression. In less than ten seconds the entire structure was reduced to nothing more than a flattened pile of debris shrouded by a dust cloud rising slowly into the atmosphere.

As the noise gradually ceased, Sky turned to take in the scene. She looked calm and controlled; very purposeful. 'Did Degsey manage to get out?' she asked Daniel. 'Have you seen her?'

He gave his head a vigorous shake. 'I've seen no movement — nothing.'

'Oh, lordy,' Jonathan bit into his lip, adding numbly, 'she must be as dead as the barn owl.'

'Don't speak like that!' Spring's eyes grew bright with unshed tears. 'That's a cruel and wicked thing to say. She's probably lying injured . . . waiting for us to help her . . . like she helped us.'

'Don't worry, Spring.' Daniel smiled to put her at ease, all the while keeping a sharp eye on the surroundings as little pockets of dust began to thin. 'If she's alive, we'll find her.'

Sky and Daniel moved forward with

Scooter at their heels. It was like walking into a dense fog and they blinked repeatedly as airborne grime stung their eyes. They picked their way carefully over the fallen rubble, holding hands to keep themselves steady as they used their limited vision to seek out any sign of the greyhound.

Scooter appeared optimistic. He'd got wind of a scent and had bounded away, barking as if to be followed. Sky tried to call him back but he just disappeared into a dense swirl of dust, his stump of a tail wagging furiously.

'I'm not holding out much hope of finding Degsey,' Sky said despondently, keeping her voice low so that Spring couldn't catch the words. 'I hate to say it, but on this occasion I agree with Jonathan.'

Daniel nodded reluctantly and squeezed Sky's hand, pointing out danger in the shape of a broken windowframe surrounded by shards of glass. They skirted round it, both now aware that a constant, freshening breeze had sprung up. It ruffled their hair and helped dissipate the dust. Suddenly, fractured slabs of concrete previously just a hazy blur, were now taking on a more definable shape.

Seconds passed — then amidst all the devastation they saw Scooter.

A pocket of dust had swirled away at ground level revealing the boxer encircling the legs of the metal-framed canteen table. Sky and Daniel exchanged incredulous glances and blinked at each other as if they had just woken up. They both held their breath in anticipation as the upper cloud of murky dust lifted and was wafted away on the breeze.

'*Degsey!*' Daniel's bruised side niggled painfully as a reflex action forced him to shout out the name. How the table had survived the bombardment was a total mystery to him — and how the greyhound still came to be lying on it was nothing less than a miracle.

Spring and Jonathan both gave a yell of delight and sprinted over the rubble to join the group. Sky was already at the table, running practised eyes and hands over the dog's head and body, checking for injuries. She had spotted a bright sheen of blood as it trailed in a lacy pattern along the back edge of the table and was now trying to trace the origin.

She said, gently and with great relief, 'All I can find is a cut just above the base of the tail — not deep enough for stitches — just a bit messy. It was probably caused by the edge of a falling roof tile.'

'Can you fix it?' Daniel asked.

'Not until we get back to Oyster Gables. I

didn't bring my first aid case.'

'Better leave it to Seamus,' Jonathan said sensibly. 'He'll have some leaves or bits of old twigs to help heal a cut. He won't want you fiddling with it.'

Tears glittered in Spring's eyes as she leaned against the table. 'I love you, Degsey,' she whispered, pressing her face against the greyhound's muscular neck and brushing her lips across the soft brindle ear markings. 'Seamus said you were a special dog . . . one who could work miracles. I know you've hurt yourself, but thank you so much for smiling.'

Degsey rested her head in the crook of Spring's arm and looked up at her with peaceful, contented eyes. Spring squeezed her tightly, flushing with pleasure as Degsey nuzzled closer.

Scooter was feeling left out of the proceedings and rubbed himself affection-ately against Sky's legs. He was rewarded with lots of playful pats and a bit of spirited horseplay from Daniel.

'How come Degsey didn't get crushed?' Jonathan threw Daniel an inquiring glance. 'By rights the table should have been flattened . . . I don't understand?'

'Neither do I,' Daniel admitted, fingering his jaw for inspiration. 'My guess is — and it's only a guess — that she surrounded herself with some sort of protective force field.'

'You mean . . . electricity?'

'Maybe.'

'Or magnetism might work,' Jonathan speculated.

'Who cares how she did it,' Sky put in. 'Let's all be grateful that she's safe — and that because of her, we're safe too.'

'Oh, so it *isn't* hocus-pocus?' Daniel put his hand on her shoulder, a mischievous query in his dark eyes. 'You do believe in Degsey's special powers?'

'I didn't,' she confessed quietly, 'especially after what happened at Scamperbuck Ring. But now I definitely stand corrected. Degsey is a greyhound with an incredible gift.'

She heaved a sigh, smiled, and looked almost relaxed as she spoke. Daniel's arm lifted and she slid under it to be drawn close to his side, her head coming to rest quite naturally on his shoulder.

Daniel ran his fingertips through her messed-up hair and glanced at the smudges of brick dust on her face. 'Ms Patakin you look terrible,' he said wryly.

'Ditto, Mr Rusk,' she responded with tender amusement.

Jonathan was puzzled by his sister's earlier words. 'Scamperbuck Ring?' he queried, blinking blue eyes. 'I don't understand. How could releasing some foxes change your mind about Degsey?'

Daniel and Sky exchanged confidential little glances but said nothing.

'Is it a secret?' Jonathan pressed.

'Could be,' Daniel hedged.

Degsey appeared to have recovered her spent energy. She stood up on the table, yawned, and stretched every tendon in her long forelegs. She looked knowingly at Spring as her left eyelid drooped in what could have been a final shaking off of fatigue, or maybe a subtle wink. Spring preferred to believe the latter.

'And Degsey's keeping the secret,' she said.

★   ★   ★

Tony Ryker's patience was wearing thin. He wasn't used to carrying out menial tasks — to fetch and carry and generally act the lackey — but that's exactly what current circumstances had forced him to do. He was dressed in overall-type trousers, tucked into wellington boots, and an old shirt buttoned tightly across his flabby stomach. The sleeves were rolled up and sweat patches stained the neck, back and armpits.

'Blast you Griggsy!' he said loudly and with feeling, letting his words echo around the walls of the warehouse.

Nobody heard him but the sudden outburst caused one of the stolen Penhill horses to turn its head and give an insolent snort. Ryker responded by yelling abuse at the animal and only just resisted hurling a broom in its direction.

The old fertiliser warehouse had been converted to hold up to twenty horses in separate stalls — and many times in the past it had been bursting to overflowing. Now, as Ryker swept the last pile of soiled bedding and manure into a muck sack and heaved the load onto his shoulder, he pondered on the unsatisfactory fact that at present it housed only three.

Thursday night's haul would have meant plenty of profit if things had gone to plan and they'd returned to Hele with the full ten-animal quota. But, as Ryker lugged the waste manure to the outside dung heap, he reflected bitterly that through his partner's inability to avoid a tranquilliser dart, the evening's work had been barely cost effective.

'Glad you're coping alright.' Griggs suddenly appeared from nowhere. He was wearing a clean white shirt, with the sleeves rolled up over his bony elbows, and neatly pressed jeans complimented by a new pair of training shoes. A smirk settled on his face as he decided to turn the tables and take pleasure in Ryker's present discomfort. 'Try and distribute the weight more evenly on your shoulder, Tony, otherwise you might drop the dung.'

Ryker swung his body as if to let the load fly in Griggs's direction. The sudden movement caused his partner to duck, but Ryker stopped short, cursed under his breath, and let the steaming contents of the sack shuffle out to add another layer to the huge manure heap.

'Tch, tch.' Griggs wagged a mocking finger at the big man. 'I thought for a moment you were going to unload that on me. Temper, temper, Tony, think of your blood pressure.'

'I was thinking more about my wallet,' Ryker replied curtly. 'This pile of dung has reached the point where it's worth fifty pounds to the local garden centre — so I'm not wasting any of it on you!'

Griggs gave a humourless chuckle. He was looking and feeling much perkier than yesterday — a fact that hadn't gone unnoticed by Ryker.

'How come you're looking so healthy, Griggsy? You could have driven the old horses to Harwich — no problem.'

'Did you manage to postpone it?'

'After a lot of phone calls and aggravation,

yes. I've put the trip back a week.'

'Good. I still feel a bit fragile. I'm in no fit state to drive the travelling box.'

Ryker gave him a sharp look. 'So how come you're out of bed and bothering me?'

'Thought I'd show willing. Maybe do a bit of housework.' Amusement edged his words as he added, 'Nothing too taxing . . . some light dusting around the home perhaps.'

'How about feeding the old horses and cleaning out the water troughs?'

'Too strenuous, Tony. You're forgetting I was shot at. I've had a terrible shock to my nervous system.'

'I wish I *could* forget it,' Ryker said, barely curbing his impatience as he strode towards the paddock. 'If you're not going to make yourself useful then stop annoying me. Go back to the mobile home and convalesce.'

'I'll stick around for a bit . . . You know, put my personal pain at the back of my mind. Partners like us should always have a caring and sharing attitude.'

Griggs was enjoying the role reversal game too much to back off now. Ryker had propped a bale of hay against the paddock's five-barred gate and Griggs watched, arms folded, as the big man gave him a glowering look and cut the string with a pocket knife. As half the bale was removed, Griggs made a generous flourish of lifting the latch on the gate and beckoning Ryker through.

'Don't overburden your strength, Griggsy,' Ryker breathed in a loud exaggerated way. 'I would hate you to add a slipped disc to the rest of your troubles.'

The six elderly horses were at the far end of the paddock when they heard the gate creak open. They all turned to look, and depending on their physical state, either managed a shambling trot or a reasonable canter in their efforts to be first to the hay. It was almost a mini cavalry charge and Mister Rafferty headed the group. Clumps of earth flew as the chestnut cob braked, pivoted, and very nearly bulled into Ryker's shoulder. Having unbalanced the big man, he tore out a lump of fodder with his teeth, before skittering away.

'Get back!' Ryker brandished the broom handle at the remainder of the snorting horses and regained his footing. As they scattered away he turned quickly to Griggs. 'I had problems yesterday with that gypsy horse,' he grated. 'The animal's a definite trouble-maker.'

Griggs's mouth quirked at one corner as he gazed at Ryker with a gleam of amusement. 'Face facts, Tony. You just can't handle 'em — you never could.'

'Don't talk rubbish.'

'You're too soft . . . I'm telling you.'

'They're a bad-tempered bunch of nags because you starve them,' he said stiffly, thrusting the half bale of hay into Griggs's hands. 'I'm aware of your devious games, my little ferret. I warned you about cutting back on their food ration and pocketing the extra money. Now shake that hay out — and make sure they each get a fair share!'

Griggs curled his lip in a gesture of defiance but the steely glare in Ryker's eyes told him the balance of power had once again shifted back in the big man's favour.

'I keep 'em hungry for a reason,' Griggs said arrogantly, watching Ryker stroll back to the gate. 'With me around they know who's boss. They respect me. One word from Griggsy and they do as they're told.'

He faced away from Ryker and puckered his lips in a shrill whistle. The sound brought five of the six horses obediently back at a very slow, wary trot.

'I think I've just proved my point,' he called out smugly, doing a cocky little walk as he distributed the hay at various feed stations around the paddock.

The point was proven — almost. The only element he hadn't bargained for was Mister Rafferty's Irish antics. The old chestnut cob

214

had cantered a full circuit of the paddock and was fast approaching Griggs from the rear. Ryker glimpsed the horse but said nothing to his partner. It was like an accident waiting to happen the big man thought, fighting down a grin as he leaned casually against the five-barred gate.

'I can't handle them, eh?' he murmured to himself. 'So let's see if you can.'

'You say something?' Griggs muttered sullenly.

Ryker shrugged and shook his head.

Griggs turned to make his way back to the gate in a dawdling fashion and began nonchalantly picking stray bits of hay from his white shirt. He wasn't really looking anywhere — certainly not to his rear — and he appeared blissfully unaware that Mister Rafferty was heading straight for him.

The gypsy cob had dragged out some hay from a feeding station and this was now streaming from his mouth as he munched, ran, and homed in on his target. Old and stiff he very definitely was, but he could still show a swift turn of foot when a devilish mood was upon him.

Griggs saw the horse — just a chestnut flash at the corner of his vision — but it was much too late to take evasive action. Mister Rafferty arrowed in, ears flattened, eyes determinedly set. He blundered solidly into Griggs shoulder-blades, hammering all breath from his body and tipping him forward into a mound of steaming, freshly dropped manure.

Griggs gurgled, coughed, and thrashed about on the ground.

'Respect? Boss-man?' Ryker threw Griggs's earlier words back at him and laughed loudly — a rich oily chuckle that seemed to come from far down below his sagging belt. 'I suggest you remind this old horse that you're in charge!'

Mister Rafferty eyed the broom in Ryker's hands and decided not to take any chances. He turned quickly on his haunches and wheeled away to join the rest of the group.

Griggs bit teeth which needed brushing into his thin bottom lip and lifted himself up on his elbows, ammonia stinging at his eyes. He cursed the dark wet stain of horse urine which was spreading across the front of his neat white shirt and frantically mopped up the streaky beginnings of a nosebleed with the back of his hand.

'Blood and pee everywhere!' he yelled at Ryker. 'These clothes were fresh on. Now look at the state I'm in!'

'I'm looking, my little ferret.' Ryker's stomach threatened to burst from his belt as he laughed raucously. 'It couldn't have happened to a nicer person. Tut, tut, what a terrible, terrible accident.'

'It wasn't an accident! You said yourself that the gypsy horse was a trouble-maker.'

'But then I could have been wrong,' he mocked softly. 'Unlike you, I'm not an expert. According to the Martin Griggs Book of Horse Knowledge — a rather slim volume I might add — I know very little about horses.'

Griggs ignored Ryker's sarcasm and exhaled bitterly as he climbed to his feet. His eyes focussed on the group of old horses and narrowed with evil intent as they settled on Mister Rafferty.

'The sooner that gypsy cob ends up as dog meat,' he spat, 'the happier I'll be!'

8

Saturday morning found Jonathan and Spring standing by the caravan watching attentively as Seamus began snipping a bandage dressing from the base of Degsey's tail.

'Hold her . . . ' Seamus's voice was a little croaky so he began again. 'Hold her head nice and steady now. Good, good, that be fine.'

Degsey didn't flinch at the scissors — just stood erect and still, switching between the trusting, affectionate gaze she kept for her master and the loving, watchful glances she reserved for her offspring.

The three pups played on the grass verge nearby, getting up to mischief by taking little nips at Scooter's ears and then using the speed in their whippy light-framed bodies to avoid the boxer's playful retaliation.

Little Degsey appeared to be growing up fast. She was far more agile than her two brothers and had the most boisterous nature. In common with her mother she seemed to fear nothing, and also possessed the uncanny ability to sense things that were about to happen — especially when Spring was close at hand. This telepathic instinct was still very much in its infancy but Spring had experienced it in a few simple ways that defied rational explanation.

She knew that she only had to concentrate very hard on the puppy's name and Little Degsey would be there to find her — to protect her from harm.

Even this morning's dip in the sea with Jonathan at Delight Cove had resulted in a type of rescue. At the water's edge Little Degsey had made a nuisance of herself by running in front of them, tripping them up, encircling their legs and making it impossible for them to swim. They had managed no more than a brief paddle before the puppy's persistent barking and frustrating blocking tactics had forced them to abandon any sort of beach activity. On the walk back to Oyster Gables Jonathan had called the greyhound an 'irritating pest' and given Spring firm instructions never to bring Little Degsey to Delight Cove again.

Only later, by listening to the local radio news, had they discovered that the hot weather had brought thousands of poisonous Orange Compass jellyfish to the Swiftly coastline. Thirty bathers had needed treatment in hospital — and only by not swimming had Spring and Jonathan avoided the possibility of a very nasty sting.

'Can you use your wee fingers to lift off the herb from me darlin' girl's tail,' Seamus was saying to Jonathan without much response. He looked up from Degsey, pushed his glasses further up the bridge of his nose and raised a wispy eyebrow. 'Are we disturbin' y'thoughts, me boy? You look t'be miles away 'n all.'

Jonathan *was* miles away. He was still feeling a bit sheepish about his earlier remarks to Spring, especially as his sister had given a blow-by-blow account of what happened on the beach to all at lunchtime. When asked for his comments he had dismissed the episode as nothing more than 'over excitement' on Little Degsey's part, coupled with 'pure coincidence' about the jellyfish. But in private he had to admit to mixed emotions.

Now, as Little Degsey gave up the game with Scooter and turned to hold Jonathan's gaze, he could see something in the puppy's eyes; an all-seeing, all-knowing twinkle which only she and her mother possessed. It was strange, inexplicable — a sort of bottomless depth around each coal-black pupil where every conceivable shade of brown merged into infinite brilliance.

'S . . . sorry.' Jonathan blinked rapidly to shake himself free of Little Degsey's scrutiny and focussed on Seamus. 'W . . . what did you ask me to do?'

'The sphagnum moss.' Seamus's watery blue eyes narrowed slightly. 'Can y'be liftin' it off so old Seamus can look at the wound there.'

Jonathan carefully removed the herbal package that resembled a distressed tea bag from the base of Degsey's tail. The cut had knitted together nicely, leaving only a thin trail of scar tissue.

''Tis mended t'be sure.' A smile wafted briefly over Seamus's face. 'Me wee girl be as good as new.'

'What is sphagnum moss?' Spring queried.

'Looks like green gunge.' Jonathan pulled a face as he examined the piece in his hand.

Seamus explained that it was a forest herb containing natural iodine and numerous other healing properties. He went on to reveal how he'd first cleansed the wound with a strong infusion of rosemary leaves and added some ground meadowsweet herb to Degsey's drinking water to help the tissue-repairing powers of her body.

'It's healed remarkably quickly,' Spring observed, running an affectionate hand over the greyhound's neck. 'I think even Sky would be surprised at the result.'

'There be many sorts o' doctorin',' Seamus

pointed out, 'but y'both know that me wee girl be used to the ways o' the gypsies. I be admittin' that y'sister be specially fine at curin' the woodland creatures of their ills — far, far better than old Seamus. 'Tis true . . . 'tis tings I've seen her do wi' me own eyes. Marvellest tings. Sewin' and stitchin', mendin' broken wings, splintin' fractured bones . . . ' He moved his head in a series of slow thoughtful nods, adding, 'Ah sure, by Jaminee, she be a saviour — a wonderful girl now.'

'Who's a wonderful girl?' Shack loomed over Jonathan's shoulder and stretched out a hand to fondle the greyhound. It was another hot day and his unfastened check shirt hung loosely over his belted jeans. 'You can only be talking about Degsey. I heard she'd been in the wars again — what a heroine! When Daniel told me how she saved your lives in the collapsing M.o.D. building, I thought . . . ' He didn't finish the sentence, just looked at the dog and gave a long whistle of admiration.

Degsey's tail flailed at the air as she gazed up at him fondly.

'Is the fallow deer all right?' Spring asked, concerned, 'I went to look for him this morning but he must have been moved.'

'He's doing well. He's in his own outside

pen now and the damaged hind leg is improving daily. With luck he'll be released next week.'

She nodded, pleasure showing in her pale-lashed eyes.

'Your busted lip's looking better,' Jonathan told him.

'It's fine.' Shack fingered the slight blemish on his mouth.

'You must have used the famous sphagnum moss cure.'

'The what?'

'Seamus used it on Degsey. It's slimy green stuff, but it healed her cut in record time.'

Shack caught the lilt of humour in Jonathan's voice and fell in with the joke. He grinned, said he'd used cold compresses on his lip, then glanced at Seamus. 'Degsey looks no worse for yesterday's ordeal. You seem to have fixed her up a treat.'

''Tis true, she be well fit. Back to her old self and no mistake.'

Shack regarded him steadily. 'And how about you, Seamus? Are you back to *your* old self?'

'I-I be fine,' he mumbled, making a determined effort to look as healthy as possible.

Seamus had always taken a pride in his personal appearance — always looking neat and well-groomed, whatever the occasion. But now, to Shack's observant eyes, there was a marked deterioration. His waistcoat had been wrongly buttoned so that one side was higher than the other; there was two day's growth of stubble shading his jaw; and the brightly coloured strip of cloth that usually fastened his pony-tail had been substituted for the convenience of an elastic band.

Shack was also aware that he seemed to have dramatically aged just in the last few days. His skin had a waxy pallor, his eyes lacked their usual lustre, and his entire demeanour was clouded over with either distress or pain or a combination of both.

'How's your chest?' quizzed Shack.

'Er . . . chest?'

'You were complaining of a burning sensation when I brought you breakfast this morning.'

He gave a little shivering movement of his head and shoulders. ''Twas nothin', young 'un, I be fussin' too much. It was a wee twinge — a touch o' indigestion m'be.' He flexed his jaws, working hard at mustering a smile and added, 'Sky's cookin' be very rich. It be so loverly that I reckon old Seamus be eatin' too much.'

His voice hinted of a weariness of spirit and he wasn't fooling anybody about 'indigestion', especially Shack.

'You can't be eating too much,' Spring announced, blinking puzzlement. 'Daniel said that you hardly touched your food this lunchtime.'

'Are you ill?' Jonathan asked bluntly.

'A few aches and pains, me boy. Old age be creepin' up fast on this gypsy. 'Tis nothin' o' consequence.'

Shack's eyes were troubled. 'Megan prepared a lamb casserole yesterday,' he said, 'but she told me you refused to even taste it.'

'I be more inclined towards veggie food now,' he replied quickly.

'Then I expect you ate the cauliflower cheese,' Spring said, delighted.

'Ay, 'twas grand. I fair scoffed the lot.'

Shack knew he was being devious — which for Seamus was totally out of character and only went to reinforce his suspicions that he was ailing far more than anyone suspected. He didn't want to browbeat the old gypsy, but he was seriously worried that he might need a doctor.

'You may have picked at a bit of the cauliflower,' Shack pressed his point home, 'but the majority of it ended up being fed to the puppies.'

Seamus was taken aback. Creases ran up his forehead and his mouth opened and closed several times, goldfish fashion.

'H . . . how you be knowin' that? You be away yesterday . . . At home, restin'.'

'And so I was.'

Jonathan and Spring exchanged puzzled glances.

'You had visitors just after Hannah brought your lunch.' Shack repressed a smile and looked at Seamus coolly. 'They came to inspect Oyster Gables and asked if they could have a guided tour of your wagon.'

'Oh ay.' He nodded and moistened his lips. ''Twas a Mr and Mrs Wilson.'

'And Mrs Wilson was very worried when she saw you giving your lunch to the puppies. She thought you appeared breathless and unwell and she blamed herself for disturbing you.'

'Never heard of people called Wilson,' Jonathan piped up. 'Do you know them, Shack? Are they friends of yours?'

'They're my mother and stepfather,' he said simply. 'They've come down from Yorkshire, touring Devon in their camper van. After Megan told them I was off sick they popped in to see me and Dad at Yelland.'

'And you talked about Seamus.'

'Amongst other things.'

Seamus's face lengthened expressively as he looked at Shack. 'You havin' lots o' names

226

be confusin'',' he grumbled, fingering his earring. 'I don't know where I be with all this choppin' and changin'.'

Spring looked at Jonathan. He shrugged.

'Not lots,' Spring pointed out to Seamus. 'Only his surname is different because his mother remarried.'

''T'ain't true. His first name be diff'rent too.'

Shack cleared his throat with an embarrassed little cough. 'I have to move off,' he said quickly, making an exaggerated effort of looking at his wristwatch. 'There's a staff meeting . . . in the office. They'll be expecting me. See you . . . er . . . later.' He finished weakly and began backing away.

Jonathan could sense Shack's very obvious discomfort and guessed that Seamus had touched a raw nerve. He reckoned there was some fun to be had at Shack's expense so he wasn't going to let the matter drop.

'His first name's Shack, his surname's Skinner,' he told Seamus, deliberately raising his voice just enough to halt Shack in his tracks. 'Nobody ever calls him anything else.'

Shack turned, waiting for the inevitable.

Seamus puffed his cheeks and continued, 'Mrs Wilson, she be askin' where she could find Cedric. 'Tis me son, she be tellin' me, and he be workin' on a trainin' scheme at Oyster Gables.'

'Cedric!' Jonathan exclaimed. His eyes lit up, then rolled comically. 'Ha! So Shack's first name is really Cedric! No wonder you were confused.'

'Fair twizzled t'be sure me boy. I be tinkin' Mrs Wilson be at the wrong animal shelter. No Cedric here I tells her, only Danny boy and Shack the donkey man.'

Jonathan laughed out loud — unable to stop. He had tears in his eyes and gripped his side because it hurt so much.

'Is Cedric really your name?' Spring looked from Jonathan to Shack and stifled a giggle.

Shack scowled and made a grunting sound of acknowledgement.

'C . . . can we call you Ceddie for short?' Jonathan was doubled up with amusement, barely able to squeeze out the words.

'No you blasted well can't!' Shack ran an agitated hand through his hair and onto the back of his neck. 'Haven't you any work to do? Like cleaning Mister Rafferty's harness? I thought that was a weekly chore?'

'Not much point, young 'un.' Seamus drew a small breath of hopeless resignation as Spring's elbow prompted Jonathan to stop laughing. ''Tis time this old gypsy came t'terms wi' the fact that his poor old cob horse be gone f'good.'

Shack walked the few steps back to the group, tucked his thumbs into the waistband of his jeans and faced Seamus. Jonathan was still grinning, but for the moment at least he was silent.

'I can't promise anything,' Shack began, his tone softening a fraction, 'but there's a possibility — a small one — that we may have a lead as to where Mister Rafferty's being kept. I don't want to raise your hopes because we might be too late. The horse may have been sold on to someone else. I think we'll know tomorrow. Trust me.'

Seamus stared at Shack, his eyes intense as he fingered his moustache. There were minuscule fluctuations in the bulb of his throat but he said nothing, just nodded amiably, letting unspoken words pass between them.

'No time to waste,' Spring announced, her whole face now suddenly alight with energy. She crossed to the rear of the caravan and opened the pan-box. She began lifting out various pieces of Mister Rafferty's harness, threading an arm through the huge coil of reins and heaving them onto her shoulder.

'I'll get the buckets, saddle-soap, silver polish and cloths from the tack-room,' Jonathan said, bobbing his head approvingly at Spring's actions. He walked quickly past Shack and kept his lips pressed firmly together, avoiding any eye contact as he struggled to hold back a grin.

Seamus realised the significance of Shack's words and was appreciative of his honesty. A warm wave of gratitude washed over him and his dulled eyes now reflected a flinty brightness that spelled hope.

'Look ... ' Shack began, taking a deep breath and jutting his jaw a little, 'this harness cleaning could all be a waste of time.'

'But you did say there was a chance?' Spring pressed.

'Yes I know,' Shack agreed reluctantly. 'But I emphasised that it was only a small one.'

Jonathan made sure he was well out of Shack's reach before risking one final retort. 'It was your idea that we do some work,' he quipped, calling out over his shoulder before making a dash for it. 'Well now we're ready . . . *Ceddie!*'

★ ★ ★

Sky gathered up the animal record cards that she had just updated, stretched her arms and switched off the shelter's computer. She turned in the work-station chair to face Daniel who was making coffee. The three

230

were in the Oyster Gables office and the staff meeting was about to begin.

'So tell us everything about last night's excursion,' Daniel prompted Shack. 'Every little detail — I'll be making notes.'

Shack swivelled back and forth in the squeaky chair behind the roll-top desk and began by giving a blow-by-blow account of his visit to the Silver Seagull at Ilfracombe. He'd travelled there with his stepfather, he told them, leaving his mum and dad at home in Yelland to catch up on each other's news.

They'd taken a mini-cab, and during the drive Shack had given precise details to his stepfather of all the recent happenings. He'd spoken graphically about Mister Rafferty's disappearance, the outbreak of horse rustling in the area, and the early morning visit they'd had from the tattooed man and his partner. He had explained about the bookmatches and the reason for the evening's outing. Everything, including the possible outcome, had been discussed and mulled over. By the time they'd picked up Sophie, Shack had decided to let his stepfather do the talking at the public house. The landlord of the Silver Seagull, he reasoned, might respond more willingly to an older person's questioning.

'So the pair of you are finally getting on,' Sky remarked, taking her mug of coffee from

Daniel's outstretched hand.

'Yes . . . amazingly. I suppose I couldn't be bothered to get to know him before — but last night we became good friends. He seems nice enough and I'm pleased for Mum . . . His name's Ken by the way.'

Daniel handed Shack a coffee, sat on the chair by the workbench and began making notes on a clipboard that was stuffed with paper.

'So how much did Ken manage to find out?'

'He did really well. They talked about golf for a bit — that's the landlord's game. There are loads of trophies and shields around the bar, so as Ken plays too he soon latched onto the small talk.'

'Were you at the bar with them?'

He shook his head. 'I got a couple of Cokes and sat with Sophie at a table nearby. Being under age I didn't want to cramp Ken's style. There was some pretty serious drinking going on, and Ken bought most of the rounds.'

Sky asked how the topic of stolen horses had entered the conversation.

'Ken made up some story about wanting to buy a pony for his daughter. He'd just bought a house with a few spare acres at West Down, he told the landlord, and he mentioned very matter-of-factly that a neighbour had spoken of a horse-trader who could sometimes be found at the Silver Seagull.'

Daniel stopped writing and leaned forward keenly with his elbows on his knees. 'Did the landlord give him a name?'

Shack inclined his head and went on to explain that several names were suggested. About four horse-traders used the Silver Seagull on a regular basis and his stepfather had listened to the comments on each, patiently playing along, and nodding in all the right places. Any one of the horse-traders, Shack commented, could have fitted the sketchy description of the big man in the mask — but everything changed when Ken casually dropped the scorpion tattoo into the conversation.

'The landlord knew immediately,' Shack went on. He named him as Tony Ryker and told Ken he had a partner named Martin Griggs. He wasn't sure where they lived — fairly local he thought — but here's the good bit . . . ' Shack sipped his coffee and paused for effect. 'They visit the Silver Seagull every Sunday for lunch. The pub has an eating area and as Ryker smokes small cigars they always sit at the only 'smoking' table. One-thirty, on the dot. They never miss. Apparently Griggs does the cooking for six days of the week, and he insists on having a break. It's a sort of tradition.'

'Griggs being the skinny one?' Sky queried.

'Mmm, red knickers — the one Daniel darted.'

Daniel grinned at the memory then began scribbling more notes on the clipboard. 'Ken did superbly,' he said. 'Now we can pin Ryker and Griggs to a definite time and location.'

'It's Sunday tomorrow.' Sky flicked a concerned fingernail against her bottom teeth.

'No problem.' Daniel sounded confident as he drained his coffee. 'My plan can be put into action at any time — besides, we can't afford to wait another week. It's possible we're already too late to rescue Mister Rafferty.'

'Which brings us to Seamus,' Shack interjected. 'I'm very worried about him. He's been complaining of chest pains. He should definitely see a doctor.'

'He's a stubborn old boy,' Daniel said. 'I've suggested it many times but he's adamant that he won't.'

'How bad is he, Shack?' Sky asked after a short silence.

'I think he looks terrible. He's a shadow of his former self . . . and I've got this dreadful feeling. I can't explain it. I just know that something is very, very wrong.'

'Mister Rafferty's the cure,' Daniel stated, drawing a long concerned breath. 'Just let's hope that the old cob's still alive.'

Sky pressed an index finger onto her lips thoughtfully. 'I agree he's pining for Mister Rafferty, but we better not take any chances. After we've finished this meeting I'll ring the surgery and arrange for a doctor to call Monday morning.'

'Thanks.' Shack looked relieved.

Daniel swung the conversation back to the rescue plan. He turned to Sky. 'Did you make arrangements to borrow a small Rice trailer?'

She nodded. 'One of our livery clients is bringing it over tonight.'

'Perfect.'

'Are we going to steal Mister Rafferty back?' Shack queried.

'No, the stealing will be done by Ryker and Griggs. They're the experts.'

'I'm not really following this?' Sky looked bewildered.

'I'll explain everything in a moment. Just remember you're the linchpin of the whole operation.'

'I've another piece of gen . . . ' Shack interjected, tapping the bridge of his nose with a knuckle, remembering. 'The landlord mentioned Ryker's make of car. He was doing his best to persuade Ken to use another horse-trader — calling Ryker 'dodgy' and suchlike — but Ken kept trying to extract more information and insisted that Ryker came highly recommended.'

'So the car . . . ?' Daniel prompted.

'Oh, a red BMW — almost new. The landlord spoke of it in case Ken wanted to meet up on a weekday. If Ryker's in the Silver Seagull, he said, then you'll always see his car parked on the forecourt.'

'Drinking and driving never mix.' Sky tut-tutted.

Daniel agreed but he was suitably impressed with this latest piece of knowledge. 'Pity we can't get a look at the car. I'd like to know if it's fitted with a tow-bar.'

'It is.' Shack was definite. 'Ken told me that Ryker uses a large travelling horse-box to go to the auctions, but for private deals he hitches a solo job to the BMW.'

'Couldn't be better.' Daniel placed some more ticks in the paper margin on his clipboard. His pencil hovered against one item and his eyes flicked to Sky. 'We'll need a couple of nets — something big and strong. Does the shelter have any?'

'There are some nets in one of the tack-room hampers. We used them once to rescue a muntjac deer.'

Sky's words were rewarded with a grateful

nod from Daniel as another tick found its way onto the clipboard.

'What exactly are you doing?' Shack fingered his chin.

'Double-checking that we have all the equipment.' He flicked over some pages, grunting and evaluating each tick. 'We do. Everything has come together just fine. We're ready.'

Shack winked at Sky and leaned forward towards Daniel. He deliberately lowered his voice to a conspiratorial whisper. 'Is it a secret or are you going to give us the details of this plan?'

Daniel hunched forward. His eyebrows were down, his face taut with concentration. 'Right,' he began, 'what we do is this . . . '

9

Martin Griggs crammed a final forkful of roast chicken into his mouth and blotted gravy from his lips with a paper napkin. His cheeks inflated as he burped a couple of times then he balled the napkin between his palms and tossed it into an ashtray. It was just after two p.m. and they were finishing their regular Sunday meal at the Silver Seagull.

Ryker looked up from his roast beef lunch and glared. 'Didn't your parents ever teach you any manners?' he rasped. 'Leave that napkin on your plate. Ashtrays are for people who want to smoke — like me. They're not rubbish receptacles.'

'Smoking is a disgusting habit. It should be banned.'

Griggs reached for a complimentary book of matches clipped to the ashtray and tore a couple out as he shifted moodily in his chair. His face held a bored expression as he struck them, letting them splutter and flare before blowing them out.

Ryker leaned forward, forearms on the table, knife and fork held upright as if to reinforce his authority. 'Okay, so what's the matter? Why the old crone act? I can always tell when you're crabby.'

'Sunday should be a day of rest,' he muttered, probing about inside his mouth with a dead match until he'd fished out a shred of chicken from a back tooth. 'I thought, just for this afternoon, we could give work a miss. I'm fed up with touring the countryside looking for horses to steal. I'm still not fully recovered. My body is telling me that I should be enjoying a lazy afternoon . . . watching a video or something.'

'Your body can be bone idle when you're moody.'

'Untrue. I'm still in the recovery stage. It's always rush, rush, rush with you.'

Ryker exhaled silently. 'Time is a luxury, Griggsy, that I can't afford to waste. I'd like to be back in Berkshire, playing golf, having a drink with my friends at the Country Club — but I'm prepared to stick it out because I've a wife who spends money like it's going out of fashion and two kids at a private school. Lazing around in your mobile home doesn't increase the wad of money in my back pocket. Horses do!'

'Well I'm getting pretty sick of horses. I smell of 'em and my clothes stink of 'em. Even the chicken I've just eaten tasted of 'em.'

'So next time have a shower before you come out. Your personal hygiene leaves a lot to be desired.'

'Ha, ha, very flippin' funny,' he replied, almost to himself. 'Have a dig at Griggsy . . . he's always good for a cheap laugh.'

'So what do you want to do?' Ryker responded. 'Break up the partnership?'

'Maybe.' He paused, his mouth surly, brooding on it. 'It's a possibility.'

Ryker was unimpressed. It was a familiar pattern and he'd heard the same old record being played many times in the past. There was only a month left before they went their separate ways, and his partner was getting bored — maybe even a little frightened. But Griggs wasn't going to quit now, Ryker told himself. He'd moan and groan, but he'd finish the season as he always did and be back for more of the same next year.

'So what will you do?' Ryker asked, still mocking him slightly. 'Go back to stealing wallets and signing on at the Social Security Office?'

'I told you — I'm thinking about it!' He glared and rose from his chair. 'I'm going to the toilet,' he added, pulling a handkerchief from his pocket. 'I can feel a nosebleed coming on. It always does when you get me stressed. Sometimes I think you do it deliberately.'

'If you have any more nosebleeds, my little ferret, your brains will fall out.'

Griggs ignored the sarcasm. 'Do you want me to order coffee?'

'Whose turn is it to pick up the bill?'

'Mine.'

Ryker's discreet cough disguised a cynical smirk. 'Then make it two coffees and two brandies.'

Griggs bristled aggressively at that. 'But I bought the drinks when we arrived!'

Ryker just looked at him with a long, unblinking stare.

Griggs mouthed some indistinct curse, turned and threaded his way towards the Gents. Ryker chuckled appreciatively, flicked the napkin ball out of the ashtray and lit a cheroot.

* * *

Sky, dressed in jodhpurs, lightweight polo-neck jumper and leather riding boots was perfectly positioned on the Silver Seagull's forecourt. She'd arrived in Daniel's Volvo with the Rice trailer hitched to the two-bar and had managed to park alongside Ryker's BMW. Following the plan to the letter she'd

241

then opened the Volvo's bonnet, propped it on its metal stay, and was now peering forlornly into the cavernous engine.

All of this was being watched by Griggs from a small frosted top window that was slightly ajar in the toilet. The Gents overlooked the forecourt, and he was perfectly positioned to spy on her every move.

He studied the chestnut horse in the trailer, experience telling him that he was looking at a classy show animal, and not a run of the mill hack.

Spring had spent several hours plaiting Sir Galahad's mane and forelock, and then weaved in eye-catching strips of coloured ribbon along the dock of his tail. Sky, Daniel and Jonathan had all pitched in and performed various grooming tasks. Body brushes, curry combs and wisps had all been used to great effect and the end result of highlighting the neck, shoulder and quarter muscles was spectacular. The final polishing had been left to Shack who had become quite an expert at 'strapping' a horse with a stable rubber. He had worked like a demon, not stopping until Sir Galahad's coat shone like the finest spun silk.

Griggs nodded his approval, gently blew his nose, and switched his gaze back to Sky. She had moved from the engine to the cab and was playing her part convincingly as she tried the ignition several times, letting the engine turn over noisily but unsuccessfully. She knew the Volvo wouldn't start because she'd switched on the immobiliser under the dashboard, but the illusion to anyone watching — and she hoped they were — was one of typical frustration shown by a motorist in distress.

Certainly, the act had fooled Griggs. He was engrossed with her every move, a faint smile playing around his lips as he heard Sky utter several loud curses and kick at a tyre with her boot. She then moved to the Rice trailer, stood on the rear ledge, and appeared to be saying a few calming words to the horse.

Unbeknown to Griggs she was having a whispered conversation with Daniel and Shack who were crouched uncomfortably under the belly of Sir Galahad.

They'd rehearsed the hiding routine with military precision last night. Nothing had been left to chance. Spring and Jonathan had guided them this way and that and told them the best posture to adopt for concealment . . . then chalk marks had been etched on the floor as a positioning aid for their feet. Luckily, Sir Galahad was big enough and the trailer compact enough for them to be neatly tucked away and screened from prying eyes. Even Degsey had been hidden from view. She was curled up in a straw-filled corner and covered with an empty bran sack.

'We're parked right next to Ryker's BMW car,' Sky told them, the words emerging through half-closed lips. 'I've angled the trailer so it's level with his tow-bar. No pun intended, but let's hope he doesn't look a gift horse in the mouth.'

'He won't.' Daniel shifted position. He lifted his head level with Sir Galahad's gaskin and grinned up at her reassuringly. 'Thumping the tyre with your foot was a neat touch . . . we could hear your loud cursing from inside.'

'I didn't think you knew naughty words like that.' Shack pulled a wry face and rubbed life into a knee that was suffering pins and needles.

A smile showed in her eyes. 'Only acting,' she said. 'Getting in the right mood for playing my part.'

'And remember,' Daniel offered some quick advice, 'don't use Sir Galahad's real name. It could be familiar to Ryker and Griggs and they mustn't suspect that you're connected with Oyster Gables.'

'Understood. From now on he'll be known as Buckingham. I thought of it last night

. . . It's regal and it suits him.' She patted the horse's rump and jumped down from the trailer's ledge.

Martin Griggs was still glued to the window. He watched all Sky's actions — saw her reach into the Volvo for a black velvet riding jacket and toss it casually over her arm. She was talking to herself, saying things which he presumed were angry grumbles about the breakdown, but which in reality were inaudible words of personal encouragement. She was trying to play down her fears and convince herself that she could carry off her part of the charade in front of strangers. She fortified herself with a long prayerful breath and strode purposefully towards the Silver Seagull's entrance.

Griggs wiped his nose and left the toilet. The bar was abuzz with laughter and talk as he shouldered his way past customers and hurried back to Ryker.

The big man didn't look up as Griggs almost fell into his chair. He swirled a brandy round in his glass and said irritably, 'I suppose you've had another nosebleed? You've been gone long enough. The drinks arrived and I had to pay — '

'Shut up and listen.' Griggs cut him off.

Ryker immediately looked up. He was startled by Griggs's directness.

'There's a girl — late teens — with a horse and trailer in the car park.' Griggs tried to keep his voice level, but it was edged with excitement. 'Her car's broken down, so she's stuck. It looks like an expensive show-horse to me. Probably worth four or five times more than the stuff we usually steal.'

'Are you saying . . . ?'

Griggs nodded and took a swig at his brandy. He swallowed too much, coughed, and hiccoughed as the raw spirit burned his throat.

'Are you saying,' Ryker began again, 'that we should relieve this young lady of her four-legged encumbrance?'

'If you mean steal the horse — yes!'

Ryker showed a lopsided smile. His jaws were set and the smile had a hard time getting through. 'That's not the way we operate, my little ferret. We always do our business under the cover of darkness. That's part of the reason we've never been caught. Going against a tried and trusted method could mean complications.'

'But this horse is being handed to us on a plate, Tony. We simply unhitch it from her car and re-hitch the trailer to the BMW.'

'I thought you were sick of horses? The smell, the — '

'I'm sick of traipsing all over the county to

246

find 'em!' His words tumbled out angrily. 'This would only take us a couple of minutes and we could relax for the rest of the day . . . ' His eyes flashed as he sucked in a noisy breath. 'Oh, why do I bother explaining . . . '

Ryker's fingers thudded a tattoo on the table. He was thinking.

'I'm surprised you're showing some initiative, Griggsy. Does this mean you're back on the firm? No more talk of severing the partnership?'

Griggs went to answer but pulled himself up. He could see Sky at the far end of the bar. She'd stopped to order an orange juice and was now picking her way towards the dining area.

'Keep your voice down. Here comes the girl.' His words were clipped with tension. He gnawed at a thumb knuckle and lowered his eyes to the tablecloth.

Sky did a very good impression of ignoring them as she strode past, her gaze fixed on a landscape picture which hung on the far wall. Five tables were being used by diners, mainly those offering a view of the harbour. There were three unoccupied and one was perfectly positioned just to the rear of the 'smoking' table.

She sat at it, placed her velvet riding jacket

on a spare chair and began nonchalantly flicking through the menu. Her eyes scanned the various dishes of the day but her thoughts were very definitely elsewhere.

Ryker was wearing a short sleeved shirt and she'd instantly spotted the scorpion tattoo on his forearm. Now, as if to reinforce his identity, a light flared in front of a cheroot as he lit it from the complimentary pack of book-matches. Sky recognised the Silver Seagull's gold-embossed cover as he slipped the book-matches into the top pocket of his shirt.

Everything in Daniel's plan seemed to be dovetailing perfectly. She was sitting at the right table, watching the right men. Of that she had to be certain, and now she was. Ryker had pocketed the book-matches and in so doing had unwittingly added weight to the fact that he had been the night visitor to Oyster Gables. And yes, she thought fleetingly, letting her gaze stray to his partner — Spring had guessed right. Martin Griggs did have evil eyes.

'So?' Griggs asked in hushed tones. 'What do you reckon? Shall we have the horse away?'

'Maybe,' Ryker said, 'I'm thinking about it. I want to be totally convinced she's genuine. No need to be hasty. The girl's the one with the problem. Let's see how she intends to sort it out.'

Sky took a sip of her orange juice and pulled her mobile phone from the pocket of her velvet riding jacket. She could feel Ryker's eyes on her face, studying the various changes in her expression as she extended the phone's tiny aerial and pressed several digits on the key-pad.

The number burred in her ear and then, as expected, Oyster Gables' answering machine clicked in. She thought briefly of Megan and Hannah attending to the shelter's animals and then listened to her own recording on the machine's opening message. She kept up the pretence of appearing worried by flicking a concerned fingernail against her bottom teeth and then launched into a one-way conversation that she'd spent most of last night rehearsing. She spoke with an affected accent, deliberately rounding her vowels in order to portray an expensive upbringing.

'Hello, daddy darling . . . yes it's me . . .' She paused momentarily, snatching a quick glance to Ryker and Griggs. They were both sitting silently, heads cocked, hanging onto her every word. She continued, 'I've got some beastly news . . . I'm not going to make it to the Somerset County Show. The car's been absolutely horrendous — you know misfiring

249

and things — and now it's given up the ghost altogether. I've had a wretched time of it, daddy, and it's left me feeling totally drained.'

'Poor sad thing,' Ryker whispered to Griggs, lifting his eyes mockingly as he sipped at his brandy. 'She sounds a right stuck up little madam.'

Sky made a pretence of listening on the phone, then went on, 'No, it's simply impossible. The dressage competition starts at three and I have to check in with the course secretary at least an hour before.' She sighed heavily as she glanced at her wristwatch. 'I know it's a ghastly state of affairs but what choice do I have? It's doubly disappointing because Buckingham would have excelled in the *piaffe*.' Another fretful pause as she tucked an errant strand of hair behind her ear, then, 'Yes, of course he's alright, and no I won't let anything happen to him . . . ' She raised her voice just a touch and delivered the line which she hoped would be irresistible to a pair of horse thieves. 'You don't have to remind me of that, daddy! I'm well aware that Buckingham cost you over ten thousand pounds!'

Griggs's eyes grew large and there was a faint glow of moisture at his temple as he stared at Ryker. 'She said ten, Tony . . . *Ten* thousand! Hellfire, you can't turn your back on this one.'

Ryker was beginning to look as if he couldn't. His lips were pursed and almost watering with anticipation as he rolled his cheroot round and round in his fingers. He listened intently as Sky began to pacify 'daddy' by naming competition venues for which Buckingham had already qualified. These included the International Show at Aachen in West Germany, and the Horse of the Year Show at Wembley in London.

'I bet there's someone on your 'private' list who will pay top money for a show-horse like that.' Griggs's lips didn't move as the words slipped silently through his teeth.

Ryker chewed on his cheroot with increased fervour. 'Maybe,' he admitted quietly. 'I dare say, with forged paperwork, I might just be able to sell it on for three thousand.'

Griggs nodded, pleased with the price . . . and so was Ryker. He had an elite clientele — a worldwide register of dishonest buyers waiting for class horses. He knew that he could easily place the animal for five thousand pounds, maybe six, but if his partner was happy to accept a percentage of a lower figure then why tax his brain with mathematics.

Sky shifted her position as a waitress arrived to take her luncheon order. She held the phone in place with a raised shoulder, pointed to something on the menu, and then continued her make-believe conversation.

'I've just ordered a smoked salmon salad, daddy . . . not that I'm hungry . . . just a morsel to pick at while I'm waiting.' She paused, listening to nothing but a hum on the line, and added, 'Yes, I'm at the Silver Seagull in Ilfracombe. Could mummy use the Range Rover to pick me and the trailer up? I'll phone for a breakdown service to deal with the car — but you know how these silly garage people can take absolute ages.'

'Oh, forever and ever,' Griggs murmured softly, his smile confident. He looked at his partner. 'Are we on?'

Ryker's nostrils arched. He nodded.

'Bless you, daddy, both me and Buckers think you're an absolute poppet.' Sky wrapped up the call. 'Half-an-hour, then . . . byeee.'

Griggs was up and away, barging through patrons as he headed for the door. Ryker took his time in draining his brandy glass, stubbing out his cheroot, and finally rising from his chair. As he turned he collided briefly with a waitress and realised that Griggs's speedy exit had meant that the bill for the meal had been left unpaid.

'Here's fifty pounds,' he said, grunting with annoyance as he fished a note from his wallet. 'It's the smallest I have and I'm in a hurry. I'll call back tomorrow for the change.'

He pushed the note reluctantly into the waitress' hands, cursed inwardly and manoeuvred his way out of the bar.

So far so good.

Things were running exactly to plan.

Sky couldn't resist a small secretive smile as she watched him go.

★ ★ ★

Degsey was the first one to hear Griggs. The bran sack slid over the contours of her neck as she lifted her head, muzzle quivering, ears vigilantly pricked.

Daniel reacted quickly by nudging life into Shack who was dozing as he rested his back against the inside of one of Sir Galahad's forelegs. He woke with a start but Daniel clamped a hand over his mouth and indicated that something was happening outside the trailer.

'This could be it,' Daniel whispered, repositioning the sack over Degsey. 'No noise . . . all perfectly still.'

253

The mood of teasing jocularity which had existed between Daniel and Shack during the drive from Swiftly had changed subtly to one of measured resolve. They waited, listening only to the sound of advancing footsteps and their own irregular breathing.

Griggs was whistling softly as he approached the trailer and Daniel tried to gauge his movements from the outside sounds. He'd be checking the Volvo first, he imagined, possibly looking at the engine before moving round to peer in the windows . . .

'Oh, heck . . . ' Daniel's face suddenly changed colour as a thought hit him. He stared at Shack, his cheeks filtering to an anxious whiteness. 'Jonathan's blue advertising sticker,' he murmured. 'I forgot to remove it from the Volvo's rear window.'

'Too late to worry,' Shack observed bleakly. 'If he's fairly observant then he's noticed it by now.'

Griggs had noticed it. His eyes had drifted over the words: OYSTER GABLES ANIMAL SHELTER — SWIFTLY . . . but the significance of the sticker hadn't registered. It should have rung huge alarm bells in his head but fortunately he was far too preoccupied with eyeing the contents of the Volvo's interior.

He had walked casually past the bonnet, which was still up, and was now peering into the passenger window. On the seat was a folder marked 'Show Documents' and a road atlas. Next to these, and all carefully packed in polythene bags, were three pairs of riding gloves, two velvet hard hats and several white shirts with black ties. Two pairs of jodhpurs and a spare black velvet jacket sat neatly on a wooden hanger which dangled from the passenger's interior courtesy hook. A wicker tack hamper labelled 'Somerset County Show' had been positioned invitingly on the rear seat.

Griggs was blissfully unaware that every article had been borrowed from the saddlery shop in Swiftly and placed in the car with the sole intention of creating the illusion that Sky was a keen competition rider. Certainly it had him fooled, and he gave a nod of approval and carried on whistling an unrecognisable tune as he edged his way round to the trailer. Commonsense told him that the clothes must have cost a fortune and were all compulsory show wear. Ryker's fears were groundless, he convinced himself. Both the girl and the horse were genuine.

Daniel and Shack exchanged relieved glances as they heard the rattle of the safety chain and the rasp of the locking pin being slid from the trailer's coupling.

'Panic over,' Shack whispered, managing a tight grin.

The tension in Daniel relaxed a notch but inwardly he was cursing his own stupidity. He'd been so meticulous in his planning, not leaving anything to chance — and then he'd very nearly tripped himself up by forgetting to remove something as obvious as a rear window advertising sticker. For a terrible few moments the world had erupted and his nervous system had been expanded to the limit of its strength.

Griggs continued to whistle as Shack and Daniel squeezed closer to Sir Galahad's underbelly, positioning themselves level with the chalk marks, expecting to hear someone's foot mount the rear ledge at any moment.

They weren't to be disappointed.

Ryker was suddenly at Griggs's shoulder. 'Does the girl's story ring true?' he asked, stepping onto the ledge and leaning over the top edge of the trailer.

'The car checks out,' Griggs told him. 'It's full of her show togs. Loads of costly stuff. She's a spoilt little rich girl alright.'

'And the horse?'

'He's no gymkhana hack. His condition is superb. I bet 'daddy' employs an army of stable staff to keep him tiptop.'

Ryker grunted, leaned further in, and ran a hand over the groomed check quarter-marks that adorned the horse's rump. Every slight shifting or scrape of feet echoed eerily in the trailer, sounding crashingly loud in such a confined space. Daniel was well tucked in and had mentally braced himself not to flinch if he caught a glimpse of Ryker's hand.

'Can't see much while Buckingham's boxed up,' the big man was saying, 'but he's short-coupled with good rounded quarters . . . and extremely well turned out, I'll give you that.'

'Reeks of money, eh, Tony?'

'Mmm, possibly.'

Daniel's stomach lurched as Ryker leaned as far over the top edge of the ramp as his body bulk would allow. Daniel glimpsed the big man's fingers dangling in front of him and took a gulp of air, holding it as he tried to ignore the diamond-studded signet ring shimmering in front of his eyes.

'Is the tow-bar fitted with a locking device?' he heard Ryker ask Griggs.

'A simple pin and chain,' came the reply. 'No problem. It was easy to disconnect.'

Ryker's fingers ceased their stroking and probing and stretched as far as they could to a point just short of Sir Galahad's stifle. The arm was now at full stretch and the scorpion tattoo was being displayed to Shack in all its memorable glory.

It froze him, and it seemed to penetrate to his vital organs. His bones chilled, and he shivered as the recollections of Thursday night's confrontation came flooding back. His tongue crept out to wet the blemish on his lip as a small voice, deep inside, held his emotions in check. Keep calm, it repeated over and over . . . remember Mister Rafferty . . . remember the plan.

'This seems too easy.' Ryker sucked on a tooth, pondering. 'It's all fallen into place so well that I'm beginning to get suspicious.'

'You think it's a set-up?' Griggs scratched the nape of his neck.

'I don't know. I've got a feeling . . . just a twinge in my stomach.'

'That's indigestion. You bolted your beef.'

'No, it's something else. Maybe I'm being over cautious but . . .'

Daniel and Shack listened nervously as Ryker began voicing the chain of events that had supposedly brought Sky to the Silver Seagull. He was verbally dissecting every element of Daniel's carefully laid plan, looking for weaknesses in the fabric, inconsistencies, any indication of falsehood.

Daniel stared at the floor, his fingers crossed tightly.

Minutes dripped by like the slow drops of perspiration trickling between his shoulder blades.

'Okay, it's all feasible . . . even though the damsel in distress bit sounds like something from a fairy tale.' Ryker wound up his analysis of events and posed a question to Griggs. 'Are you sure the stuff in the Volvo looks authentic?'

'I'm sure.'

'Perhaps I should double-check.'

Daniel traded swift glances with Shack. Martin Griggs had failed to make the connection with the sticker, but they both knew that the mistake would not go unnoticed by Ryker's shrewd scrutiny.

'No need.' Griggs huffed indignantly. 'I've done it and I'm satisfied. You'd simply be wasting your energy.'

Ryker looked at his watch. 'Alright, time's pressing so let's get on with it.' He snapped out the order, his voice reverberating around the inside of the trailer.

'Phew! That was close.' Shack shuddered with relief and Daniel exhaled gratefully as the big man lifted his arm from view. There was a small metallic groan as the trailer's springs relaxed from the extra weight and Ryker stepped from the ledge.

With the danger gone, Degsey's eyes,

gleaming and lustrous, appeared from under the bran sack. Her whole presence radiated wisdom as she looked from Shack to Daniel and up to Sir Galahad. She understood everything, Daniel thought. Her gaze was nerve-tingling, inspiring, provocative, and nothing ever escaped her attention. He guessed that she'd recognised Ryker's and Griggs's voices from their early masked visit the other morning — and possibly even before that. It now seemed highly probable they had also been responsible for her shoulder injury, and if this was the case then the incident was far from forgotten. The look in her eyes told him that seeing them brought to justice for their crimes was at the very forefront of the greyhound's mind.

'He's shifting the BMW into position,' Shack whispered the words as the smooth purr of an engine percolated through the trailer's walls.

Daniel nodded, feeling a shudder of movement ripple through the floor as the towing arm was uncoupled. The switching of vehicles would be easily accomplished, he reasoned; just a case of Griggs manhandling the trailer clear of the Volvo and re-hitching it to the ball socket on Ryker's tow-bar.

Daniel could now feel a movement in the

trailer's tiny wheels — possibly two revolutions. He listened carefully to every sound, going through the various manoeuvres in his mind until finally the trailer stilled and there was a hollow clunk.

'We're coupled up,' he said to Shack, knowing it was now safe to ease his cramped body into a more vertical position. He unhooked two large nets that had last seen action rescuing a muntjac deer and handed one to Shack. 'Did you remember the rope?'

Shack nodded and tapped the back pocket of his jeans.

'Okay. Then it's time to get ourselves organised.'

10

Sky had positioned herself by an outside staff door and was observing the forecourt activity from beneath a leafy overhang of branches that provided shadowy cover. She waited until the trailer was well on the move, watching the red BMW exit the car park before crossing with all haste to the Volvo.

She shut the bonnet, flicked off the ignition immobiliser, and spun the front tyres as she negotiated her way past a few straggly parked cars. The Volvo bounced over a traffic hump as she swung left out of the Silver Seagull's forecourt before joining a one-way system that would take her along part of the High Street.

The pavements were bustling with Sunday sightseers and vehicle movement was heavy. There was a bus, a van, and four cars in front, all slowing her progress — and to make matters worse she was heading due south with the sun blazing into her eyes. She pulled down the driver's visor and snatched a look down every side-turning she passed, just in case Ryker had slipped free of the main stream of traffic.

No sign.

She was clear of the High Street now and three cars and the bus peeled off at the next road junction. That left one car and what she now identified as a baker's box van in front of her. She gave a shaky sigh as she realised she was fast approaching a set of traffic lights with a right-hand filter. Now she had the BMW and trailer in her sights. They were stationary, caught on the red filter light. Suddenly she didn't want to be this close. The main lights were already green and she knew that if she took that route she would have to double-back, which in all probability meant losing them. If she decided to turn right and use the filter she would be sitting directly behind them, just begging to be spotted.

The lights were closing fast and she had to think quickly. She took one hand off the steering wheel, letting her fingers flutter nervously in front of her lips.

Luckily, the baker's van solved the dilemma. As the car in front flashed through on the green, the van indicated right, giving her the cover she so desperately needed.

'Thank you, thank you,' she heard herself saying, braking and waiting, glimpsing the logo on the van's rear doors. 'I promise I'll always buy Bosworth's bread from now on.'

Seconds passed and then the filter light changed to green. Ilfracombe was behind her but she was looping back to the sea on a narrow country road signposted: HELE BAY. Farmers' fields flashed past for the next two miles as she hugged the van's rear end, catching the odd glimpse of the trailer as the tight bends forced it to fishtail and swing wide.

Habitation now; a dozen or so houses and a variety of small stores. Sky eased off on the accelerator as the baker's van indicated its intention to pull into a slip road by the shops. She drifted the Volvo to the kerb and came to a halt behind the partial cover of a bottle bank and a parked motorbike.

She had a clear view of the red BMW car and trailer. They were some two hundred metres ahead of her and climbing a fairly steep hill. She'd wait until they reached the brow, she told herself, and then follow at a safe distance.

The waiting was unnecessary. Without giving a signal the BMW and trailer veered off to the right and disappeared from view. Sky immediately engaged a gear, swung clear of the parked motorbike and revved the Volvo's engine.

The turning was barely visible from the road. Sky cruised up the hill and only spotted it because she knew it had to be there. It stood well back from any passing traffic; an inconspicuous unmade track where brambles were left to their own devices and thrived on the permanent haze of roadside exhaust fumes.

The suspension grated its displeasure and the steering wheel vibrated in Sky's hands as the Volvo bounced through a cluster of potholes. The width of the track had increased over the years by the constant journeying of Ryker's travelling horse-box. During the spring and summer months the large vehicle would scythe back the under-growth leaving a single raised strip of diseased grass running up the middle of the track and deep earthy tyre indentations either side.

Sky struggled to control the steering as the Volvo pitched in and out of the ruts. Suddenly the track divided and she decided to fork left for no better reason than it looked less bumpy. Now she found herself heading up an incline and a blind bend lay ahead. She slowed to a crawl, not knowing whether to get out and walk or press on and maybe risk being seen. The safety of the estate car appealed more, so she eased the Volvo gently round a curve and breathed a sigh of relief as the track gradually fanned out to reveal a large ramshackle building.

Suddenly, carried on the wind, she heard somebody shouting instructions.

'A bit more . . . Easy, easy! Hold it . . . that should do you!'

She immediately jerked on the Volvo's handbrake and switched off the ignition. The estate car's front windows were open and although the voice was faint — a very long way off — she instantly recognised it as belonging to Griggs. There was a fair bit of revving, which she guessed was coming from Ryker's BMW, and she hoped this had masked any noise of her arrival.

Her ribs were cold with moisture but her mouth was prune-dry as she calmed herself to take stock of her surroundings.

She had halted close to some barbed-wire fencing at the rear of what appeared to be an old warehouse. It was a tall building and the fierce afternoon sun was bouncing off the roof and casting long shadows across the Volvo.

She couldn't be seen, she decided, grateful that she'd taken the correct fork in the track. Whatever action was now taking place was happening at quite a distance on the other side of the warehouse. She opened Sir Galahad's hamper of tack and pulled out a bridle, keeping her fingers wrapped tightly

266

round the snaffle bit to stop it from rattling.

Exiting the car she trampled through dried bracken as she made her way awkwardly along the rear of the warehouse. Nettles and brambles clawed at her jodhpurs as, still concealed by the cloak of shade, she ran the length of the building's wooden cladding to a corner vantage point.

She pulled her phone from her jacket pocket, letting her eyes roam over the property's six acres. The paddock for old horses, the mobile home, and the corrugated iron structure which housed the travelling horse-box were all now visible.

And so were Ryker and Griggs.

The trailer had been backed under the leafy camouflage of some huge oak trees but both men became visible as they stepped out of the shadows and into the sunshine.

'Do you want Buckingham put in a stall?' Griggs was saying. 'Or shall we let him stretch his legs in the paddock?'

'I want the horse in the warehouse and out of sight,' Ryker replied, climbing out of the BMW. 'The girl's probably reported him stolen by now.'

'What about the trailer?'

'We dump it. The police could come sniffing around and I don't want it found on the property.'

Daniel and Shack could hear the conversation clearly as they crouched motionless against the inside of the trailer's ramp. They held their nets loosely, ready to spring into action, their eyes steadfastly set on the inside keepers that located the exterior bolts.

They could hear Ryker puffing on a cheroot. When he spoke, the smoke caught in his throat and the words rattled like gravel. 'Okay, drop the ramp and get him out. I'll put down some fresh bedding in one of the stalls.'

Daniel cursed as a thin brew of unease began to percolate in his mind. He turned to Shack, adding softly but firmly, 'We need them together. If Ryker and Griggs separate we've had it.'

Shack pointed to the metal chains that ran either side of the trailer's interior. They were there to give added strength and support to the ramp when it was lowered — but they could also have another use. Shack gripped the chain at his corner tightly and by using sign language prompted Daniel to do likewise.

He nodded, following Shack's actions.

Breaths were held as Griggs started whistling yet another unrecognisable tune and the bolts were slid free of their keepers.

Two stringy hands with badly bitten nails wrestled to release the ramp. Shack and

Daniel took the strain on the chains. They rattled but the ramp didn't budge.

'What's up with this,' Griggs grumbled. He turned and called out to Ryker. 'You'll have to give me a hand, Tony. The blasted thing's stuck!'

Shack lifted a thumb to Daniel and grinned. The ploy with the chains was unscripted but it was having the desired effect.

'Can't you handle anything on your own?' Ryker was saying irritably, striding back. 'That lunchtime brandy must have dulled your senses. Are you sure the bolts are off?'

'Of course I'm sure. I'm not stupid.'

'That's open to debate, Griggsy.'

Daniel swallowed hard and Shack nibbled on his lower lip as Ryker checked the bolts before his big sturdy hands joined forces with Griggs's.

They pulled at the ramp together and the strain on the chains was enormous.

'On the count of three . . . ' Daniel said on a raw whisper, exertion twisting his features. 'One . . . Two . . . '

'*Three!*' Shack added his voice to the count, and both chains were immediately released.

The ramp flew open, rocking on its hinges and leaving everybody's ears ringing as it crashed to the ground with the noise of a small explosion.

Suddenly there was pandemonium. Everything happened simultaneously.

In one lithe, ultra-fast movement, Daniel and Shack jumped from the trailer, their nets billowing in their hands . . . Ryker and Griggs stepped backwards, unnerved, confused, shrouded in a carpet of dust thrown up by the ramp. Sky broke cover, running at full tilt . . . Degsey leapt out . . . and Sir Galahad, frightened by all the din swayed sideways, muscles rippling violently in his quarters as his head went up and he snapped his halter.

'What the . . . ' Ryker's lips moved back sharply on his teeth. The net had engulfed him but he was still lashing out at Daniel with manic strength, like a trapped and incensed wild bear.

Griggs was ensnared too. His eyebrows flew up in sudden terror as Shack dived at him, bringing the net down over his head and bony shoulders and forcing him to his knees. The netting clung to his face, distorting it, making his eyes bulge hugely as, totally disorientated, he wriggled and squirmed against Shack's strength.

'Lie on the ground!' Shack discarded the net, and twisted the collar of Griggs's shirt like a tourniquet. 'Don't even *think* of escaping!'

'W-who . . . ?' Griggs gave a strangled little cough as a bubble of saliva puffed from his lips and popped. 'A-are you police or something?'

'Or something,' Shack affirmed, nudging Griggs's thighs further apart and forcing him face down in the dust. He pulled some rope from his pocket and began tying Griggs's wrists and ankles, looping the two ends together so he would be trussed up like a chicken.

Daniel was having far more of a problem.

He'd managed to get a grip around Ryker's thick waist and was holding his own — until fate and Sir Galahad intervened. Sky was reaching to grab the loose horse's head-collar when its hindquarters blundered heavily into Daniel.

The impact jarred all breath from his body. Suddenly he had no air, no voice, and his lungs were burning. He staggered sideways, somehow managing to remain upright as he fought to regain his faculties.

Ryker had disentangled himself from the net and intended to exploit Daniel's predicament to the full. Grunting heavily he body-charged Daniel, knocking him to the ground and sending sparks pinwheeling before his eyes. Ryker paused briefly for the dust to clear before balling his fists and moving forward as if to finish the job.

'Leave him!' Dried sweat stiffened Shack's hair as he confronted the big man. He stood with arms folded, legs set aggressively apart.

Ryker's eyes suddenly flashed as he remembered every detail of Shack's face. 'Well, well, if it isn't the kid who tangled with me at that Oyster place at Swiftly. You've done well, sonny — you set me up and I fell for the lot ... the trailer breakdown, the show-horse, the girl with the plummy accent ...'

'I've made a call on my mobile phone,' Sky chipped in, hot-eyed and flushed. Her hair was damp and mussy as she knelt by Daniel. She was still holding Sir Galahad by the broken halter. 'The police and RSPCA will be here at any minute.'

Ryker's gaze was on her. 'So what would you like me to do, Miss Plummy Voice — *stay*?'

Sky felt a surge of anger, but she controlled her voice. 'You can't get away. Your horse rustling days are over. Both you and your sickening trade are finished.'

'Nobody tells Tony Ryker what he can and cannot do!' His face darkened dangerously. He took a deep breath to calm himself before smiling at Sky indulgently. The corner of his mouth curled up and she shivered slightly as he went on, 'You animal welfare people make me sick. You're an irritating bunch of do-gooders with empty lives. I can set up again . . . anytime, anywhere. And believe me — I'll be long gone before the police arrive.'

'We've got your partner,' Shack reminded him, tilting his head towards a wriggling Griggs. 'He won't be going anywhere.'

'So keep him. He suffers from nosebleeds and he's more trouble than he's worth.'

Ryker took a couple of sideways steps towards the BMW.

'Don't make for the car,' Shack warned, 'or I'll — '

'You'll what?' Ryker focussed on him sharply. 'Set the dog on me?'

Degsey was lying by the paddock gate, motionless. She seemed very cool and assured and she was watching Ryker diligently. Mister Rafferty stood on the other side of the gate, sniffing briskly at the air. He had been reunited with his old friend and he capered and pranced excitedly behind the woodwork.

'I wouldn't pin your hopes on the dog,' Ryker went on, laughing mirthlessly. 'That greyhound could barely manage a growl when we last met.'

Daniel leaned against Sky as she helped

him to his feet. His chest was heaving and he let out a wheezy groan as he clung to Sir Galahad's neck for support. Shack's eyes flicked briefly towards the group. It was a foolish lapse of concentration and time enough to allow Ryker to seize his escape opportunity. He lunged suddenly for the BMW's driving door and had his fingers curled around the handle and was yanking it open before the movement had even pricked Shack's awareness.

He reacted but it was too late. Much too late.

He tried to compensate by hurling himself at Ryker in a cannonball dive — but the big man had anticipated the move and swung the half-open car door into his path. It crashed painfully into Shack's side, lifting his legs from under him and sending his breath hissing through his teeth. He righted himself, clutching his ribs, hearing the BMW's engine throb into life and a noisy grating of gears as Ryker floored the accelerator.

'He's getting away!' Sky turned her gaze to Daniel, her voice shrill.

Daniel could only watch helplessly, waiting for his strength to return as he clung to Sir Galahad's mane.

There was a smell of rubber in the air as a wave of dust surged from the car's powerful wheel spin. Shack managed to stagger clumsily away as he felt a wisp of air from the trailer's slipstream caress his face. The tiny wheels rumbled past his feet; the still-lowered ramp bouncing and rattling over the uneven surface.

Degsey was now standing by the paddock gate. She stretched and shook life into her taut muscles, knowing exactly what she must do . . .

'Can I have some help with this?' Sky released Sir Galahad's head-collar and was struggling both to hold the horse and attach the bridle.

'I'll do it,' Shack's voice rasped with dryness. He was still rubbing his side but looked in far better physical shape than Daniel.

Degsey sprang forward like a cork leaving a bottle, adopting her powerful racing stride as she flew past the group's legs. Shack, who had never seen her at full stretch before, let out a soft whistle of amazement.

'Jeez,' he murmured, the whistle causing his bruised ribs to grate painfully under his denim shirt, 'that's one heck of a fast greyhound.'

'The best.' Daniel straightened his back, taking gulps of air as he worked life into his shoulders.

'Gypsy devil dog . . . ' Griggs jerked out the words in a strangled undertone as he wriggled against the ropes, twisting onto his side. A nosebleed had erupted, the redness caking his nostrils and trailing thinly to his lips as he corkscrewed his neck to glimpse Degsey.

'She's going after your boss,' Sky told him, accepting a leg-up from Shack and vaulting onto Sir Galahad's bare back. 'She'll have something planned — you can bet on it.'

'And you?' Daniel asked, the colour returning to his face. 'What are you planning to do?'

Sir Galahad was gusting breath, one hoof pawing impatiently at the ground. 'Catch Mr Ryker,' Sky said simply.

Daniel moistened his lips and exchanged apprehensive glances with Shack, but neither spoke. They could both see that Sky looked determined, her eyes direct and steady, full of plucky spirit — and they both knew there wasn't a word they could say that would stop her.

She gathered the reins and tapped her heels firmly against the horse's flanks. Sir Galahad sprang forward, knowing she meant business as he effortlessly changed his gait from canter to full gallop in one graceful movement.

Ryker was weaving a hazardous course

around the property's perimeter track. He was hampered by the trailer; the ramp rumbling and jolting, creating resistance and destabilising the BMW whenever the route narrowed or he encountered a sharp bend. He'd rattled past the corrugated iron structure which housed the travelling horse-box and was now on the other side of the paddock — surging away from the mobile home and heading towards the warehouse. If he reached the fork in the track unhindered, then he was away and clear.

Sky spanned the paddock fence on Sir Galahad, cutting a swathe through the startled old horses as she thundered across the patchy turf, using the shortest route possible before bracing the muscles of her back and cresting the fence on the far side. Riding without a saddle wasn't easy but she kept her seat secure, forking her body tautly, tightening her legs around the horse's ribs.

She continued to cut every conceivable corner, using her eventing skills to coax the chestnut horse this way and that, spanning ditches and jumping barbed-wire fences in an attempt to head off the BMW.

The task was too great. Ryker was watching her in the rear-view mirror and he had no intention of being out-manoeuvred.

'No chance, Buckers,' he murmured

through clenched teeth, stamping hard on the accelerator. 'Compared to the car you're sadly lacking in vital horsepower.'

The warehouse loomed ahead. Ryker gave a grunt of satisfaction, dropping down a gear as he approached the fork in the dirt track.

Suddenly his vision blurred over . . .

His fingers tightened compulsively on the steering wheel.

A penetrating light was searing at his pupils, boring into them with such severity that he fumbled frantically to flip down the car's sun visor. It jammed — he pulled — it broke off in his hand.

'What . . . ?' Through screwed-up eyes Ryker could just make out the shape of a greyhound. It was standing immobile where the track forked, muzzle drawn back, head tilted upwards towards the sun. A pinpoint of bedazzling light radiated from one of its teeth, growing, expanding, and enfolding him. Its strength blanketed the car, shimmering through the windshield and blinding him with a halo of brilliance.

'No! No! I can't see!' His voice was clipped as he yelled the words at Degsey, cupping a hand to his forehead.

A welter of emotions criss-crossed his twisted features as Griggs's warnings about the dog flashed into his thoughts. A gold tooth? Was it possible? Is that what he'd seen in the headlights on the journey back from Marshwood? Is that why he'd swerved? Griggs had always claimed that it was a devil dog. Now, as Ryker's apprehension tightened several notches, he was beginning to wish he'd heeded his partner's warnings.

He began to sweat as he spun the steering wheel this way and that, hoping to break free of the energy-sapping beam.

No reaction — his efforts didn't alter his course and the wheel ran free in his hands. The car had suddenly developed a will of its own ... dictating a very definite route, accelerating under its own resolve and putting him on a collision course with the warehouse.

He felt dizzy. His heart palpitated fast.

Degsey was unmoving. Silhouetted against the sun. She held her position and blinked ...

There was a frigid click as the BMW's central-locking system snapped involuntarily on, sealing the doors. Ryker heard the noise and knew what was happening. His unsteady fingers fiddled with the electric window switches — wrenched frantically at the driver's door-handle.

No response.

He was panicking now ... real white-faced panic ... stamping on the foot-brake in an attempt to stop the car. He pumped at the pedal, hoping to find a reassuring resistance as brake fluid found its way to the cylinders — but there was just a soft hissing sound and the hollow slap of his foot making contact with the floor.

'*Try the handbrake, try the handbrake . . .*' The words strummed hotly in his head, running like quicksilver through the veins bulging between his forehead and ears. In a last-gasp effort he fumbled for the lever, almost wrenching it from its metal housing. Once again there was no pressure, no tension. Only slackness. It slopped about impotently, as if the cable had been cut.

He cursed loudly and dementedly. In the past he had always been in charge of whatever situation presented itself . . . prided himself on always being in control. But now he had never felt so helpless in his life. Helpless, weak and ineffectual. The wooden facade of the warehouse was closing by the second . . . and he knew he was going to crash.

Blind that dog's eyes! Send that greyhound to hell!

Ryker wrapped his arms around his face as the red BMW slammed mercilessly into the warehouse doors. Wood splintered in a deafening crescendo as the building's heavy metal locking bar buckled under the thrust of the car's radiator grille. It lifted and spun, punching a spidery hole through the BMW's windshield as it lanced past Ryker's shoulder and embedded itself into the leather upholstery. Tiny arrowheads of glass rained onto Ryker's lap as the car ploughed on.

Ahead were the stalls — empty apart from the three stolen Penhill horses. They were tethered to securing rings and these twisted jarringly as the animals whinnied and snorted, their eyes bulging in panic as they tried to skitter away from the impending danger.

Ryker's knuckles whitened on the steering wheel and he heard the crack of one shifting in its socket as he braced himself. His eyes were squeezed tight shut as he waited for the impact of the car striking horseflesh — waiting for the inevitable bloodshed which would surely follow.

Only it didn't.

The brakes came on.

The tyres screamed for traction, lurching Ryker forward and causing his ribs to bounce against the steering wheel. Four molten black strips of tortured rubber licked across the warehouse floor as the red BMW slewed sideways and came to a shuddering halt.

The engine stuttered and died. Only the noise of Ryker's loud, wheezy breathing could be heard above the hiss of steam escaping from the car's ruptured radiator.

Sky, on Sir Galahad, trotted through the gaping aperture and into the warehouse. The horse was lathered, foaming, and shining with sweat. It quivered and trembled still as Sky gentled it before swinging a leg over the withers and sliding to the floor.

The sound of a police two-tone siren began to gain in intensity. Ryker felt his heartbeat quicken knowing he was only minutes away from arrest.

He yanked at the door handles but they were still firmly locked. Glaring at Sky he thumped a fist against the dashboard. 'Caught by three cocky teenagers and a gypsy dog!' He coughed out the words, wiping spittle from his mouth and giving her a look that trawled the very depths of her flesh; evil and brutal.

'We didn't catch you, Mr Ryker,' Sky said, quietening the Penhill horses as she gazed at him through the ragged hole in the windshield. 'Greed did.'

* * *

Seamus Horrigan's whole body was shaking with delight. His proud, sensitive mouth had curled into a huge smile and this had caused his crease lines to dive and take refuge under the tangle of his iron-grey moustache.

'Praise be to God and Mary, Peter, Paul and Patrick,' he said, tears of relief smarting his eyes. He fondled Mister Rafferty's ears and blew gently against the chestnut cob's muzzle. 'I be full o' gratitude to you all. Me heart be fair burstin' wi' the joyestest o' feelings . . . 'Tis a fact I never thought I'd be seein' the old rascal again.'

Mister Rafferty lifted his head and whinnied jubilantly. He rolled back his top lip and exposed well-worn, slightly brownish teeth.

Jonathan, dressed only in surfer's shorts, ran a hand over the old cob's coarse, uneven mane and exchanged a delighted grin with Spring.

It was early evening and Daniel, Shack and Sky had arrived back at Oyster Gables. Their faces held a look of triumph, but their bodies were racked with muscle fatigue brought on by the afternoon's events. They had each given statements about Ryker's and Griggs's horsenapping activities to the police and then assisted the RSPCA inspectors in sorting out the stolen horses. The three from Penhill were easily identified, but the six old animals from the paddock proved more difficult to classify. Eventually five were matched against the

Society's computerised records of thefts — and of course Degsey had no trouble in establishing Mister Rafferty as the sixth. Both the old cob and the greyhound were inseparable.

'Where's Sir Galahad?' Jonathan asked, standing by the trailer and running a finger over the dents and jagged scratches that scarred the ramp's leading edge.

'We only had room for Mister Rafferty,' Daniel explained. 'The RSPCA will drop him off later when they return the Penhill horses.'

'You've hurt your face.' Spring indicated a plaster that covered a small graze on Daniel's temple. Both he and Shack had received first aid treatment at the local police station.

'Was there lots of fighting?' Jonathan's eyes lit up as the questions tumbled out. 'How many were in the gang? Did they use weapons? Was there lots of blood and spit and stuff?'

'There wasn't any gang,' Shack said, fingering the strapping that now hugged his bruised ribs. 'Although sometimes it felt like it.'

Degsey was showing everyone her pleasure at being reunited with Mister Rafferty. She stood under the cob, looking up at him as she weaved in and out of his legs. It was a game they had played many times in the past and

284

the old horse hadn't forgotten the routine. Whenever Degsey's wagging tail presented itself he would turn and dip his head, trying to knock her off balance.

'I expect Mister Rafferty has lost a bit of weight,' Sky remarked to Seamus, smiling at the animals' antics as she leaned into the Volvo and folded the borrowed riding clothes neatly over her arm. 'We'd better put him on a special diet for a week to build him up.'

Seamus said nothing, just looked slightly embarrassed as he toyed with the strip of brightly coloured cloth that secured his pony-tail.

'You will be staying for a bit?' Spring fixed him with apprehensive eyes.

''Fraid not. I be doin' a lot of tinkin' and it be best if old Seamus be makin' a move.'

He spoke the words so calmly that Jonathan could only stare open-mouthed until he realised he was gaping and closed it. He cleared his throat. 'You're leaving . . . what now?'

'T'morrow mornin', boy — after breakfast. Ireland be callin' this tinker's name. 'Tis time me and me family be on our way.'

Daniel, Shack and Sky traded glances. They knew only too well that once Mister Rafferty had been found there would be nothing to keep Seamus at Swiftly; but

285

hearing talk of his sudden departure still came as a blow. They had all become entwined in his life, his problems, his mysterious ways — and all of them had gained so much from the experience. Life at Oyster Gables would undoubtedly go on — the way it had in the past — but with Seamus gone, a marvellous little chink of colour would always be lacking from their lives.

'You'll be sadly missed,' Daniel said, 'by all of us.'

'And I shall be missin' all o' you.' Seamus's watery eyes crinkled as he looked at each face in turn. 'You all be me family . . . me very special family — and Mister Rafferty, and me darlin' Degsey will be tinkin' o' you with every roll o' the wagon's wheels.'

Spring's face was intense, the tears gathering heavily in her dilated eyes and overflowing slowly down her cheeks as she swallowed noisily. She was looking at Degsey, trying to blot out thoughts of never seeing the glorious greyhound again.

Seamus caught her look and glanced furtively at Sky. 'Can I be askin' a special favour?' he said, puffing out his cheeks. 'Me babbies be growed so big that there barely be room in me wagon to keep the wee rascals . . . So I be wonderin' . . . '

He paused, rubbing his sandpapery jaw.

'You were wondering . . . ?' Sky prompted.

Spring blinked away her tears and stared at him hard, her pale lashes rolling back widely from bright, acute eyes. She hoped desperately that the words she wanted to hear would finally emerge.

'Ay, Seamus be wonderin' whether Jonathan and Spring would do him the favour o' keeping Little Degsey.'

In a breathy voice, Spring asked, 'For always?'

'Ay, for always.'

'Brilliant!' Jonathan gave him a jaunty salute.

Spring had already climbed the caravan's steps to the footboard and was peering over the top of the porch doors. A source of warmth and joy coursed through her body as Little Degsey jumped up to greet her. Her smile was delighted, infectious, as she turned to blow Seamus a kiss.

Shack moved forward to take the halter from Seamus's hands. Tonight, at least, Mister Rafferty would be spending a safe night in Oyster Gables' stables.

Daniel followed behind the old horse with Sir Galahad's hamper of tack. Seamus smiled at both of them, thanking them quietly for their help and their courage and telling them he'd say his 'goodbyes' in the morning.

Daniel thought the old gypsy seemed to be at peace with himself. His face had noticeably lightened and for the first time he looked relaxed — free from the anxieties which the past week had presented.

Even Daniel's bodily fatigue had lessened. Mister Rafferty was safe and that's all that mattered — that's all that had ever mattered. Every bruise, graze, ache and pain had been worth the effort.

Shack turned, glancing over his shoulder. 'Good to see the old boy looking so happy. All's well that ends well, eh, Daniel?'

Daniel smiled. 'Amen to that,' he said.

11

Staff and helpers usually arrived in stages for breakfast at Oyster Gables but this morning was no ordinary morning and Sky had her work cut out to cope. Due to Seamus's departure everyone was appearing at seven on the dot.

Shack and Daniel had finished their mucking out and cage cleaning duties and were at the large butler sink sharing a joke and washing their hands. Megan and Hannah had made a point of coming in early to help with the animal feeding and were now slicing bread ready for the toaster. Spring was clicking on a timer as she prepared to boil herself two fresh eggs . . . and even Jonathan, who was always an hour behind everyone else, was generally getting under Sky's feet as he played with Scooter.

'So the police phoned here last night and asked if we could offer an explanation . . . ' Daniel chuckled to Shack as he dried his hands. 'They couldn't shift Ryker because all the BMW's doors were *welded* shut. They said they'd never seen anything like it. In the end they had to use cutting gear to get him out.'

'What about the smashed windshield?' Jonathan posed the question.

'What about it?'

'Couldn't they pull him out that way?'

'He was too bulky. They tried but he got jammed.'

Shack caught his breath in a rueful giggle. 'Did you tell them Degsey was responsible for the doors?'

'Would you have told them?'

He grinned and shook his head.

'My thoughts exactly. The true story would have got me an appointment for brain treatment!'

Sky had resorted to using two large frying pans. One sizzled away appetisingly with sausages, bacon, frying bread and tomatoes, whilst the other was ready with heated cooking oil to accept seven free-range eggs sitting in a nearby rack.

'Nice smell, Miss Plummy Voice,' Daniel mocked softly, enjoying her closeness.

'Thank you Mr Rusk.' Sky grinned mischievously and put on her practised Silver Seagull accent as she joined in the game. 'Cooking breakfast is a frightfully tiresome business, but one appreciates being appreciated.'

His warm breath touched her earlobe. 'I wasn't talking about breakfast. It's *you* that smells delicious.'

Sky laughed, tilting her head to look at Daniel and letting the great, soft masses of her hair fall back from her face.

'Who's Miss Plummy Voice?' Jonathan broke in, the question interrupting Daniel's thoughts.

'Er . . . It's a sort of nickname,' he explained. 'Invented by one of the horse thieves.'

'There seems to be a lot of this nickname stuff going on,' Jonathan responded, flicking a glance to Shack. 'I mean who would have thought — '

He stopped abruptly as Shack glared at him and made a throat-slitting gesture.

'Thought what?' quizzed Sky.

'Oh,' he swallowed, having to think quickly. 'That . . . that horse thieves should have a sense of humour.'

'Takes all sorts,' Shack said, his features relaxing.

Sky asked Daniel if he would try to persuade Seamus to join them for breakfast. 'As it's his last morning,' she added, 'it would be nice if we could all eat together.'

'He always has his meals in his wagon.' Jonathan stated the obvious.

'Make yourself useful, Jonathan.' Sky said the words firmly, her eyes dark and direct. 'Please set the table for eight.'

'Seamus won't come. He's far too stubborn.'

Sky gave him an implacable stare. She opened the cutlery drawer and just pointed.

'I'll see if I can manage a bit of arm twisting.' Daniel made his way to the door. 'But you know Seamus — it won't be easy.'

'Tell him I've prepared a packed lunch to eat on the road,' Sky added, remembering.

'And ask him if he'd like some cans of dog food for Degsey and the pups,' Spring said brightly, helping herself to a yoghurt from the fridge.

'Will do.'

'And Daniel . . . ' Sky stopped him in his tracks.

'Yes?'

'Don't be long. Breakfast is nearly ready.'

Sky's mouth had softened, the corners turning gently upwards into a warm, open smile.

Daniel paused to look at all the genial, familiar faces. He felt a glow of contentment spread through him; a keen sensation of physical well-being. He wanted to rekindle the feeling of Sky's lips on his own; to touch and caress. He knew things had finally come right between them and he felt wonderful. He closed the door softly at his back, stretched, and stepped out into the misty early morning sunshine.

Crossing the forecourt he almost half expected to see Mister Rafferty in the caravan's shafts. He knew Seamus was an early riser so it wouldn't have surprised him if the old cob had been collected from the stables and tacked up, ready for the long journey ahead.

No horse, but the caravan's pan-box was open and some pieces of harness lay in a disorderly tangle on the ground.

Not only harness, but a man's shoe. An old-fashioned leather brogue that Daniel recognised as belonging to Seamus.

Suddenly his spine felt chilly and his stomach was tight.

Something was very, very, wrong.

'*Seamus!*' he shouted the name, ducking under one of the shafts and scooting up the steps to the porch.

The porch doors were wide open, revealing the three pups huddled together on the skin rug. They looked up at him, shivering — not with cold — but with an all-embracing fear of the unknown. His eyes travelled past them to the bunk bed beneath the rear window, where hazy sunlight filtered in through the Venetian-style shutters.

He saw Degsey first, standing on the

patchwork quilt which lay crumpled on the floor . . . and then he saw Seamus.

The old gypsy was sitting loose-limbed on the bunk, his face waxen, his head lolling unnaturally sideways. He was fully dressed apart from one missing shoe and his lifeless blue eyes were staring unseeingly at Degsey.

Daniel crossed quickly to the bunk, hearing the greyhound give several throaty whimpers as she stretched her long neck, nudging persistently at Seamus's arm, trying to wake him.

Daniel knelt, checking the gypsy's pulse and breathing; knowing inwardly it was hopeless, but going through the motions nevertheless. Seamus's leathery skin still felt slightly warm to the touch as Daniel closed the old man's eyes with a sweep of his hand.

Degsey nuzzled closer to Seamus, sniffing and gently licking at his fingers, the pupils of her eyes wide and midnight black, willing her master to waken.

Daniel wished it could all be fiction, a fragment of a night's bad dreaming. He suddenly felt salt tears on his lips and knew he must have been weeping without knowing it. He looked at the greyhound and took a shuddery breath.

'Seamus has gone, Degsey,' he said softly, brokenly. 'Your master is dead.'

The words had a stunning, unnerving effect.

She immediately lifted her head to the window, catching the slatted rays of the sun across her face . . . and then she howled. At least, Daniel assumed it was a howl. He'd never heard anything so extraordinary before, and never wanted to hear it again. It was an eerie, quivering wail which when it broke free, tore open the silence, shooting through his senses like an explosion and causing him to reel backwards as if someone had struck him. It grated painfully against his ears and plucked at the raw edges of his nerves.

Every muscle in Degsey's body was bunched and strained as she stretched her neck higher, her Adam's apple working furiously as if to burst free of her larynx. The gathering of black skin around her muzzle lifted and rumpled back to reveal her gold canine tooth. Set against the glistening pinkness of her gums, it was strobing with an overwhelming brilliance.

Daniel shielded his eyes, squinting through fingers that had developed a definite tremor. For the first time he was feeling real fear. He had minor palpitations. He sweated.

The wailing continued, raw and intense. It bubbled in the greyhound's throat and forced Daniel to cover his ears.

Something was happening to the tooth, which in turn was causing the weather outside the window to change dramatically. Clouds were suddenly massing darkly overhead.

It was as if both were inextricably linked. The gold was slowly disappearing and the sunshine was noticeably fading. Daniel watched open-mouthed as a single finger of the now-weakening sun's rays enfolded the tooth, sapping, bleeding, leeching the gold away; spinning round it like a vortex as it licked at the precious metal and replaced it with a hard milky whiteness.

Degsey's special powers were ebbing away . . .

A scribble of lightning briefly lit up the caravan's interior, followed by a loud clap of thunder. Large droplets of rain began to bounce on the leaded roof, hitting the outside chimney stack and resounding down to the old Colchester stove.

Degsey was quiet now. She looked a trifle weak and she was panting softly. Her muscles were free from spasm as the final remnants of sunlight evaporated from inside the caravan. She placed her chin on Daniel's thigh, focussing on him, the deep grief of losing Seamus emanating from the depths of her much-too-human soul and reflecting in her eyes.

Inside, Daniel knew she was crying. She couldn't weep openly but was the rain on the window her tears? He guessed that it was. The water spattered behind the velvet curtains and ran in rivulets down the expanse of rearwindow glass.

Tears of sadness, he convinced himself, stroking her long, beautiful face.

Tears for Seamus.

His mind was still numb and his actions almost mechanical as he put a finger to Degsey's muzzle and lifted the soft flesh to glimpse the tooth. No bright sparkle of gold, no serendipity, no mystical powers — they had all died along with the old gypsy. Now there was just a strong, healthy white canine in the lower jaw. Degsey was back to being a normal greyhound. How it should be, Daniel supposed. How, without Seamus to protect, it was always meant to be. Suddenly the finality of what had happened no longer frightened him.

'Mr Rusk?'

Daniel turned towards the porch steps, sucking in a startled breath. The rain had stopped as suddenly as it had started and the early morning sunshine had returned.

'Yes . . . Who . . . ?' He squinted towards the silhouette of a tall, male figure standing on the footboard.

'My name's Doctor Becker. I've been to the house and Ms Patakin sent me here. She phoned the surgery on Saturday asking for an early Monday morning call.'

Daniel's brain tilted. With all the happenings of late, Shack's request for a doctor to see Seamus had completely slipped his mind. 'I'm sorry . . . Yes . . . Come in . . . He's here.'

'The patient is a Mr Horrigan I believe?'

Daniel nodded, distress showing in his face. He stood up and coaxed Degsey to one side, leaving a clear view of the bunk. As the doctor removed his rain-soaked jacket he glimpsed Seamus and the situation became only too obvious.

'I found him like this,' Daniel said in hushed tones. 'I'm afraid he's dead.'

Doctor Becker rolled up his sleeves and sat on the bunk. He had iron grey hair and iron grey eyes to match. He opened his medical bag and took out some pieces of equipment.

Daniel heard the sound of feet on the caravan's wooden steps. He crossed quickly to close the bottom half of the porch doors just as Jonathan reached the footboard.

'Sky sent me,' he said, his blue eyes scanning Daniel's face. 'She's going ballistic. You were expected back ages ago. Your breakfast will be all yucky and dried up.'

'Tell Sky I'll have some toast later. I have to stay with Doctor Becker.'

'Is Seamus alright?' He shook rain from his anorak, pulling the hood back and trying to crane his neck past Daniel's deliberately blocking shoulders.

'Can you take the pups back to the house?'

'I suppose I can.' He looked suspicious. 'What's up? Why are bits of Mister Rafferty's harness dumped by the pan-box? And what's that shoe doing there?'

'Don't ask so many questions, Jonathan.'

'I bet he's poisoned himself with all that herbal stuff he keeps in the table-top cabinet.'

'No he hasn't.'

'Well let me see him.' He pushed at the porch doors.

Daniel had his foot jammed firmly against them. 'He's with the doctor. Just take the pups — alright?'

'Let me in and I will.'

Daniel turned and called the pups to him. There was a scramble as he opened the porch doors just enough to let them squeeze through.

Jonathan stifled a sigh. 'At times you can be really weird, Daniel. Are you sure Seamus is alright?'

Daniel evaded answering. 'Tell Sky I'll join her as soon as the doctor leaves.'

The sun was coming through quite strongly now, and pale patches of hazy blue were showing overhead.

'You're as weird as the weather,' Jonathan went on. 'Was that some sort of freak storm or what? It only lasted a minute. We don't get crazy stuff like that back home in Sussex.'

'Thank you for the weather statistics, Jonathan. I'll see you later.'

He walked backwards down the steps and gathered the pups around him. 'Seriously weird . . . ' he said again.

Daniel closed the top half of the porch doors and pushed home the bolt.

Doctor Becker had finished his physical examination and was now going through the contents of the veneered table-top cabinet. He opened tiny containers stuffed with twigs, bark and leaves, and sniffed curiously at the vials of oil.

'You don't think any of those are to blame?' Daniel spoke with more ease than he felt. 'I thought they were harmless.'

'Oh, absolutely. They're just the normal assortment of herbs and curatives used in folklore. I thought I'd better just check — having overheard the boy's observations.'

'Yes, of course, so . . . ?' Daniel moistened lips that were suddenly too dry to finish the sentence.

300

'A heart attack killed him, Mr Rusk. He's been dead about an hour. I saw the harness and shoe when I arrived — so putting all the pieces together I'd say it's very probable that he overtaxed himself getting the harness from the box. He more than likely collapsed, losing his shoe in the process. He's a very old man — middle to late eighties, I'd say . . . but he was wiry and being the outdoor type probably as tough as old boots.' He paused, then added in a quiet, controlled voice, 'It's my guess that after Mr Horrigan collapsed he dragged himself back into the caravan to die.'

'To be near his darlin' Degsey.' Daniel deliberately used Seamus's words as he patted the greyhound, a pale smile piercing the preoccupied stillness of his face.

Doctor Becker began replacing the containers of herbs in the veneered table-top cabinet. 'Ms Patakin explained that he was a traveller spending some time in Swiftly. Did he have any relatives?'

'He never spoke of anyone.'

'Mmm.' He paused to close his medical bag and glanced at Seamus. 'Well, things have to be done. Would you like me to take care of the initial arrangements?'

'Moving him you mean?'

'Yes, until his affairs get sorted out.'

'Thank you, I'm grateful.'

Doctor Becker had replaced all the containers and vials but the drawer was jamming as he tried to close it. He fiddled for a while without success, then decided to pull it out from the cabinet to find the obstruction.

'There's something catching at the back . . . ' he began, placing delicate fingers around a large rolled up envelope which kept uncoiling itself. 'Here we are . . . got the culprit.'

He flattened it, placed it on top of the cabinet, and closed the drawer.

Daniel stared, his face intense as he glimpsed his own name. He was baffled as to why the foolscap envelope should be addressed to him. But there, in black ink, and written in beautiful copperplate writing were the words: MR DANIEL RUSK.

Doctor Becker was watching Daniel's eyes. He tapped the bridge of his nose with a knuckle and said, 'I think you should open it. It could be important.'

Daniel nodded and looked at Degsey as he swallowed uneasily. He tore open the manilla flap and pulled out the contents. It contained one large double sheet of thick paper, folded lengthways, and a brass key with a label attached.

'Locker seat opposite the policemen.'

Daniel read the words on the key tag aloud.

'Policemen?' Doctor Becker gave him a searching look. 'Does that mean anything to you?'

He indicated with his eyebrows. 'The old Colchester stove,' he responded, as the breath caught in his throat. He felt his pores snapping shut in shock as he glimpsed the central heading on the document. It read: *'This is the last Will and Testament of me Seamus Horrigan.'*

Daniel cleared his throat. 'Grief,' he said, handing the document to Doctor Becker. 'I've never had to read one of these before. Why the heck is it addressed to me?'

The doctor's eyes scanned the first page. Same black ink. Same copperplate handwriting. 'Mr Horrigan must have trusted and admired you a great deal. He's named you as sole executor of his will.'

Daniel had heard the term before — he remembered that his father and uncle had both been executors of his grandmother's will, but he still wasn't exactly sure what it meant.

'You're the trustee of Mr Horrigan's estate,' Doctor Becker explained. 'It will be your job to make sure that his last wishes are carried out to the best of your ability.' He turned the document over and glanced at the

303

date and accompanying signatures. 'This was signed and witnessed only a few days ago. It's a perfectly legal and valid document.'

'But Seamus never had any money . . . Well, I mean, he never *spoke* of having anything.'

'Perhaps he'd found the fabled pot of gold at the end of the rainbow.'

'Perhaps he had.' Daniel smiled in a lack-lustre way, stretching out his fingers to stroke Degsey, knowing that the doctor's words weren't a million miles from the truth.

'Anyway, this isn't for my eyes — it's for yours.' Doctor Becker placed the will back in the manilla envelope and gathered up his jacket and medical bag. 'When you've read it go and see a solicitor. They will apply for what's known as a Grant of Probate.' He extended a firm hand for Daniel to shake. 'Good luck, Mr Rusk.'

Daniel thanked him and opened the porch doors, watching as he strode briskly across the forecourt to his car. Daniel waved a goodbye, then turned back to face Degsey.

'So what's this all about?' He showed the greyhound the tagged key. 'What mystery is this going to unlock?'

Degsey padded behind him as he crossed to the Colchester stove. He knelt by the locker seat and turned the key easily, sliding open the dark red polished mahogany doors.

It seemed to be full of neatly stacked blankets and towels but when Daniel shifted these to one side he found a cardboard box containing two brown paper packets tied securely with thick string and daubed with sealing wax. On the smaller packet was written a number two, on the larger packet a number ten.

He blinked in total mystification. 'Your master has given me a few surprises this morning,' he murmured to Degsey. 'We'd better go back to the house and sort some of them out.'

During the examination Doctor Becker had fixed Seamus into a more pleasing position. He was now lying fully back on the bunk, his head on a pillow and the patchwork quilt covering his legs. The complex tracery of lines and broken veins of his skin seemed less deeply etched and he looked to all the world as if he was sleeping.

'Time to leave, girl.' Daniel spoke coaxingly to Degsey as he gathered up the will and the brown paper packets. He edged towards the door.

The greyhound was unmoving. She had returned to the bunk and was resting her head on Seamus's chest, her eyes growing round as they flicked from Daniel to the splendid brass lamp fixed to the window jamb.

Daniel followed her gaze and comprehension dawned.

The Angel lamp.

Seamus would have wanted it lit and Degsey was prompting him to do just this.

Seamus's pipe and matches were on the chest of drawers. Degsey's eyes tracked Daniel's every move as he collected the matches and crossed to the Angel lamp. She watched him check that the ruby red oil reservoir was full before he removed the globe and the chimney and put a match to the wick.

He closed the wooden window shutters and adjusted the burner so that the lamplight rippled over the lower bunk. Seamus was bathed in the glow. He looked perfectly at peace.

'Is that what you wanted?' Daniel turned to Degsey. The greyhound blinked contentedly as she looked into the light. She left Seamus's side and followed Daniel to the door.

★ ★ ★

'Ten thousand pounds?' Shack stared at Daniel, slack-jawed, his eyes reflecting his consternation. 'How on earth could old Seamus save that amount of money?'

It was long past breakfast and Daniel, Sky, Shack, Jonathan and Spring were now seated in the Oyster Gables' office. Earlier, when Daniel had broken the news of Seamus's death there had been lots of silent tears and woeful faces, but now — gradually — the atmosphere had lessened to sombre disbelief and everyone, in their own way, had come to terms with the situation.

'I expect the money represents a life-time's savings,' Daniel said in answer to Shack's question. 'Seamus told us he used to do odd jobs during his travels . . . well this was probably accumulated over sixty or more years.'

Everyone was looking at the various denomination banknotes that were spread on the desk in front of Daniel. They were the contents of packet 'ten' and comprised English, Irish and Scottish currency.

Daniel ran his finger along a handwritten bequest in the will, telling all that it was Seamus's last wish that the money should be spent on rebuilding the stables.

'I wasn't aware that he'd ever seen the stables.' Sky's eyebrows drew together in a quizzical frown.

'I probably put the idea into his head.' Shack looked a little guilty as jigsaw images floated out of the past to tease him. 'It was the night we were all sitting round the fire listening to the story of Degsey and her gold tooth. Seamus mentioned that he did basket weaving to gain a few pennies, and I joked that he should teach us the craft. That way, I said, we could earn some extra money to repair the stables.'

'They are very shabby,' Daniel stated. 'It's a wonderful gesture.'

'Thank you, Seamus,' Sky said softly to herself. 'Thank you for thinking of us.'

'There's a clause relating to the bequest.' Daniel struggled with some of the misspelled words and the phrasing written in Seamus's inimitable way. 'Me old cob, Mister Rafferty,' he read aloud, 'will be allowed to live out the rest of his natural life at Oyster Gables. He will be used to pull me wagon whenever it's agreeable.'

'Is the caravan a bequest?' Sky asked.

Daniel's eyes dropped back to the copper-plate writing. He nodded. 'The wagon and 'all belongin' to it' has been bequeathed to the shelter.'

'We could rent it out for short breaks,' Shack said, liking the idea and nodding his head decidedly. 'Caravan holidays are incredibly popular in Devon. Families would love it and we could use the extra income to buy new equipment for Oyster Gables. Everyone would benefit.'

'Especially Mister Rafferty,' Jonathan observed.

Spring had been sitting tight-lipped and pale, her eyes loaded with unshed tears, her clenched hands braced on her knees. Only now, was she managing a smile.

'He would be back between the shafts — travelling again. Seamus would have wanted that. I think it's a brilliant idea.'

'It will need careful planning,' Sky said, resolutely down-to-earth. 'We'd have to run a proper advertising campaign.' She paused to give Shack a nod of approval. 'But yes, Spring's right. It is a brilliant idea.'

'And it's a proper wagon,' Jonathan emphasised, 'not a modern piece of junk you see in most holiday brochures.' He cleared his throat and did his usual bad impression of Seamus. 'Ay, she be a genuine Reading, built in the early nineteen-hundreds and weighin' thirty hundredweight.'

'It is a classic,' Daniel agreed, relaxing a little. 'A piece of history. Oyster Gables is very lucky to inherit it.'

Shack swallowed deeply. 'Whenever it's rolling we'll be reminded of Seamus. His memory will always be with us.'

Spring's eyes were glistening. Shack

didn't attempt to fill the short silence. Any further comment would have sounded trite.

It was left to Daniel to intervene quickly. He returned to the will and tapped the packet numbered 'two' with a pencil. 'Seamus has also left two thousand pounds to cover funeral expenses. He's requested that he be buried in Ireland at the village church in Knockgrafton.'

'At the foot of the Galtee mountains . . . ' Animation entered Spring's tense little face as she remembered the story of Degsey's birth. 'He wants to be near Deggoran Odyssey. He wants to go home.'

'I think you're right.' Shack gave her a rallying smile, glad to focus on mundane matters. 'Seamus will be resting in one of his favourite places.'

Sky nibbled on her lower lip as a thought suddenly struck her. She turned to Daniel, her face showing a bewildering mixture of emotions.

'May I see the will?'

'Of course.' He handed it over, a furrow appearing between his eyes. 'Something bothering you?'

'Just curious about the witnesses. As Seamus rarely left his caravan I was wondering — '

'A Mrs Helen Wilson and a Mr Kenneth Wilson,' Daniel said from memory, anticipating the question. 'You'll notice they've given a Yorkshire address — tourists I suppose.'

She turned to the back page and shrugged pensively. 'I've never heard of Mr and Mrs Wilson.'

Jonathan's eyes were fixed on Shack. He moved his head to avoid their point of focus.

'They're my mother and my stepfather,' he said eventually, clearing his throat with an embarrassed little cough. 'They called in at Oyster Gables last week — unaware that I was off sick. They told me later that they had looked over Seamus's wagon, but I didn't know they'd witnessed his will.'

'Well, that solves the mystery.' Sky looked reassured.

'Names can be confusing,' Jonathan said pointedly, pursing his lips as he strolled casually to the computer and back. 'I know they had old Seamus confused.'

'Not now, Jonathan,' Shack cut in with strenuous patience.

Jonathan returned to his chair and folded his arms as Spring changed the subject.

'Any mention of Degsey and the pups?' she asked.

'A request that Degsey should live at

Oyster Gables,' Daniel told her, 'and the pups be found good homes.'

'They'd probably make excellent racers . . . ' Shack began, then caught an audible breath as he pulled himself up. He shook his head as if to rattle some sense into it. 'What on earth am I saying? That's the last thing Seamus would have wanted. What was it he told us round the camp-fire? Degsey and the pups should . . . ?'

'Run free to chase the wind,' Daniel said.

'And so they shall,' Sky promised. 'Mum and dad have agreed that Spring and Jonathan can keep Little Degsey and I know I can place the other two in caring homes.'

'And big Degsey?' quizzed Shack, deliberately throwing a note of humour in his voice. 'Surely we don't want her hanging around . . . flashing her gold tooth and getting in the way.'

'I'm afraid we do.' Sky's lips actually curved. Her first smile. 'She'll live here just as Seamus requested.'

'She'll be company for Scooter,' Jonathan said.

'And she'll bring you good fortune,' Spring put in, visibly brightening. 'I bet her tooth brings you masses of serendipity.'

Daniel's expression was haunted, flustered, as he swivelled uncomfortably in his chair. So far he had made no mention of the gold evaporating from the tooth and he wasn't relishing having to recall the event to all the faces now looking at him. He sat forward, marshalled his thoughts, and explained in detail what had happened.

As the full implications of this body-blow sank in, everybody was silent, and Daniel continued, 'So Degsey's back to being a normal dog again. She can't influence things any more. From now on she's just an ordinary pet greyhound.'

'She'll never be ordinary.' Spring's eyes became fixed, her expression melancholy. 'She'll always be special.'

'I suppose it couldn't last forever,' Sky remarked.

'We were very lucky she had her powers when we needed them,' Shack added.

Jonathan, exhibiting ageless wisdom, said, 'She's going to need a lot of extra affection now Seamus has gone. She mustn't be allowed to feel lonely or she'll pine. We'll all have to put in some extra effort — do our bit — show her that she's loved and wanted and that Oyster Gables is now her new home.'

His words caused shadows of faint surprise to drift across Sky's face. She blinked in an exaggerated way at Daniel.

He finished placing the packets of money

in a cash-box and turned the key. 'Some-times, Jonathan,' he said, with a hint of dry humour, 'you never fail to surprise us.'

'Why, what's up?' He scowled. 'What have I said now?'

Daniel let the tangled tension of the morning unwind a little before answering. Everyone was trading small, swift smiles.

'Probably what all of us wanted to hear . . . A lot of good commonsense.'

Sky grinned at the rather pleased look on her brother's face as the desk telephone trilled for attention. She leaned across and lifted it from its cradle.

The grin rapidly disappeared and her breathing quickened as a small tinny voice vibrated from the phone's earpiece. 'Oh, no,' she said with an audible groan, 'that means the whole of the north coastline will be at risk.' A long, listening pause, then, 'Yes, Oyster Gables has the basic washing facilities. We've coped before; we'll cope again. Yes, we'll be ready. Thank you for the warning. Goodbye.'

All eyes were on Sky.

'That was the Coastguard,' she said evenly. 'There's been an oil spillage — an Atlantic collision — and a tanker has ruptured one of its tanks.'

'That means lots of gummed-up sea-birds,'

Shack observed bleakly.

Sky nodded and shifted in her seat. 'We'd better get prepared. They reckon the wind's on the turn and the oil slick will hit Swiftly by morning.'

12

Life at the animal shelter became increasingly hectic which helped ease the trauma of Seamus's death by focussing everyone's minds back to the business of wild animal welfare.

The oil slick had invaded parts of the North Devon coastline and the long stretch of Swiftly beach had been one of the worst hit areas. Oyster Gables, along with other wildlife and bird rescue organisations, had pooled their resources in order to cope with the huge clean-up operation.

Jonathan and Spring had spent the remaining four days of their holiday helping to wash and groom the vast quantity of sea-birds which had been collected by volunteer helpers and delivered to the shelter. They comprised gannets, cormorants, razor-bills, kittiwakes, terns, guillemots, storm petrels as well as the more common black-headed and herring gulls. It had been tiring, round-the-clock work, with everyone toiling through long shifts in order to minimise casualties. By the time the weekend arrived the number of new admissions was down to a tiny trickle and many hundreds of oil-free sea-birds had been boxed-up and collected by national welfare agencies. They would all be transported and released along the non-polluted waters of the South Devon coast.

Gradually things slipped back to normal and Saturday morning found Daniel and Sky at the stables. In about an hour Sky would be driving Spring and Jonathan back to the family home in Sussex so she was enjoying a brief break and combining the leisure time to check on the cleanliness of Delight Cove. Five miles of local coastline had been given the all-clear by the Department of the Environment, and the oil dispersal teams had moved on to tackle more stubborn contamination elsewhere.

'Race you to the beach.' Daniel swung into Sir Galahad's saddle and the horse sniffed the air briskly as he gathered the reins.

'I'm exhausted.' Sky yawned as she sat astride Excalibur. Her muscles felt stiff and aching, her eyes gritty. 'I couldn't manage more than a slow trot. My body's telling me it could sleep for a week. If you want to race then pit your riding skills against Degsey.' She gave him a teasing smile, adding softly, 'I bet you can't beat the dog.'

Degsey had now established herself at the

shelter better than anyone had hoped. Not that it had been easy at the beginning. The first couple of days had been worrying, with the greyhound refusing food and steering clear of the house, preferring to spend her days and nights huddled on the caravan's footboard. Everyone had taken it in turns to sit with her, to talk to her, but no amount of patience and affection would coax her away. Daniel had reluctantly padlocked the porch doors but she didn't attempt to enter the wagon's interior by the flap-like aperture. She knew Seamus was no longer inside — she'd watched the old gypsy being taken away by three men in a black limousine — but her intellect was such that she wouldn't relinquish her territory until the oil in the Angel lamp had exhausted itself. Only then, when the flame had finally dwindled and died, did she accept the finality of the situation.

She was now circling the two horses as they made their way to the paddock. She didn't weave in and out of their legs — that trick was reserved solely for Mister Rafferty — but she was enjoying the companionship, and never strayed very far from Daniel's side.

'I'm so pleased Degsey's settled.' Sky yawned again as she stood up in the stirrup irons and made a pretence of lifting the metal-keeper on the five-barred gate. 'I'm sure she's accepted us as her new family.'

Daniel was about to agree when Sky unexpectedly tightened her reins, cribbing Excalibur's head movement and wheeling the mare around.

'Hold up . . . ' Daniel's breath came in a jerk as Excalibur's haunches flexed and quivered, clipping Sir Galahad's quarters and nearly unseating him.

Sky whooped a laugh as she veered away, applying pressure with her legs and pushing Excalibur into a canter. 'You caught me like this soon after you arrived,' she yelled back, her voice thin against the wind. 'Now I'm turning the tables!'

As Daniel's fingers fumbled to free the keeper on the five-barred gate he could only watch in astonishment as Excalibur, without fear or hesitation, breasted the fence. Sky performed the jump with such perfect harmony of balance that she was barely conscious of the slight jolt on landing.

'Exhausted, are you?' Daniel mouthed the words soundlessly, his heels immediately urging Sir Galahad into a canter. 'Couldn't manage more than a slow trot . . . Ha!'

Degsey streaked ahead of him as soon as the gate swung inwards. Spirited in pace and manner she flashed across the open turf, easily outflanking the horses.

Excalibur was now at full gallop, the mare extending her neck and flattening her ears to counter the drag of the wind. She was a good four lengths clear of Sir Galahad who was responding boldly to the surge of pressure from Daniel's legs.

There was no chance of Daniel significantly closing the gap. The paddock was too short and the beach gate was already in view. Both riders saw Degsey crest the obstacle, tucking in her forelegs and raising her hind legs just sufficiently to cruise over the woodwork without faltering. Such was the power of the jump that she somersaulted on landing; tumbling over twice before her paws splayed for grip in the damp sand.

Sky was only a few seconds behind, her concentration steady, her eyes fixed on the wooden obstacle as she drove hard and straight at it. Excalibur took the jump smoothly, the hooves of the mare's forelegs tucked into her chest, her hind legs using every muscle in her thighs, effortlessly lifting her bulk in a perfect take-off as she spanned the gate. Sky reined in and glided to a halt beside a heavily panting Degsey.

Sir Galahad followed in the mare's slipstream. Daniel kept the reins taut, holding them only millimetres from the animal's neck, but as they crested the woodwork he mistimed the jump and the gelding jarred slightly on landing. Clumps of moist sand flew at the impact of juddering hooves as Daniel stiffened his spine, bracing himself back into the saddle and braking to a dead stop alongside Excalibur.

Sky was flushed with the pride of her performance. The salty air whipped her hair into her eyes as she pranced the mare about in front of him and smiled, teasing. 'A pretty convincing win, wouldn't you say?'

'For Degsey, yes.' He wiped a fine film of moisture from his forehead. Inwardly he was taking the 'win' in good part, but outwardly he was keeping up an air of playful annoyance. 'You cheated. There's no way you would have beaten me in a fair gallop.'

She threw her head back and laughed, her pulses still racing.

Daniel's jaw jutted. 'Okay, you've had your joke. So if you're not too exhausted I suggest we check the state of the beach.'

The two horses trotted side by side, weaving in and out of the rock pools with Degsey scampering behind. She would pause to sniff at the tiny crabs stranded until the next tide in pebbled hollows, flicking an inquisitive paw at the crustaceans and sending them crawling for cover. It was a harmless game which had her spinning madly round in circles and left Sky and Daniel laughing aloud at her antics.

The sheltered bay of Delight Cove was surprisingly clean. A few remnants of black sludge still glistened with dispersal fluid as it clung stubbornly to the wooden uprights of the breakwater, but the beach was almost back to its silvery colour. The foamy breakers at the water's edge were crystal clear and tinged with blue as they slushed against the horses' fetlocks and nudged at a line of seaweed on the wet sand.

A cormorant spiralled in soundless circles above them. They rested the horses for a moment, squinting through the heat-haze which cloaked the sea, watching the airborne manoeuvres.

'That's what makes all the hard work worthwhile,' Sky said, after a moment's reflection. 'We've given life back to over five hundred sea-birds.'

'Jonathan and Spring were a tremendous help,' Daniel responded. 'I'd reckoned on a lot of moans and groans, but they really got stuck in with the dirty jobs. I expect the oil spillage was quite a climax to the end of their holiday.'

'I shall miss them.'

'Me too.'

'They've both grown up a lot.'

'We all have.'

Sky let her feet dangle free from the stirrup irons and swung one leg across Excalibur's withers. She leaned nearer to Daniel, swaying against his chest. He kissed her briefly, then more leisurely, and hugged her.

Degsey lay close to the horses, missing nothing. She blinked contented eyes as she stretched languidly in the sand.

Sky caught the dog's gaze and glanced at Daniel with mock suspicion.

'Nothing to do with the greyhound this time,' he pointed out defensively. 'That kiss was the genuine article. No prompting whatsoever. Go check her tooth if you don't believe me.

'I have and I do.'

They both laughed.

Sky reached up and kissed his temple, her lips lingering on the pulse that beat there. She closed her eyes for a long moment as he held her.

'I love this place.' Daniel sighed reflectively, breathing out the taste of oil which seemed to have clung to his lungs for the last four days. He drew in a deep breath of the salt-fresh air. 'Swiftly, Oyster Gables, Delight Cove, Scamperbuck Ring . . . all of it.'

'I love it too. I couldn't live anywhere else.'

Daniel was deep in thought. He tented his

fingers and pressed them against his lips.

'Penny for them?' Sky said.

'The past couple of weeks have flown by. They seem more like a couple of minutes.'

'The months will fly even quicker and then you'll be at university.' Sky traced the outline of his brow and cheekbones with a finger, gently, lovingly. 'Exeter's only an hour's drive away. Promise me you'll visit us every weekend.'

He tipped up her chin until they were looking into each others' eyes.

'You just try and keep me away,' he said.

* * *

'Well, goodbye, Ceddie!' Jonathan thrust his right hand towards Shack. 'I expect we shall see you in October. It's half-term so we're down for a week.'

'I shall count the days.' Shack's eyes regarded Jonathan with intense scrutiny, but inwardly he was having problems holding back a smile. His grip was firm and cordial as they shook hands.

Daniel carried the cases to the Volvo, stowed them safely, then erected the dog-guard. He had volunteered the use of the estate car as it was more comfortable on long journeys than the van, and it would also keep Little Degsey securely housed.

'Goodbye, Daniel . . . Goodbye, Shack.' Spring reached up to give both of them a hug and strove to keep her voice steady as her blue eyes misted a little.

Degsey and Scooter didn't need any prompting when it came to farewells. They had boundless energy and were using it to dash around the forecourt, skimming as close to the youngsters as possible in a display of canine showmanship.

Both Jonathan and Spring crouched, letting the dogs fly into their arms. Each were fondled individually, then swopped to be given endless hugs and pats.

'Goodbye, Degsey.' Spring knelt and pressed a moist cheek against the hollow of the greyhound's neck. Her eyes were closed as she whispered, 'I promise to take care of Little Degsey and bring her to visit whenever I can.'

The sun was hot, the sky cloudless as Daniel leaned against the Volvo, tanned arms folded, watching the show of warmth and attachment. He could see the trusting look in Degsey's enormously dilated eyes as she listened to the softly spoken words. She rested her head affectionately on Spring's shoulder.

'Are we all ready?' Sky exited by the side-door.

There was a glow to her skin and in her eyes which accentuated all that was feminine and lovely in her. She looked freshly showered and her abundant unruly hair was worn loose, swaying across her face as it was caught by the breeze. She clutched a small overnight bag in one hand, and held Little Degsey on a lead with the other.

'Luggage is in,' Daniel told her, 'and you have a full tank of petrol.'

'Right, kids, let's go.' She ushered Spring and Jonathan into the Volvo. 'Wind your windows down or else the heat might upset Little Degsey.'

Shack got to grips with the greyhound puppy and lifted her into the hatchback, setting her down on a car rug. She gave a small throaty greeting as she spotted her mother padding briskly towards her.

'See you both tomorrow morning.' Sky beamed a smile to Daniel and Shack as she slipped on a pair of huge sunglasses and settled herself in the driving seat. 'The RSPB should be here in an hour to collect the remaining seabirds. You'll find a fresh supply of cardboard carrying-boxes in — '

'The storage shed,' Shack interjected.

'Sorry.' Sky briefly pressed her lips together. 'Am I behaving like a mother hen?'

'Yes, you are. Now enjoy your night away.

Oyster Gables won't fall to pieces in twenty-four hours.'

Daniel was standing to the rear of the Volvo watching Little Degsey respond to her mother's caresses. He'd always been intrigued by the amazing resemblance, and none more so than now. Little Degsey appeared to be growing bigger by the day and her mother really had to stretch from ground level to reach her. Apart from the indistinguishable body markings their facial expressions also seemed uncannily alike. It was like looking at a mirror-image, Daniel thought. The pair were as one; so close it seemed they shared mutual heartbeats.

'Bye, all!' Sky adjusted the rear-view mirror and turned the ignition.

Daniel closed the hatchback and Degsey briefly placed her front paws on the bumper so, for a moment, both mother and daughter had their noses pressed each side of the rear window.

'See you tomorrow,' Shack shouted out. 'Drive carefully!'

Daniel called Degsey to heel.

Spring and Jonathan were both waving enthusiastically as Sky eased the Volvo out of its turning circle, past Seamus's caravan, crunching over dusty gravel as it headed towards the two huge conifer trees which flanked the driveway.

Shack and Daniel raised their hands in farewell as they watched the departure.

Little Degsey was standing up, looking back at the receding view of her mother, panting in the heat and swaying with the movement of the vehicle.

Daniel suddenly blinked. He felt his mouth drop open. The car's rear window seemed to glow and turn opaque as it was caught by the slanted rays of the sun. It glowed, then cleared, and for a bewildering millisecond Daniel was certain that he'd witnessed the glint of gold in Little Degsey's lower jaw.

The Volvo swept past the trees and disappeared from view.

'Did you see . . . ?' Daniel gulped at the craziness of his own thoughts.

'See what?' Shack frowned.

'Little Degsey . . . The tooth . . . It was shimmering.'

He gave a strangled laugh. 'Very funny, Daniel. I expect she's inherited it from her mother.'

'I'm not joking. I saw it.'

'But Little Degsey hasn't got a gold tooth.'

'I know. Am I sounding completely stupid?'

'You're not making much sense.'

Daniel held his breath, unsure whether to be glad or frustrated.

'You saw a trick of the light, maybe,' Shack added sensibly.

'It could have been that, I suppose . . . ' He paused, swallowed, as the doubts crept in. 'You really didn't see *anything*?'

'Nothing.' Shack was adamant.

'But I was sure . . . '

'I reckon you're suffering from lack of sleep. We all are. It's been a hectic week.'

Daniel nodded. He suddenly felt embarrassed. Of course Shack was right — it must have been a trick of the light. He cursed his stupid gullibility in believing otherwise.

Degsey hung back but Scooter plodded ahead as Shack turned towards the house.

'Shall we make a start?'

'Sorry . . . ?' Daniel blinked, slightly at a loss.

'You're the boss until tomorrow, Mr Rusk.' Shack grinned widely. 'Assistant manager and all that. I await your instructions.'

Daniel's mind was still running in little swirls of confusion, numbing his senses. He looked at Shack blankly.

'Sea-birds,' he prompted, placing a strong hand on Daniel's shoulder. 'Cardboard boxes. RSPB. One hour. Remember?'

'Of course.' Daniel's voice was more positive as he dragged it past the dryness in his throat. He drummed up a smile and fondled Degsey's velvety ears. She was still standing just behind him. 'Work to do, girl,' he said. 'Let's go.'

Daniel didn't look back as he and Shack strode purposefully towards the house. Had he done so he might have noticed the slight swagger in Degsey's step and the rhythmic swing in her tail as her gaze shifted from the dust trail left by the Volvo and settled briefly on Seamus's caravan. A whimsical, very private twinkle lurked in the depths of her eyes.

THE END

Other titles in the
Ulverscroft Large Print Series:

STRANGER IN THE PLACE

Anne Doughty

Elizabeth Stewart, a Belfast student and only daughter of hardline Protestant parents, sets out on a study visit to the remote west coast of Ireland. Delighted as she is by the beauty of her new surroundings and the small community which welcomes her, she soon discovers she has more to learn than the details of the old country way of life. She comes to reappraise so much that is slighted and dismissed by her family — not least in regard to herself. But it is her relationship with a much older, Catholic man, Patrick Delargy, which compels her to decide what kind of life she really wants.

THE SANCTUARY SEEKER

Bernard Knight

1194 AD: Appointed by Richard the Lionheart as the first coroner for the county of Devon, Sir John de Wolfe, an ex-crusader, rides out to the moorland village of Widecombe to hold an inquest on an unidentified body. But on his return to Exeter, the Coroner is incensed to find that his own brother-in-law, Sheriff Richard de Revelle, is intent on thwarting the murder investigation. But Crowner John is ready to fight for the truth. Even faced with the combined mights of the all-powerful Church and nobility . . .

SHOT IN THE DARK

Annie Ross

When an elderly nun is raped and murdered at a drop-in centre for drug addicts, the police decide it's a burglary gone wrong. Television director Bel Carson sees pictures of the body, and is convinced that this was a ritualistic murder, carried out by a sadistic and calculating killer. Then he strikes closer to home, and Bel determines to track him down. As she closes in on the monster, she senses that someone is spying on her home. And, in a final, terrifying twist, she finds herself caught in the killer's trap . . .

SAFFRON'S WAR

Frederick E. Smith

Corporal Alan Saffron, ex-aircrew, is desperate to get back into action, but instead he's posted to Cape Town as an instructor, along with Ken Bickers, a friend about as hazardous as an enemy sniper, who considers Saffron a jonah for trouble. Within half an hour of arrival, Saffron's jonah strikes, and he makes an enemy of Warrant Officer Kruger, who turns Saffron's cushy posting into total warfare. With recruits as wild as Hottentots, obsolete aircraft, and Cape Town's infamous watch dog, Nuisance, Saffron's sojourn in South Africa becomes a mixture of adventure, danger and pure hilarity . . .

THE DEVIL'S BRIDE

Penelope Stratton

Lord Rupert Glennister's luck at cards and his tireless sexual appetites were thought to be the work of satanic forces. An outraged society made him an outcast until he could redeem himself by marrying a woman of virtue. Calvina Bracewell was a parson's daughter but was bullied into servitude by her 'benefactors'. Rescued by Lord Rupert, she found herself agreeing to his shocking demand that they should marry that very night. For a while, Calvina was happy but then attempts on her life began. Only one man could want her dead, and that was the husband she'd grown to love.